AS USUAL, CHANGING WAS UNPLEASANT.

And as always, it was viscerally satisfying. Through it all, in a corner of her brain, Lee kept control. The steady vision in her mind's eye remained calm sculpting the gross matter of flesh and bone, weaving the finer tissues of muscle and nerve. It took its time, oblivious to the racking pain in the body it manipulated. The first spasms had been the bold lines of a rough sketch. Then, as the work was done, the changes became smaller and less painful. Finally, the change was like a rough massage, a kneading of skin surfaces, a few brutal pinches and stretches.

When it was over, she let the dizziness subside before she opened her eyes. . . .

ROC

ROC BRINGS THE FUTURE TO YOU

☐ **THE IMMORTALS by Tracy Hickman.** The United States in the year 2010—ravaged by disease and slowly stifled by martial law. Though fear runs rampant across the land, one man, Michael Barris, dares to challenge the government's tightening grip. This powerful cautionary tale paints an engrossing portrait of the near future. (454022—$19.95)

☐ **KNIGHTS OF THE BLACK EARTH by Margaret Weis and Don Perrin.** Xris, top human agent of the Federal Intelligence Security Agency, finds himself joining forces with his oldest enemy in a desperate attempt to halt the seemingly unstoppable Knights of the Black Earth—a fanatical group determined to sabotage the current government and revive Earth supremacy. (454251—$18.95)

☐ **DEATHSTALKER by Simon R. Green.** Owen Deathstalker, unwilling head of his clan, sought to aovid the perils of the Empire's warring factions but unexpectedly found a price on his head. He fled to Mistworld, where he began to build an unlikely force to topple the throne—a broken hero, an outlawed Hadenman, a thief, and a bounty hunter. (454359—$5.99)

Prices slightly higher in Canada.

Buy them at your local bookstore or use this convenient coupon for ordering.

PENGUIN USA
P.O. Box 999 — Dept. #17109
Bergenfield, New Jersey 07621

Please send me the books I have checked above.
I am enclosing $_____ (please add $2.00 to cover postage and handling). Send check or money order (no cash or C.O.D.'s) or charge by Mastercard or VISA (with a $15.00 minimum). Prices and numbers are subject to change without notice.

Card #_____ Exp. Date _____
Signature_____
Name_____
Address_____
City _____ State _____ Zip Code _____

For faster service when ordering by credit card call **1-800-253-6476**

Allow a minimum of 4-6 weeks for delivery. This offer is subject to change without notice.

POLYMORPH

Scott Westerfeld

A ROC BOOK

ROC
Published by the Penguin Group
Penguin Putnam Inc., 375 Hudson Street,
New York, New York 10014, U.S.A.
Penguin Books Ltd, 27 Wrights Lane,
London W8 5TZ, England
Penguin Books Australia Ltd, Ringwood,
Victoria, Australia
Penguin Books Canada Ltd, 10 Alcorn Avenue,
Toronto, Ontario, Canada M4V 3B2
Penguin Books (N.Z.) Ltd, 182–190 Wairau Road,
Auckland 10, New Zealand

Penguin Books Ltd, Registered Offices:
Harmondsworth, Middlesex, England

First published by Roc, an imprint of Dutton Signet,
a member of Penguin Putnam Inc.

First Printing, December, 1997
10 9 8 7 6 5 4 3 2 1

Copyright © Scott Westerfeld, 1997
All rights reserved

Permission for the excerpt from *The Explicit Body in Perfomance*,
copyright © by Dr. Rebecca Schnieder, 1997, Routledge,
granted by the author.

Cover art by Peter Gudynes

 REGISTERED TRADEMARK—MARCA REGISTRADA

Printed in the United States of America

Without limiting the rights under copyright reserved above, no part of
this publication may be reproduced, stored in or introduced into a
retrieval system, or transmitted, in any form, or by any means (electronic, mechanical, photocopying, recording, or otherwise), without
the prior written permission of both the copyright owner and the above
publisher of this book.

BOOKS ARE AVAILABLE AT QUANTITY DISCOUNTS WHEN USED TO PROMOTE
PRODUCTS OR SERVICES. FOR INFORMATION PLEASE WRITE TO PREMIUM MAR-
KETING DIVISION, PENGUIN PUTNAM INC., 375 HUDSON STREET, NEW YORK, NEW
YORK 10014.

If you purchased this book without a cover you should be aware that
this book is stolen property. It was reported as "unsold and destroyed" to the publisher and neither the author nor the publisher has
received any payment for this "stripped book."

To Thomkat

Thanks to all of you who read this book when it was a short story, an unfinished novel, and unpublished first novel. Here it is, again.

Extra thanks to: Nicky for the wattage of her insights. Kathleen for her fierce wisdom. Rebecca Schneider for letting me poach from and misquote her wonderful book, *The Explicit Body In Perfomance*, Routledge Press, New York (1997).

And for my parents, so much love you would need buckets.

PART I

The Principle of Safety

CHAPTER 1

Payday

Sometimes, someone would come home with her (or him) and would be amazed at the closet. It was the larger of the apartment's two small rooms. Clothing on hangers was suspended from a wire stretched diagonally across the room, between eye hooks buried in the white plaster walls. The eye hooks were uneven, and the force of gravity packed the clothes together at one end. The hangers held a collection of dresses, skirts, trousers, jackets, coats, suits. Some guests would assume that there was a roommate, as the clothes were for both sexes. But the clothes were too numerous and varied in size and style for only two wardrobes. Eclectic and somewhat shabby, they looked more like the start of a secondhand clothing store.

Milk cartons (the illegal kind) were wired together with garbage bag ties to make shelves in the two free corners. They were stuffed with T-shirts, scarves, underwear, gloves, trousers, shorts, and socks. The floor was littered with shoes paired off in tight embraces, their mingled laces wrapped around them.

This collection (no, definitely not a wardrobe) ranged across current and defunct street styles: a black jumpsuit, a silver Mylar jacket, combat boots; a white dress shirt hung under a tweed jacket, a snakeskin tie; a red evening dress and black feather boa. Some guests would notice that in the smaller room (which was bedroom, kitchen, and living room) a full-length mirror hung. They would smile to themselves. It was a collection of costumes.

Tonight it was hot in the apartment. The cool breeze from the two windows stalled against the heavy air inside the closet. She was digging through the milk cartons one by one, ignoring the heat. Sooner or later she would break a sweat. As each item was selected, she threw it into the bedroom. She picked among the shoes in the darkness under the hanging clothes, knowing them by feel. They were always the hardest decision.

At last, a pair of red hightop sneakers flew toward the stack in the other room. They were a prized possession, stolen from a lover. She let her bathrobe slip to the ground and kicked it into a carton. She ran her fingers through her hair. It was still wet, but the relief of the shower had already faded into the hot, sticky night.

Dressing in the other room, she was careful to avoid her reflection. The tank top was heavier than she would have liked, but the dark khaki was necessary to balance the red pants. They were military issue: many-pocketed and the iridescent coral that jump troopers wore. She Velcroed them tightly at the waist and ankles. This might be her last chance to wear them. This week, she had seen the bright-red color in a store window on West Broadway. Once SoHo legitimated a trend, it lost its currency in the clubs. She pulled a white headband down around her neck so she wouldn't forget it. Better to get the hair right first.

She didn't lace the sneakers yet, they were too large anyway. Her fingers felt weak as she put them on. With a shortness of breath, a faint tickling in her loins, and a fresh bead of sweat running down her side, excitement was growing quickly.

As usual, changing was unpleasant. As always, it

was viscerally satisfying. She squatted, her back to the mirror, and breathed slowly and deeply to calm herself. First came a looseness in the gut, like a hasty elevator descent. The feeling expanded and she rocked forward, knees hitting the floor. Her hands balled into weak fists. A ragged cough escaped her lips. Her lungs weakened, until they seemed barely able to expand. The emptiness in her belly became a dull ache, and then a fiery pain that shot up into her head. The pain played across her face as it probed and pushed her features. Vision swam, the room warping. The roots of her hair burned.

Through it all, in a corner of her brain, she kept control. The steady vision in her mind's eye remained calm; sculpting the gross matter of flesh and bone, weaving the finer tissues of muscle and nerve. It took its time, oblivious to the racking pain in the body it manipulated. The first spasms had been the bold lines of a rough sketch. Then, as the work was done, the changes became smaller and less painful. Finally, the change was like a rough massage, a kneading of skin surfaces, a few brutal pinches and stretches.

When it was over, she let the dizziness subside before she opened her eyes.

She rolled over and stood at the mirror. There was the usual disorientation as her new reflection mimicked her. She readjusted the Velcro on her pants, which had grown too tight. The shoes fit better now and laced snugly. The khaki tank top, as predicted, complemented her now darker skin. The face was more beautiful than she normally liked, but the nose was strangely Roman, and the incongruity threw things off balance. The face was taken from a young girl, a child from a large Chinese family who lived in her housing project. She never used faces from magazines or films.

The neck was thin and elegant. It was modeled on

a young Polynesian transvestite who worked an after-hours club downtown. The boy was a hustler, who had come home with her (or rather, him) in an ecstasy daze one night, no charge. She touched the neck intimately, remembering. The shoulders she regarded critically; too masculine. She shrugged them.

She combed her damp hair, pushed the headband up to frame her face, fussed with her hair until it gave the impression of an expensive cut. Arms at her sides, she regarded herself.

She was beautiful, statuesque, definitely Asian. Door workers for the clubs tended to favor Asians, whom they assumed to be more affluent and more ready to spend than whites. The clothing was wrinkled, but stylishly so.

Something was wrong, however. She was beautiful, but not . . . striking. Even with the odd nose, she still looked like a picture in a magazine. That was the kind of face she hated: the kind that rolled off printing presses by the millions, unthreatening, lovely, and unreal. She considered wreaking havoc with the nose, but then she would just look like a rich Japanese girl who had been the victim of cheap westernization surgery. She sat down on the bed.

There was a row of anatomy disks on the floor along the wall. Among the pages of paperware indexes were receipts, Post-its, business cards. These scraps of paper marked pages where a bar code or catalog number was highlighted. Each corresponded to a picture or video on one of the disks, where a diseased skin texture, a strange limb, or the line of a cadaver's exposed muscle had caught her eye. The change had heated her up, and she was anxious to leave the hot apartment, but she wanted to make one more adjustment. The image that had been in her mind's eye was too perfect, too clean. She thumbed through the paperware volumes quickly and distractedly, like a young girl leafing through a fashion magazine.

In the index to a medical journal downloaded from the public library, she found what she wanted. The page had been marked months ago with an invitation to a long-defunct club. She flicked on a power strip, and found the corresponding disk before her little machine had finished booting. The article took a few seconds to come up. Her graphics card was Canal Street cheap and always struggled to downgrade images from library-quality disks to a format it could handle.

The pictures were as she remembered, digitized black-and-white photographs of an exquisite pair of hands. They belonged to a woman who had lived in Oklahoma. The fingers were almost normal, though strangely tiny compared to the palms. They were delicate and fine, like precision instruments. The thumbs jutted out almost perpendicular to the fingers. At first she thought the thumbs were short, but they were normal length, simply embedded too far into the hand, as if attached to the bones of the index fingers. She studied the pictures, six views and a navigable X-ray, carefully. The text fields were cluttered with jargon that her two years of anatomy classes couldn't penetrate.

When the image had formed in her mind, more solid there than in the flat pictures, she closed her eyes. She breathed deeply, quickly, and it began again. The pain, though contained in her lower arms, was sharper than usual. It struck suddenly, with a blinding flash of red behind her eyelids. It felt like someone was pulling her thumbs back relentlessly. The bones inside snapped, rejoined, and snapped again. She let out a cry, and there was a brief moment of panic. Perhaps she had gone too far too fast in her impatience. A familiar thought occurred to her: there were no doctors who could fix her. She remembered her mother's horror when, as a child, she would bend in impossible ways. *"You'll get stuck that way!"*

She had quickly learned to curb her transformations and to practice the slow-developing art alone and in secret. Now she calmed herself with the memory of those slow, erotic experiments in which she had first changed her shape, her face, her sex. In a quiet, flashlight-lit closet in her mother's apartment, feeling her bones and organs dance as if they were just tardily developing muscles.

Gradually, panting and with eyes screwed shut, she gained control again. Her instinctive sense of her hands' shape came to match the image in her mind. The hands throbbed with dull pain, but they felt whole. They flexed smoothly, but with a queer feeling, as if the skin were stretching in an unfamiliar way. She opened her eyes.

She liked them better than the Oklahoman's hands. Their deformity was not twisted or bizarre, merely alien. The fingers flexed with a kind of liquid motion, like the legs of an upended tarantula. The thumbs were articulated in three places, the fingers syndactylic, a web of skin between them taut when she splayed her hands. The hands ached dully. She filled the sink with cold water and soaked them in it, wondering at their new shape. She had experimented with ugliness before and with shapes that simply hadn't . . . worked. But never had a deformity seemed so fit. What was a mutant called in biology? A hopeful monster.

When the pain subsided, she dried the hands. The everyday motion had to be reinvented. She washed her face, suppressing a shudder as the hands first touched it, and primped in the mirror again. She blew herself a kiss, borne on an alien palm.

The elevator wasn't working, as usual. She preferred to avoid it anyway. The other tenants in the project might eventually wonder how many people lived in her apartment. It was only ten flights, and exercise helped to break in a new body.

The stairway was crowded. Kids were playing tag in it just above her floor. Halfway down, an old white couple rested with a full grocery cart, their eyes quietly sad. Below them, a Hispanic mother scolded her son, who had a tubercular cough. She wondered if they had seen her hands. There was no reaction from any of them. Of course, little was shocking in the projects. The wall of the ground-floor stairwell was blackened where a small fire had been set.

The pavement outside still radiated heat. White dust was falling: burn-off from the HARD plastics plants in the Bronx Free Enterprise Zone. They said it couldn't hurt you. It was just fancy carbon. HARD plastic was inert; that's what made it hard. But she had heard a woman on TV, a senator, say it wasn't that simple. The dust was accumulating in the pavement cracks like the first flakes of a snowstorm. She smiled. Real snow hadn't fallen as far south as Manhattan in four years.

She walked along Delancey toward the river. Silent cars swirled the dust in the gutter as they passed.

Her club of choice was called Payday. It appeared every week or so, always at a new location. The door workers, the DJs, and the crowd were the same, but the site of the club might be a warehouse, a wealthy patron's loft, an abandoned subway station. She felt a kinship with Payday. It maintained its identity without being trapped in a single unchanging shell. Tonight, Payday inhabited a crumbling amphitheater in East River Park.

The park snaked along the eastern coast of Manhattan, bounded by the FDR Freeway and the river. It faced demolition to make way for a light-rail line, a project that had been stalled by the usual protests.

The friction between the park's homeless inhabitants, their extremist advocates, and the police had drawn Payday to the spot.

After a ten-minute walk, she reached the pedestrian bridge that spanned FDR. From its center she saw the amphitheater toward downtown. It was bathed in pink light, Payday's trademark. On the shoulder of the freeway, a parked city bus was half filled with sleeping police officers. The saurian shapes of heavy construction equipment slumbered in the dark wreckage of a baseball field. Uptown from the machines, the concrete, earth, and trees of the park were a twisted ruin. She crossed the bridge and entered the baseball field hesitantly. A few yellow ribbons that read POLICE LINE—DO NOT CROSS fluttered from the construction machines. As she passed through them, a mercury spotlight sprang to life high in one of the machine's cabs, finding her. A police radio popped. She waved one of her strange new hands, tried to smile, and kept walking hurriedly. She reached a row of orange cones softly glowing with chemical light, past which the grass was untouched. The spotlight wavered and disappeared.

Beyond the border of destruction's arrested progress, the PWHs and their defenders were encamped. There were several circles formed around fires set in rusted garbage cans. The People Without Housing kept together, away from the protesters. Except for a skinhead beating a plastic box to the rhythm of an aimless chant and a group of women passing a bottle, the camp was asleep. Past them was a dark no-man's-land and then Payday. It seemed safe enough to cross the lightless expanse to the amphitheater. Payday didn't usually manifest in so forbidding a locale. She was starting to wish she had taken a cab.

Trees and a few benches populated this part of the park. A few bodies, almost lifelessly still, lay on the benches. She assumed they were sleeping PWHs who didn't like the company of the radicals in the camp. The pink light from Payday cast long, soft shadows through the trees. The city's silhouette was smeared by the orange mercury-vapor glow lighting the dust-fall. The only other visible lights were those of the Domino Sugar factory across the river.

She heard him coming at the last second, turning just in time to take the force of his charge with her shoulder. She went down on her back, the breath knocked out of her. He pinned her arms, straddling her and immobilizing her legs before she could kick him. He was bearded, strong, and smelled of stale beer and cologne.

She relaxed, fighting the release of adrenaline before it took control from her. Her muscles slacked and she closed her eyes. Breathing stopped, and her attention moved to the tiny junctions of her capillaries and the beating of her heart. Gradually, she contained the stress hormones that panic had thrown into her system. She altered her adrenal gland to produce noradrenaline, which was easier to control. Her energy built, but remained latent.

The man seemed to take her lack of resistance as surrender. He was still breathing hard. He maneuvered one of her arms so that it was pinned under his knee, and took her by the throat with his free hand.

Her panic suppressed, she breathed again, careful to start the change slowly. She felt a prickling in her stomachs. It was the release of her own unique hormones.

He kept saying, "Real pretty, real pretty." He leaned closer. The alcohol on his breath filled her nostrils. He released an exaggerated sigh and said: "We will not act civilized in this fucking city." The anarchists' motto. He laughed, as if it had been a witty thing to say, and began to touch her.

Blotting it out, she concentrated on subtle shifts in the bones and sinews of her face. The jaw needed extra muscle. The lips could be thinned and hardened, but only slightly. The change was not even painful. It was trivial compared to her earlier exertions. The last, precise step took only a few seconds.

By the time she opened her eyes, her teeth were razor sharp.

His hands were crudely fondling her breasts. He was still breathing hard and mumbling something to himself, eyes closed. She struggled one hand free and tapped his shoulder. His eyes opened.

"Kiss me, you fool," she said.

Ten years before, there had been a man named Carlos living in her mother's building. He never seemed to leave the projects, occupying the front door stoop from morning until the yellow parking lot lights came on at dusk. At this signal, she had to run back home from the project's playground. Seated on a folding chair too small for his bulk, Carlos would smile as she squeezed past him. Then one afternoon Carlos had found her alone, playing under the broken solar panels on the building's roof. He had assaulted her. In her panic and confusion, her body had done things to Carlos that made this look like child's play.

The teeth sliced in so cleanly that he probably didn't feel it, at first. As she turned to spit a warm mouthful of flesh to one side, she felt his blood running warm onto her neck. He started to say something, but it came out wet and meaningless, turned into an animal mewling as she pushed him off. She kicked him in the stomach, and he made a single low sound like a cough and stopped moving; she was very strong. She walked steadily away. There would be nightmares later, maybe the clean wash of tears, but in suppressing her panic she had for the moment switched off everything inside that could be shaken. Changing also had that effect: it pushed emotions back into some nether region, turned her focus to the needs and pleasures of the body.

She went on toward the club. A little alcohol would kill any viruses and wash away the taste.

The usual crowd was outside Payday. There were kids from New Jersey, white-faced and anxious, who had parked their parents' big ethanol cars on the broad shoulder of FDR. A group of suits, slumming, looked at their watches as they waited for the door workers to check them out. The crowd was fairly small, and nobody was getting in.

A long limousine, a clumsy old gas-burner, pulled in off the freeway. The driver got out to have a quick word with the door workers and then returned to open the door of the car. A beautiful young couple in full evening dress emerged, and the crowd parted for them.

She straightened her hair and approached the red velvet rope. She recognized Louis and Carol, Payday's door workers for two months now. Carol checked her out first. The coral jump pants brought a sneer to her lips. Carol turned to Louis with pursed lips and pointed.

As Louis took a terse look at her, she splayed a hand on her chest in a *Who, me?* gesture. His eyes widened at the hand's strange outline, and he made a quick computation in the obscure calculus of door workers. He dropped the rope.

Inside the ruined amphitheater, soft blue halogen lights bathed the graffitied and broken stone. The entrance opened on what had been the audience area, the seating formed by wide concentric steps that led down to the stage. A few dozen Paydayers had arranged themselves in small knots. A bar was set up to her right. The entrance faced a half-collapsed concrete band shell. Behind it, inside the structure that had served as the amphitheater's backstage, Payday's familiar dancebeat pulsed.

The arch over the stage bore a reminder of her encounter in the park. It read: WE WILL NOT ACT CIVILIZED. . . . in meter-high letters. The last phrase was overgrown with weeds. Rumor had it that the amphitheater had once witnessed the sacrificial rites of the Missing Foundation, an anarchist cult that had mutated out of an extremist homeless advocacy group. On the other hand, she had also heard that there was no Foundation, or that it was just a stalking-horse for real estate interests, the police, and authority in general. For her part, she liked to believe that there were many Missing Foundations, spawned one from another like rumors in a long, hot summer. She doubted that the man who had attacked her was part of any of it. He was just a man.

She avoided the bar and the stench of the chemical toilet behind it. Descending the steps to the stage, she saw a few people she had met before. Some, she knew well. Of course, there was no recognition in the glances they returned. Stairs led up either side of the stage into the dance area behind it. The stone floor vibrated with the beat. Inside, harshly colored lights moved and strobed, and the music was cruelly loud.

Payday's dancebeat extended well into the infrabass. Most of the sound was too low to really hear, but it provoked an urgent physiological response. Her confidence had been riding on delayed adrenaline from the attack, but as she crossed the dance floor her gut tightened, her knees weakening. She could still taste the man's blood. She hoped she hadn't swallowed any. She looked down and gasped: The slick dance floor was transparent. Below a rock-steady sheet of HARD plastic was garbage accumulated from decades of abandonment. Rain-soaked leaves and magazines, rotting food, tattered clothes, feces, even a used condom were flattened by the dance floor like butterflies pressed under glass—Payday's conservative aesthetic at work. The club altered its environs as little as possible. Rather than clean up the detritus collected over years of ruin, Payday had preserved it, serving it up like some pagan delicacy.

Something brushed her shoulder. She started and turned. Billowing above her in the constant breeze of a wind machine was a long silver bolt of cloth. In the high windows of the building, silhouetted against the night sky, two muscle-builders, a man and a woman, posed. An occasional flash of light revealed that they were naked except for single sashes of cloth across their shoulders. Each sash was ten meters long. The sashes were as shiny and fluid as lamé but the wind lofted them as lightly as tissue paper. As she stared, she realized that the man and woman were slowly moving, their pose shifting almost imperceptibly to the frantic dancebeat. She noted their overdeveloped musculature with pleasure. Their forms had the clean lines of synthesized muscles, artificially exercised by small jolts of electricity. She strained her eyes as a strobe began to flash and tried to see the tiny scars where the generators had been surgically implanted. She could see very well when she wanted to.

In the midst of this revelry, something cold and hard was pressed into her hand. She looked down. It was a Rolling Rock. Smiling at the boy, she tasted the beer cautiously. It seemed all right. The boy also seemed all right. He wore a collarless silk jacket over a white tee. A pair of brightly shined dog tags twinkled on his chest. His haircut looked expensive. He was white. He watched her expectantly and sipped his beer.

Finally, he inclined the neck of his bottle toward hers and said, "You drink Rock?"

"I do."

"To Rock!" He toasted so hard she thought for a moment that the bottles had broken.

There was another expectant pause. It was easy to talk in Payday, even on the dance floor. The dance-beat was loud, but most of the frequencies of human speech were high enough to be heard over the pulse. This boy, like many males, sounded nasal here on the dance floor, the lower register of his voice drowned out by the infrabass. She had cultivated a voice that cut through the dancebeat clearly.

The boy was uncomfortable. She waited, keeping eye contact. There was a nervous energy about him, as if he was slowly building up to another burst of conversation.

There was a flicker in his eye before he spoke.

"Freddie," was all he said.

"Lee." It was one of her standbys. She never decided in advance what her name would be.

"Where are you from?"

"I'm from Seoul, Korea," she lied.

"What's it like?"

She thought for a moment. "It's exactly like New York City."

He let out a burst of laughter.

"No fuckin' way. There's no place like New York City!"

"Why not?"

"People wouldn't stand for it." They laughed together.

She decided to tell the truth. "I was born in New York. Projects. Loisaida girl."

He stroked an imaginary beard, as if contemplating this revelation. She saw that he wore a brace on his right forearm. It started at some point inside the jacket, covered the back of his hand and his palm but left the fingers free, separating only the thumb. As they talked, she stole guilty glances at it, wondering whether it compensated for a deformity or a broken bone. It looked like the braces worn by roller bladers to keep their wrists from snapping when they fell, but those were usually made of black plastic and trimmed with fluorescent green or red. The boy's brace was the dirty beige of an Ace bandage.

He was from Nevada. His mom had been a telemarketer, laid off during the mid-nineties bank failures and still out of work. No dad was mentioned. The boy had the self-assured talk of the young men who had arrived in New York in time for the city's renaissance at the turn of the century and had made good, or at least better than the rest of the country. He also had the self-deprecating manner of immigrants when they meet a native. He was vital but not dangerous. Refreshingly, he did not paint, act, or play music.

She said little about herself. She was good at drawing others out. Constructing a new body for the night was hard enough without creating a new history as well. Her body, whatever its form, was solid and real. For any personal stories to make sense, she would have to fill them with lies.

It didn't take much to draw Freddie out. He offered his ideas about the park's demolition. He admitted that the planned light rail was already obsolete, since even the Canadians were building mag-lev lines now, but he had little use for the protesters. He didn't mention the PWHs. He took her to task, as a native New Yorker, for the city's exploding steam pipes and crumbling bridges. Things would have to change, and soon. Fortunately, he said, a complete reworking of the city's infrastructure was at hand. He explained that planned obsolescence had a silver lining. The things built in New York two hundred years ago—the bridges, the roads—were built to last two hundred years. Things built a hundred years ago—the tunnels and housing—were built to last a hundred years. He asserted that nothing built in the last twenty years could possibly last more than twenty years—and the federal housing built since the turn of the century, no more than five. Thus, the diminishing life spans were converging. Soon, in a colossal crash coordinated by humanity's shrinking foresight, everything would fall apart at the same moment. The city would be left as flat as Belgrade after the Intervention.

"And then," he paused for effect, "we start over. Just like they did. New factories, new roads, new housing: New York!"

"When?" she asked. Naturally, the idea appealed to her.

He looked at his watch gravely, and they laughed.

He liked to find solutions for things. He was a technophile, but practical in a serpentine way. His opinions were long and complex, turning aside from obvious conclusions, contradicting themselves. She was soon comfortable with Freddie. When the beers were gone they finally accepted the music's insistent call, dancing until they broke a solid sweat. The DJ was punctuating the music with sudden pauses. Short sampled phrases, sound bites lifted from the president's latest reelection ads, stabbed into the silences. Out of context and isolated, his rhetoric sounded emptier than usual. As they danced, she noticed that Freddie was also listening.

The music slowly elided into a more Gothic beat, until the infrabass shudder became unnerving. She bought a round, with cash, and led Freddie down to the water's edge behind the amphitheater. A few hundred feet of the park had been fenced off and incorporated into Payday. They watched an ancient F train lumber across the Manhattan bridge.

She took his hand, the one without the brace, in hers. He looked puzzled, rubbed his fingers across her palm, and caught her eye. One of his nervous pauses began. She waited. Then he slowly lifted her hand into the light and stared.

"That's extraordinary." He said it with simple awe.

"You only just noticed?"

He didn't answer, splaying her fingers and staring at the hand like a child with a strange animal. He looked at the other hand. "It's the same."

"It's the opposite," she said, grinning.

He didn't smile.

A waitperson came by and Freddie bought a pair of shots. She saw that the edges of Freddie's smartcard glinted with optical circuitry. It was probably from one of the more upscale companies. He whisked it through the waitperson's hand-held reader with great care, as if the card were new and prized.

They did the shots and were silent for a few moments. She felt her stomachs roil as the tequila hit them. Her stomachs were quite small, but she had crenulated their walls to increase their surface area. They absorbed alcohol very quickly. She took a deep breath as the tequila hit her bloodstream.

She heard the chirp of Freddie's phone in his pocket. Freddie looked at his watch and bit his lip. He took the call, for a moment turning toward the water. He spoke for a few moments and pocketed the phone.

One of his pauses passed.

He said, "I've got to go to work." Another pause, in which she found herself disappointed. Then, to her surprise, he added: "You want to come?"

"What do you do?"

"I'm an animator."

"OK." She had no idea what he meant.

It was still dark out, with nothing in the sky except the orange glow of mercury-vapor streetlights. Only a few cabs were queued up outside. She picked a taxi whose driver was pirating electricity from a lamppost that stretched over the freeway. The cab was one of the new Croatian ones that the *Times* said weren't safe. The driver pulled the recharge cable from the lamppost and let it reel back into the trunk with a rude snap. Freddie opened the door and pulled himself to the other side. She got in, her tall frame cramped in the little car.

The cab's card reader was broken, and the driver had to type in Freddie's number on a dashboard keypad, propping his door open to keep the light on. The driver, whose Slavic name crowded the license card posted on the dashboard, listened disinterestedly to Freddie's directions, then nodded vigorously. The little car accelerated onto the freeway quickly, with the eerie silence of foreign electrics. The driver said, "Hot," and the windows slid down with a whine. The cab was suddenly filled with a warm, chaotic wind. Her hair whipped annoyingly and she cursed it. It was the one part of her body she had no control over.

Her limbs still rang with echoes of Payday's dancebeat. They sat in silence. She reached out and grasped Freddie's right arm. A flash of desire struck her as she felt the hardness of the brace through the jacket. The metal inside the bandage ran from elbow to palm, on the underside only. His arm was bound tightly to it with three Velcro straps so that the wrist couldn't bend. She moved down the length of the brace until her fingers touched his.

Freddie worked in one of the long warehouses of the old meatpacking district on the West Side. Many of the old buildings had been converted to living co-ops in the early nineties, before the crashes, and now they stood empty and desolate. A few prostitutes haunted the old truck-loading docks, tall and gaunt. Most of them were dressed as women, but all were men. Her grip tightened as she watched their faces, collecting any nuances she could from this errant margin of desire.

Freddie misinterpreted her excitement. "Don't worry. It's safer than it looks around here."

He guided the cabbie down a side street. They stopped before a lamplit stairwell. While Freddie verified the tip, she climbed the stairs and read the buzzer plates:

ICON TACT LEGAL SEARCH SERVICES
HIRACHI INT.
ACNET
VERITY CORP.

She had no idea which would need the services of an animator.

Freddie came up behind her and ran his card through the door's reader. The door buzzed and swung open easily at her push. A tiny camera hummed as it tracked them across the lobby. The elevator doors opened. The building was sparse and efficient, finished in the direct and shiny style of the information industry. Inside the elevator, Freddie pushed 3. The button bore the AcNet logo.

The elevator doors opened directly into an office occupying the entire floor. She counted fifteen ranks of six desks each, stretching back along huge industrial windows that overlooked the street. Each desk had identical hardware: a flatscreen monitor on a swivel mount, a desk lamp, qwerty bracelets, and a handrest inlaid at a slight angle. No one was there. The only movement came from a small cleaning robot rolling slowly and aimlessly in one corner.

Freddie led her toward the rear of the office. Each desk bore a personal touch: a tea-stained and illustrated mug, a cartoon pixelated by fax transmission, a set of small photographs in Lucite frames, a fuzzy animal with suction-pad feet stuck to one monitor—

the various effluvia of quiet desperation. The monitors were on. Each showed intermittent bursts of color that exploded like tiny fireworks from random corners of the screen. From Freddie's desk in the last rank, all the monitors were visible. The combined effect of the pyrotechnic display was spectacular.

"What the hell is all that? Are those the animations you do?" she asked.

He laughed. "That's just the screen saver."

"Don't you ever turn the monitors off?"

"They're part of the System, and the System is designed to stay on all the time." He said it with respectful finality.

Freddie put on his qwerty bracelets, winding the fingerclips around his brace expertly. The explosions on his screen cleared away. A small menu appeared. Four names: Turbo, Action Jackson, C.C., and Cosmo.

"What the hell do you do for a living, Freddie?"

"I animate." He peeled off his jacket, selected one of the names by touch, and began qwerting. The brace was beautiful against his pale skin. He qwerted in short, nervous spurts. He was incredibly quick. As he talked, his fingers kept up their dancing in the air. "AcNet started out as a database for actors and other theater types. Casting calls and what productions were running. We had biographical data about directors, producers, whoever. There was also a chat line, where people could type in messages to each other in real time. That was a big deal twenty years ago, and it was the only part of the service that made money."

His sudden bursts of qwerting flew by as text on the screen, each character corresponding to a different position of his fingers. There was a small *snick* of sound from the monitor confirming each letter. He had the capslock key down. He made errors in every line and didn't bother to correct them. "So they forgot about the database and made the chat line national. Actors used it to gossip, bitch about being actors, and talk about whatever. 'Cause actors don't have money, it was cheap. So when the net went voice and visual, AcNet didn't really have the cash to upgrade; it stayed text-only."

"Do actors like to type that much?"

"Nope. There aren't a lot of actors anymore. Now it's the old hackers, the technical types who didn't like it when the net got user-friendly. Our motto is, Everything sucks but ASCII. All those faces on-screen made everyone too polite. The AcNet customers still like to flame and gender-surf and generally be assholes. They also stay here 'cause it's one of the last places with all technical users. It's a great place to pick up tips. But mostly, I make sure things stay animated."

"You talk to them?"

"I chat. I animate. When boring guys like Turbo and Action Jackson are on the line, someone has to provide some interest or everyone just signs off."

"You know these guys?"

"I know everyone. I'm on eight hours a day."

"So you're sort of like a host?" she asked.

"Not really. I'm what you might call a shill. They all think I'm another subscriber. Most of them think I'm a young NYU drama student named ME."

"ME?"

"That's my user name, anyway. The stupider the user name, the better."

She began to catch up with the frenetic pace of the text on the screen and saw snatches of conversation. It wasn't just one dialogue, however. Short exchanges from several different conversations were interleaved among each other. Each conversation moved forward, disappeared and was replaced by another, and then returned, having advanced a step in the meantime.

"You're talking to more than one person."

"I'm chatting with all of them. Look." His qwerting paused, and he pointed at the screen. "Each time I send, the computer takes me to the next conversant who's sent a message to me, the one who's been waiting the longest for a reply. It shows me the last thing I said to him, which I probably wouldn't remember otherwise, and his reply to me. I qwert in my response, and *pow!*"—he bent both thumbs at once, evidently the SEND function—"I'm on to the next one."

He started qwerting again. "I'm conversing with each of the four users who are on-line. A couple of them have separate conversations going with each other, but ME is the one holding their attention and, more important, keeping them on-line."

She bent closer to the screen. As she halfway listened to him, the babble on the monitor began to make sense to her. Turbo was definitely a man, and he was coaxing Freddie to reveal the breadth of his sexual experience. But it wasn't buddy-to-buddy talk. Turbo was flirting, making lewd puns with ME's callname, but the humor had a straight sensibility. Then she realized the obvious: Turbo thought ME was female. Freddie was playing ME as a woman, a shy but curious young student. Freddie's responses to Turbo's suggestive queries were evasive but not dismissive. It was as if ME was intrigued by Turbo's leering questions, and was playing a coy game at the arm's length of the qwerty bracelet. ME tended to answer questions with more questions, and Freddie sprinkled her messages with wows and multiple exclamation points. She realized why Freddie kept his capslock key down. In addition to speeding his qwerting, the uppercase letters gave ME's correspondence the breathless excitement of an innocent.

Intercut with this dialogue were exchanges with the other three conversants. One seemed to have a faster response time than the others; almost every second message the computer prompted Freddie with was marked "C.C." Freddie said she was a woman. Her messages were filled with the misspelled homonyms of a speech recognition transcriber.

Either C.C. was telling ME about a pornographic fantasy she had entertained or she was a shameless liar. Her messages were long and rambling, and ended in the middle of sentences. Sometimes the dangling thoughts were completed in the next message, sometimes they weren't. Freddie barely read them before responding with over-excited filler like TELL ME MORE!!! or WHAT HAPPENED THEN???!!!

Freddie explained that Cosmo and Action Jackson were chatting to each other, so their messages to ME came less frequently. Cosmo, who Freddie figured to be a man, used New Age jargon and was playing old-timer to ME's youth. Freddie took more care with his replies to Cosmo, in which ME held forth on the emptiness of life. Freddie's fingers wove cliché after cliché of adolescent angst. He chuckled as he did so, seeming to enjoy wallowing in ME's existential swamp. Cosmo was hooked, tirelessly offering his hackneyed formulas to cheer ME up. Action Jackson and ME discussed baseball, and made fun of Cosmo behind his back.

Soon she was able to keep track of the four different sets of messages simultaneously, and she began to comprehend the conversations as if they weren't interrupting each other. She felt her mind splitting its attention as it adapted to the task of tracking four parallel lines of thought. At the same time, she saw that Freddie sometimes let ideas jump across conversations. Touching the screen with his good hand, he would highlight a comment from one conversant and send it to another. The meaning of the comment might shift when placed into another stream of context, but that seemed part of his intent. He used other techniques, almost too fast to see. Groups of words popped up when he struck any of the thick double row of function keys across the top of his handrest. They were apparently configured to deliver common phrases with one key stroke.

As the distinct personalities of the four conversants became clearer, she began to see a pattern in Freddie's responses. There was an easy grace with the way he dispatched Turbo's advances, always gently enough that the man kept on trying. From a screen full of C.C.'s ramblings, he could pick out and respond to a telling phrase in seconds, turning it around on her so that it drove her erotic narrative to new heights. Freddie assaulted Cosmo's New Age serenity with ME's relentless depression, but Cosmo kept arguing, hooked by the dialogue.

Freddie's dexterity amazed her. She thought of all the lovers she had taken in her various shapes; men and women, gay and straight. The organic metamorphosis she used to remold herself for them suddenly seemed crude. Freddie was changing identities from second to second, re-creating himself constantly to play to the weaknesses and imaginations of his conversants. Her own encounters in her anonymous city had always been physical, visceral. She kissed her lovers, held them, penetrated and was penetrated, even tore them, as she had her attacker in the park. Her prehensile nervous tissue could breach the skin and mingle with another's in the sweaty, half-conscious aftermath of sex. The body shapes she took to perform these connections were as fleeting as the encounters, which only increased the intensity. But Freddie made the same anonymous, exquisite connections through the slender link of text on a screen—uppercase text only. There was a razorlike efficiency to it. He moved among the needs and frustrations of his conversants with a kind of inhuman lightness. It was as if in ME he became an omniscient, nameless confidant, effortlessly innocent and wise. She realized she was drunk.

As Freddie managed the four interleaving sets of messages, he kept up a fifth conversation with her. She was too rapt with the information on the screen, however, and murmured unfocused answers as she watched.

A prompt box that read Special J came up, and Freddy said, "Hello. Here's someone I haven't met before." He sent out a message introducing himself. The response came back: *You mean you're ME!? I've been trying to find myself for years!*

"Heard that one a million times," said Freddie tiredly, but responded with another ME joke. They sparred like this for a few exchanges.

"The ME thing is always good for a couple of minutes," he said. "I've got all the jokes hard-coded in my brain. Easy money."

"Easy money?"

"Real easy. Subscribers pay fifteen cents a minute to stay on-line. When I'm animating them, I get thirty percent of that for the time they spend chatting to me."

"That's how you get paid?"

"Yep. Six or seven at once and it's good money. These days, text-only is the boutique market, so the bastards who own this place really clean up." To emphasize his point, he paused to wave an arm at the dozens of computers assembled. At his gesture, a few random characters popped on-screen like a censored curse in the comics. She looked up at the rows of flickering screens and imagined an animator at each one, adopting multiple personalities as they flitted among conversations with unknowing strangers. She felt vaguely nauseated by the promiscuous enormity of it all. Another anarchists' motto, which she'd seen painted on the aluminum-only dumpster behind her building, occurred to her: *It's been said before: Any god's a whore.*

She sat down on the spindly ergonomic chair next to him. Her eyes ached from hurriedly reading the phosphorescent text. The dry air and fluorescent lighting of the office were starting to take a toll on her energy. The small clock in the corner of his screen said 04:26. Normally, she would be leaving Payday now for an after-hours club.

He noticed her detachment and said, "There's coffee."

In a tiny kitchen near the front, she poured a cup of water from the red spigot on the refrigerator. She stirred in coffee and experimented with a white powder that she hoped was cream. In the bright light of the kitchen, the blood under her fingernails was evident. She picked them clean absently, Freddie's qwerting clattering in the distance like a light rain.

When the coffee was cool enough to drink, she bolted it down. It was mundanely awful. She concentrated on putting the caffeine to work without delay. She found the switch for the kitchen overhead lights, turned them off, and sat for a moment in the indirect glow of the office lights outside. The caffeine and the remains of the night's adrenaline moved through her limbs as she relaxed her muscles and performed a few superhuman stretches.

When she returned, Freddie looked up and smiled. He was sitting awkwardly in the small chair, shoulders hunched a little. His eyes were steady as they looked into hers, his fingers pausing for a moment. She moved behind him and pushed her fingers deep into the knots in his shoulders. The muscles were rock hard. He relaxed, hit a function key, and stopped qwerting. He groaned as she roughened her massage. He pointed at the key he had just struck.

"I just sent them all the same long joke. I macroed it earlier today. It's a good way to buy a few minutes and get them all on the same subject for a while. It's an all-purpose joke. Want to hear it?''

"No." She experimented with her new hands. The radically opposed thumbs provided extra leverage, and could push under the shoulder blades hard and tirelessly. He was a good subject, appreciating a fierce, uncompromising massage. She idly wondered if someone with hands like hers would need special qwerty bracelets.

As she kneaded his shoulders, he unlocked the brace on his arm with the loud rip of new Velcro. The skin on the forearm was a sun-starved white, and he flexed the wrist tenderly.

"Hurts like shit," he said, tentatively spreading the fingers. "The brace keeps me from bending it all day."

"What's it for?" she asked.

"Carpal Tunnel. It's an RSD."

"A what?"

"Repetitive Stress Disorder."

"Ah. You get it from qwerting, right?"

"Anything like that: typing, assembly-line work, pushing a mouse. It's neural damage from doing the same damn thing all day."

"Why don't you use speech recognition?"

"Too slow," he said. "With SRT you can't manage more than sixty words a minute. I can qwert almost two hundred. Besides, my voice'd give out in two hours. Probably just get carpal of the throat."

"Speaking of speech, don't these people *ever* use voice and visual? It's cheaper."

"Anonymity is bliss; you can say what you want. AcNet may be more expensive than a regular on-line, but it's cheaper than a shrink."

A thought came forcefully to her: *He understands.* It was the incorporeality of text that let him transform himself, that gave him his power.

She said, "Well, if you get carpal from doing the same thing for too long, let's do something else."

He grinned, tilting his head back to catch her eye. "Anything you like."

"I'll show you . . . what I like." She strengthened her grip on his shoulders, rotating them in their sockets. Then she slowly extended her massage down his arms. He resisted a moment when she knelt and took the damaged arm in both hands. As she gingerly probed it, he relaxed, but not completely. Maybe his arm felt vulnerable out of the brace, or perhaps he was still uncomfortable with the bare touch of her mutant hands. She kneaded the forearm carefully to avoid hurting the under-used flexor carpi radialis and tendons. The bones and muscles were fine. Whatever damage he had sustained was in the nervous tissue. Helping him would have to wait. She stood up.

"Let's go."

There was another taxi ride, very short. The driver, also Eastern European, followed Freddie's directions to Chelsea. Freddie didn't want to walk the ten blocks at this time of night. She smiled and let him pay.

A large and tattered CONDOS FOR SALE banner was draped across his building. The sign bore the logo of a bank that had crashed explosively the year before. The buzzers were ripped out and the hall lights were dark. Freddie didn't bother to wait for the elevator. He took out a small flashlight and started up the crumbling stairs. He explained that the building's electric bill hadn't been paid for months. The building was stalled in its second generation of co-dominium. The original tenant group had folded, and while the guaranty bank was selling off the empty apartments, the bank had folded too. Freddie's ownership of his apartment remained in some under-regulated limbo.

He shrugged it off. "I bought it in the waning days. They didn't make me put too much down."

Inside, the electricity worked. The apartment stretched, four rooms long and claustrophobically thin, from the front of the building to the back. The bare wooden floors creaked with every step. The kitchen was floored with crumbling white hexagonal tile. From a plastic two-liter bottle, he offered her iced coffee with a Japanese brand name. She took it and they locked eyes. He reached for her shoulders and kissed her a little feebly, then backed away. They drank the coffee, which was sweet and absurdly strong, from robin's-egg-blue mugs decorated with a corporate logo.

He was nervous now. His speech returned to sudden, sporadic bursts. She asked for a tour. As they walked, she absently rubbed his back with one hand. There was the familiar thrill of entering someone else's domain. The bedroom was small and spare; the bed on the floor. A study held only a metal chair and desk. On it, a Sony computer was jury-rigged to use his Manhattan Cable VTV. She knew that was illegal, but that a lot of people did it for the high resolution.

The front room was the only one that Freddie had bothered to decorate. Two wooden bookshelves looked freshly oiled and out of place. Maps filled the walls. They were world maps, strange projections that warped the shapes of the continents. She remembered that the New York school system had adopted one of them; its peculiar geometry meant to compensate for the old Mercator map that had favored the Northern Hemisphere. The result had been a short, patriotic controversy drummed up by the tabloids.

There was also a stereo. It had a turntable for playing the old oversized disks that she remembered were called Long Playing, even though they didn't play for long at all. Freddie had a stack of these disks in their cardboard covers. She suddenly realized why microdisks were called micro. The old disks were huge.

He leafed through the stack nervously. The best way to calm a man was to talk to him about his toys.

"You collect these old things?" she asked.

"Yeah. LPs, they're called." He pulled one out of its cover. She took a step forward and grasped the disk, pulled it closer. He tensed a little.

"It seems a little . . . dark. Is it plastic?"

"Actually, you're not supposed to touch them," he said, a bit too loudly. He added lamely, "It's vinyl, actually." He held the disk as if it were fragile, by the edges. It had a circular paper label in the center and a tiny circular hole within that. She squinted and manipulated her eyes a little, adjusting their focal length. The record had grooves, or rather, a single groove that spiraled from the inside out to a smooth band around the circumference.

"How does the laser read vinyl? It's not very reflective, is it?" she said. She let her eyes relax, and the room slowly came back into focus.

"It's not an optical medium. It's mechanical." He put the disk on the turntable. A small robot arm jerkily picked up from beside the turntable and swiveled until it was over the disk's circumference band. The arm ended in a tiny pin that she assumed was the read head. It was odd seeing the workings of the machine out in the open. It made her slightly nervous. At least MD players were contained. After a moment's pause, the arm lowered. She was alarmed for a second, thinking it was going to miss the disk altogether, but it made contact on the outer edge and the speakers suddenly sprang to life. The sound was a kind of low static, bright with tiny pops.

"Isn't this great? It's called surface noise."

She looked at him a little quizzically. "But—"

The music started. It had a distant, haunting qual-

ity, like the cry of a seagull. She had always heard
that LPs were tinny, but this was not just lack of
fidelity. It was as if the musicians were far down the
hall of an old house. The quality of sound was familiar and comforting. It was, she realized, the melancholy sound-track quality that filmmakers used to
signify nostalgia. There were saxophones and drums,
and some sort of bass that was barely distinguishable
above the rumble of the speakers.

"My dear, I offer you the Ink Spots." Freddie was
suddenly much happier.

They danced, slowly, their bodies pressed together.

They were about the same height. His arms
wrapped around her. She reached through them to
feel the muscles of his back and his tight shoulders.
Her cheek rested against his, and she could smell the
sharp scent of amphetamines on his sweat. So that
was why he was so damn nervous. She kissed his
ear and murmured into it.

"How does it work?"

"What?" His voice sounded dry.

"The LPs. You said they were a mechanical medium. What does that mean?" She kept up the massage of his shoulders. As his mind shifted to the
explanation, he began to relax.

"Well . . . it means not digital. The disk has an
analog of the sound waves pressed onto it."

"Yeah?" She slowly worked her hands toward the
muscles around his sharp shoulder blades.

"Yeah. So the music is stored as undulations in a
long sinuous groove on the surface of the record."

"Mmmm. Tell me more."

"And as the record rotates, the stylus—that's the
read head—slides along the groove. . . ."

"Are you making this up?" She smiled at him as
he reached for the light. Her massage reached his
flanks, his hardened groin.

He continued. "And the stylus moves with the undulations. Its vibrations, thousands per second, go to the speaker, which reconverts them."

"Into?"

"Into music."

They kissed, deeply and for a long time. Their dance stopped and her breath was arrested. The Ink Spots sang in a sweet harmony blurred by the ancient medium. After a long moment, a salty taste entered her mouth from his. She broke from him and felt her teeth with her tongue. One of them, a canine, was still quite sharp from her transformation in the park. She tensed and quickly smoothed it. She had cut his tongue. He didn't seem to have noticed.

She kissed him again. A few drops of blood were nothing after what had happened in the park.

The stereo and its power strip gave off a red glow, but it was dark enough. She was wary of making love in the light. Sometimes at climax her face contorted inhumanly. It wasn't the sort of thing lovers should see. Freddie was nervous enough about her alien hands. He took a sharp breath the first time she touched his cock. His advances became more frantic after that, and his breathing deepened, but it wasn't just fear. Freddie knew how to channel his nervous energy into passion.

He was naked first. She was drawn to his pale, damaged arm. As she kissed it, she breathed the strong odor of speed. The smell of the bandage and of contained sweat sharpened the scent. He lay back a moment, as her lips brushed his nipples and the hairs on his belly. She went down on him deeply, the taste of his blood still in her mouth.

Soon her clothes were off, and they had exchanged places. Thinking of his bleeding tongue, she kept him from going down on her. Despite her abilities, there was risk of transmission through the vaginal walls. She had tangled with viruses. They were hard to beat. There was a moment apart as he searched for a condom in his strewn clothing.

The synthetic rug was scorching as it rubbed against her back. She gave into the exquisite torture for a few minutes, but it began to drown out the wet friction between her legs, and she took Freddie by the shoulders and put him on his back. She straight-armed him, holding him steady against the abrasive rug. She slowed their rhythm. Now she could concentrate.

She strengthened and articulated the muscles of her groin. Pressing Freddie deep into her, she contracted her vaginal walls in a slow, undulating wave. He groaned, and his shoulders went slack under her hands. Freddie's face glowed with sweat in the red light, his mouth open slightly. He pushed up into her, his buttocks and stomach rigidly taut.

Her vaginal muscles gradually gained in articulation, and their lovemaking slowed to a crawl. She brought her knees together, squeezing his trunk with her legs. She sat back onto him, and he groaned, deep and guttural. Her hands slid down his flanks to anchor him at the waist. Inside, her muscles clamped hard at the base of his cock, holding it steady. She stroked the length of the member with hard and slow compression waves. Freddie was panting in short, sharp breaths. His eyes closed, he shuddered. She broke a sweat, concentrating to bundle nerve and muscle and form a small, prehensile clitoris deep inside. Tender at first, it moved carefully toward Freddie's trapped cock. It pushed against the glans, gaining in strength and confidence. He cried out as, through the thin film of the condom, it penetrated his urethra. She held it there, undulating, and drank in the pleasure that went with controlling someone else's pleasure. For minutes, the two of them were almost motionless except for their ragged breathing.

Then she released him, and they moved against each other again. Her legs still grasping him tightly, she leaned forward so that she could move faster. Their chests came together wetly. With the scent of his sweat in her nostrils, she allowed herself to come to a long, shuddering orgasm. She arched her back to shoot the fire up her spine, her fingers digging cruelly into Freddie's flanks. She drew in a huge breath, expanding her lungs superhumanly until the light-headedness of hyperventilation was a soft, warm cloud around her. As her motion slowed, Freddie came with a kind of relieved, injured sigh.

The disorientation of bliss faded slowly, and she let her temporary changes subside. She did a slow internal census to make sure none of her vital organs had been too badly wrenched in the passion. She massaged her beautiful new hands, which were sore. She disengaged herself from Freddie and lay alone for a moment before opening her eyes.

Freddie's eyes were still closed. Her mouth and her throat were dry from panting. She reached up to the stereo top and retrieved her mug of coffee. She filled her mouth with its cool and bitter dregs, and leaned over to kiss Freddie. He responded with barely parted lips, and she let half the coffee run into his mouth.

He swallowed thirstily, his eyes opening. She smiled and kissed him again. He grinned weakly and closed his eyes again. She laughed and rose to a kneeling position, running her arms under his knees and back. He was surprisingly light, and the bedroom was only yards away. The effort reminded her of the beer and coffee in her bladder.

His bathroom was clean for a man's.

After pissing, she sat next to him on the bed and drank from his mug of coffee, which he had hardly touched. It was still cold from the refrigerator. The sliver of sky visible through the windows of the front room was reddening. She contemplated Freddie's right arm.

She turned it over, and ran her finger down the thin blue line of the venus cephalica. Freddie did not react. He was deeply asleep.

Although she was tired from the brutal lovemaking, a well of subtle energy had been tapped by it. Also, the coffee was extremely strong. Freddie liked his stimulants.

She took his arm and laid it out straight on the bed, palm up.

The skin of her right palm fit tightly against Freddie's wrist. She held it there, its pores sweating until there was no air in the spaces between their skin. Her other hand encircled his forearm, ready to pin him. Things could get very messy if he woke up and started to thrash.

When she was set, she shifted into a squatting position, her feet on the solid floor. Her breath slowed and deepened. The change started.

The loose feeling in her gut was heightened by her coffee-washed, otherwise empty stomachs. She was dizzy for a few moments, the looseness slow to turn to pain. When it did, it moved up into her chest. Her breathing slacked, and she coughed away the air in her lungs. Then the pain grew hot and mean, and split into her shoulders. Her breath returned, burning and ragged.

The pain burned its way toward her hands, spreading down her arms like a lover's sharp, splayed fingernails cutting into her. It concentrated in her palms with redoubled fury, scalding enough that it flashed between cold and heat. A childhood memory reared up among red spots behind her eyelids. Snow had last fallen in Manhattan when she was sixteen. Without gloves, she had thrown snowballs until her hands were bright red and had grown hard to move. Thinking she had frostbite, she rushed into her mother's apartment and thrust the half-frozen hands under a stream of hot water. It had felt like this.

She maintained control. She had done this before. The fire concentrated itself in the thick complex of nervous tissue in her right hand and began to pulse. At first the pulse was attuned to her own heartbeat, which was faster than two beats a second. Then it slowed as she moved her nerves toward the surface of her palm. By the time the first nerve strands broke the surface, agonizingly tender in the sweaty medium between their skin, the pulse was matched to Freddie's heartbeat.

Her nervous tissue began to penetrate the flesh of his wrist. She bit her lip viciously with the pain of it, forcing the tissue forward into Freddie's body. Millimeter by millimeter, she was burned by the raw input from her naked nerves. She was careful to avoid his veins and arteries. Finally, after a few breathless moments, the first signals from Freddie's nervous system rose like a subtle itch. They were connected.

There was jazzy electricity from the remains of the speed he'd taken, a flicker of a dream sending phantom commands to his limbs, and, under it all, the calm deltas of deep sleep. There was also a background hum of fresh pleasure from the natural opiates of their passion. Her pain remained, but slipped sideways into some uncaring portion of her mind. As more of her tissue followed and the connection broadened, she felt the phased beats of their two hearts align. He was very fit, his heartbeat quite slow. The messages from his kinesthetic sense briefly dizzied her, and she tipped forward from squatting to kneeling. His brain waves washed against hers, pushing her toward a half-sleep. She shook her head and nudged him carefully closer to consciousness, so that the connection wouldn't drag her down into his sleep.

She ignored the information flowing through his nerves, and felt the tissues themselves. Carpal Tunnel was new to her. The nervous tissue was badly swollen, its expansion constrained by the lines of muscle, bone, and blood that crowded the wrist. Under the stress of his brutally quick and nervous qwerting, Freddie's nerves had bloated and were starting to die.

The mass of the damaged tissue was small. She was glad of that. She could spare the tissue. She always made her hands overly sensitive. The healing required no direction, happening at the edge of consciousness. Slender strands of her tissue spread through his, exactly tracing the swollen nerve paths. A network of her nerves slowly built up that shadowed his own, gradually replacing his damaged tissues. With a more conscious effort, she took control of his excess tissue and drew it out bit by bit into the salty spaces between their skin, where, disconnected, it writhed and died. An hour went by in this dreamlike exchange.

When it was done, her nervous tissue that remained in him drew back of itself. She was taken by a small shudder of surprise when the last connection faded and her body was again distinct and alone.

Her bitten lip was sore. She wiped blood off her face with her left hand. Through the front room, the light blue of early morning was visible. Freddie, who had REMed throughout the process, slipped back into a full sleep. She was exhausted. Setting a small time bomb of adrenaline to wake her in five hours, she curled into a fetal position in the corner of the futon. She tossed and turned, her brain buzzing with caffeine and the strange, disowned images that had slipped into it from Freddie's thoughts. She often wished she could control her mind as well as she could her body. At last she slept a sleep full of alien dreams.

When the natural alarm went off and pushed her to the surface of consciousness, her eyes were strangely dry. She was still tired. Short sleeps were usually enough for her, but she never slept well in someone else's bed.

As she dressed, her right wrist hurt like hell. It felt weak and inflamed, probably close to what the symptoms of carpal felt like. She poured a glass of water and drank it standing by the sink. Then poured another. She went to Freddie and took his pulse from his right wrist. His arm seemed fine. The pulse was strong, and he was close to waking up. She sipped the water, flexed her sore wrist, and considered staying until he awoke. But she had no way to explain what she had done.

Before she left, she took Freddie's brace from the kitchen table and strapped it to her wrist. The Velcro pulled tight and supported the sore muscles. The wrist felt better, and she liked the look of the brace on her strange hand. Freddie wouldn't need it anymore, and her nervous tissue sometimes took days to regenerate. She smiled. She could add the brace to her collection.

She took Freddie's card from his wallet, locked the door behind her, and slipped it back under. It was an old trick for letting sleeping lovers lie.

Outside, the sky was cloudless, and there was a hint of morning chill in the air. She bought some orange juice at a Korean. It was painfully acid in her stomachs. Workday traffic choked the streets.

She decided not to take a taxi. Home was about thirty minutes' walk, and the possible routes were many.

CHAPTER 2

Snips and Snails

Halfway home, a fine mist began. As she walked, it gradually shifted to sprinkling, and then a steady rain. The HARD plastic burn-off from the night before turned to mush in the gutters. It had the consistency of soggy confetti. She avoided 14th, where some kids were pelting each other with damp and heavy snowballs of the congealed ash. Rainwater pools formed over the sluggish drains on Houston, glistening with oily rainbow snakes. The downpour let up suddenly as she turned onto Allen Street, one block from home.

The elevator was working again.

She threw the red jump pants onto the shower stall floor, hoping the harsh rainwater had faded them. She kneaded them with her feet as she showered. Squeezing the last of a tube of FDA Acid Rain Wash into her palm, she shuddered. You weren't supposed to use it on your hair. Her wrist was painfully sore. She dried her forearm carefully when she stepped out, then strapped the brace back on.

The rain hadn't diminished the humidity in her apartment.

She regarded herself, naked except for the brace, in the mirror. Among the disks strewn on the floor were two cans of illegal spray paint, one silver and one black. She considered spraying the brace silver, taping off a crosshatch pattern, and then adding the black. But the constant throb in her wrist reminded her that the brace wasn't decoration. Its dirty beige color, medical-looking and darkened a little by the rain, gave it a seriousness she liked.

She toweled her hair as dry as she could with one hand, then pulled the blackout blinds down over the open windows and tried to sleep. A hot breeze stirred the blinds occasionally, allowing scalene shafts of sunlight to probe the two rooms. She lay atop the sheets, limbs splayed to radiate her body's heat.

At the remote edge of her attention a faint buzz lingered, a leftover from her connection with Freddie. It was the hum of his amphetamines imprinted on her nervous system. Under the speed's airy echo was a deeper buzz: Freddie's inherent restiveness. It kept her off balance as she fell toward sleep. It would steal up just as she slipped into unconsciousness and jolt her awake. The shocks pushed her sideways from sleep, into a state where she floated with alien sensations; strange daydreams that pulsed to Freddie's unfamiliar rhythms. She had connected her nervous system with lovers before, but somewhere in the interchange of tissue, Freddie and she had penetrated each other more intensely than she had expected. He was built of sudden ideas, instantly grasped meanings, jolts of emotion. He shifted to new perspectives unhindered by residue from the old. She reflected that in an era without computers he would probably be useless to society.

As she lost consciousness, the individual sparks of their connection coalesced into a single presence. She slept, again in his embrace.

She woke to the mournful, staccato cry of heavy equipment moving in reverse. Surprised to be alone, she reached for one of the blackout blinds. At her touch it flew out of her hand, rolling up to reveal a sunset so red and mottled that the sun itself was indistinct. She'd read an article in the *Times* that said these sunsets were getting more common, and more lush. She put on dark glasses and placed a Rolling Rock in the freezer, twisting the ancient analog timer built into the stove to twenty minutes so the beer wouldn't explode. Waiting by the window, she watched shadows climb the new Kings County jail up on Houston.

Her wrist still hurt like hell, but the sharp stabs of pain had subsided into a dull ache. She slipped the brace off and rotated the wrist in slow and exquisite agony, swearing out loud. She kept up the exercise with dogged determination, filled with the perverse pleasure/pain of pulling the bandage off a scab. Once in a while a reluctant breeze would push a shallow breath of air into the apartment, tainted with the smell of the city. Soon she broke a sweat.

Her body still buzzed faintly with the nervous residue of her connection to Freddie. The feeling had stabilized, its tiny shocks replaced by a warm glow. She wondered if Freddie was back at work, casting a net of interaction with the bored and lonely shut-ins of the electronic city. She considered what it would be like to log on to the AcNet chat line and anonymously converse with ME. But there was no modem on her deck. For that matter, she didn't have a phone, and she hardly had the money to pay Ac-Net's steep connection fees. But she found herself thinking of him.

By the time the timer rang, the sunset had diminished to a finger-width streak of blood red.

Beer in hand, she toured the closet in the reddish half-light. It was Monday, and the Glory Hole was open tonight. There were really only two choices: extravagant evening wear or her rumpled Mets shirt. With her pretty Asian face, she preferred not to do the lipstick dyke routine. It would be overkill. She slipped the Mets shirt on without putting down her beer and sought out a pair of mercifully cool pin-striped pants that tied at the waist. Somewhere, she found a blue pair of deck sneakers. They fit after she flattened her arches a few centimeters. She tried them with socks, but it was too hot.

Her hair was a frizzy mass of angst. She ran her good hand through it and considered the dog trimmer she had bought on Canal Street the week before. It could be set in centimeter increments and could buzz the whole fucking mess away before her beer got warm. As she had several times since purchasing the trimmer, she pulled it out of its black vinyl case and threatened the unruly hair. It was no use. Contemplating an irreversible change in her appearance was almost impossible. She was too used to editing her appearance, refining and redacting until it matched an image in her mind's eye. But, she consoled herself, her nerve was slowly building. One day soon.

She tied a red bandanna around her neck and combed a palmful of Stiff Stuff into her hair. The synthetic-smelling goo partly tamed it. With her hair combed back, she looked more masculine.

But the face was still too pretty. The crowd at Glory Hole was too rowdy for the angelic, rich-looking Chinese girl who stared back at her from the mirror. She contemplated a small shift of her skull to make her brow more manly, but the thought of it gave her a headache. In the last twenty-four hours she had done enough shifting for a week.

What did monomorphs do at times like this? In one of the milk cartons in the closet was a cluttered box of makeup implements stolen over the years. She rarely used them. A tube of black lipstick seemed hopeful, but what made Anglo girls look tough made her Asian face look like a geisha's. She wiped it off. The makeup box also held a switchblade. She flicked it open a few times before the mirror, posing with it between her teeth. It put an edge on her soft appearance, but she could hardly carry it openly.

She ran the flat of its blade down her white and perfect cheek. The answer was obvious, really.

Her stove was the ancient gas kind that could still be found in the projects. It heated the apartment noticeably, but it boiled water faster than a microwave. Once the water was bubbling, she swished the knife blade in it until its metal handle grew hot. She sat down in front of the mirror, having collected a handful of tissues from the box beside her bed. Even though she knew the pain would be trivial compared with a change, it was hard to get started. She blocked the nerves of her right cheek as best she could and made an inch-long cut. The blade was duller than it looked.

The pain seemed far away, but it had a nasty, throbbing edge that she wasn't used to. She let it bleed freely for a while, watching the blood surface and run with morbid fascination. It had the tardy pace of violence in an old western, welling and dripping down her face like slow motion. After half a minute, she turned her concentration to sealing the cut while she wiped her neck and chin dry. She dulled the red of the scar a little to make the wound look older.

Her face was perfect now. The thin line of the scar added the touch of asymmetry she had been searching for. The wound toughened the angle of her high cheekbones and made her dark eyes seem wiser and older. It made it easier to wear the expression she preferred in the Glory Hole: wicked and vulpine.

She reached into the ashtray beside her door, pocketing her smartcard and a few dollar coins. She ignored the condoms. As she pulled the door open, her wrist gave a sharp pang, and she remembered to put on the brace. She took the stairs leisurely. It was a couple of hours before the Glory Hole would open.

One last wrinkled *Times* was left at the corner bodega, and there was a free table in the Paradise Lounge on Houston. By the time her bean soup arrived, a soggy mountain of rice rising from the center of the bowl, her hands were streaked with the *Times'* bright pastel hues. The heavy food had soon soothed her stomachs.

As she walked toward the West Village, there were traces of relief from the heat. The streets were still wet from the day's intermittent rain and a breeze off the East River had broken the humidity. The traffic on Houston was light, even for a Monday.

Soon she saw why. West Houston was ripped up for construction. Deep, muddy gouges in the street bared the subterranean complex of the city's sewage, heating, and communication systems. She saw an old steam pipe and thought of Freddie's theory of simultaneous decay. The concrete pipe looked ancient and decrepit beside the fluorescent color-codes of the fiber-optic PVC tubing piggybacked along it. Surely the wiring, fibering, and piping couldn't all go bad at once. But the notion of a city rebuilt from the ground up still appealed to her.

They were widening Houston to add a high-occupancy transport and freight lane where the median had been. It was designed for trucks and busses from the West Side VTOL port. The sidewalks were open to pedestrians, though the big machines were still at work in the harsh glare of halogen floodlights. The machines were awesomely loud, their gas-driven engines enveloping the street in a thick cloud of fumes. She turned uptown. The club was a few blocks north of Houston, on what native New Yorkers still called Sixth Avenue.

* * *

The floor of the Glory Hole was tiled with the likeness of a chained dog. The mosaic was crude and Roman-looking. The club's theme was Pompeii: revelry before the eruption. The cover was twenty dollars. She knew from experience that there was no arguing with the doorwomen. She usually didn't pay covers on principle, but the club was only open once a week, and at least there was no waiting around outside to be checked out. Not for women, anyway.

As always, there was a mixed crowd inside, the atmosphere more densely erotic than Payday's. The plurality of choices and the lack of division into exogamous camps complicated the possible scope of arrangements. In short, anybody could go home with anybody. And with little air conditioning, it was very hot.

Rolling Rocks were five dollars. The bartender, who wore a nose ring, smiled at her.

In the corner by the pool table were a group of women who looked like they belonged to the row of Harleys parked outside. They wore black leather chaps over dusty blue jeans, their collapsed helmets dangling from straps around their wrists. They were heavy on neck bands; the drivers wearing slender black leather around their necks, the backseat riders ornately studded chokers. Even with her scar, she didn't feel up to joining them.

Along the back wall was a row of venerable pinball machines. Countless generations of digital arcade machines had never completely supplanted the old mechanical games. Especially in a bar, nothing could duplicate the physical connection between the player and the encased ball. A few lipstick types leaned into the machines, or stood by, smoking cigarettes in long holders. They were all in bright dresses, high heels, and stockings. Someone's kid walked unsteadily under the pinball tables, short enough to stand upright under them. He was dressed in a little sailor's suit. One or two of the women looked intriguing, but she felt a little intimidated by all the high fashion. She stayed by the bar. The women here were dressed like her—loose pants, T-shirts and halters, baseball hats turned sideways. Everyone had a ready smile. They were free of the rough posturing being played out at the pool table or the cool composure of the lipsticks.

Before her beer was half finished, a tall Italian woman named Bonita had said hello and introduced her friends: two more women and a man called Blake. There were always two or three men here, and, like Blake, they were always safely gay. Once again, she decided her name was Lee. They were nice people, though the music was too loud to do much but stand and exchange glances. It was a kind of old-fashioned acoustic jazz. Lee's ears picked up some of what Freddie had called "surface noise," and she wondered if there was an LP player here. The music's feel was very loose, but the rhythm was undercut by a heavy-handed beat coming through the floor from the dance room below. Bonita asked Lee if she knew the club, as she didn't look familiar. Lee laughed and dodged the question with her own: "Come here often?" Bonita laughed and grasped Lee's braced hand. The contact lingered for a moment, Bonita feeling the short, alien fingers before letting go.

A onetime lover of Lee's named Kathy came past. Lee smiled and waved. Kathy waved back. Lack of recognition was no problem for Kathy; she'd forgotten more lovers than most people remembered. The others knew Kathy too. Everyone did.

The music changed downstairs, and they all wanted to dance.

At each step down, the air thickened. It was more crowded here. To the left was a sunken pool, about four meters to a side. Usually it was empty of water, but tonight it had been filled. She paused at the rail. Two dark-haired women, one with eyeglasses on, embraced in the meter-deep water. The heady vapors of heated chlorine caught her breath. A large, shirtless woman splashed into the pool, and a small wave splashed over Lee's sneakers. She rejoined her new friends and danced, keeping her eye on the stairs in case Kathy came down.

Bonita smiled at her again and split their dance off from the group, standing a few centimeters closer to make it private. Her eyes were light green, an uncanny color that was probably contact lenses. Her neck was long and thin, her hair cut short as if to show it off. She caught Lee's stare and posed for her a few beats, neck arched seductively, eyes closed, lips pouting, and then laughed. Lee reached for her hand and returned the squeeze. Bonita was prettier than the sort of person she normally liked, but her broad shoulders and muscular arms had caught Lee's eye. The taut skin across Bonita's collar bone revealed sharply defined sternal muscles, and the ridge of her spine was sensuously apparent through her tight black T-shirt. Lee idly wondered what Bonita would look like with the shirt off.

Kathy appeared and said, "Have you seen the pool? It's filled again."

Lee answered, "Pompeii."

Kathy said something about either license or *a* license. The three of them danced.

The music here was less sophisticated than the dancebeat at Payday. It followed a formula as old as the drum machine: a cavernous bass drum on one and three, a snare like a car door slam on two and four, the shuffle of a tight high hat struck four times every beat. As music, it was as good-natured as the crowd, as free of pretense as Payday was drenched in it. It was music so simple and literal that anyone could dance to it, and everyone did.

They were soon all glistening with sweat. Bonita was very fit, the energy in her step unwavering. Lee was starting to tire when a few seconds of brown-out, common in the summer, briefly interrupted the music. Kathy stopped dancing and headed down a hallway toward another room. Lee followed her, Bonita close behind.

The space had been changed since the Monday before. There was the new-paint smell of recent construction. Small doors with coin locks lining the tight hallway. Lee assumed they led to back rooms—small, dark closets for private encounters.

In the far room, which had another bar, an air conditioner labored with a heavy whine. A fire exit leading up to the street, propped open to let in the cooling night air, was much more effective. Lee was drenched with sweat. She fanned the hem of her shirt, and the cold air rushed up and hit her chest like a cool shower. She was glad she'd worn the Mets shirt instead of evening clothes.

A tall blond woman with a seat at the bar bought Kathy a White Russian. The woman's friends were all drinking White Russians. The press of bodies in the hall muted the music from the dance room, and it was quiet enough to talk. Introductions were exchanged. The tall woman and her friends were from New Orleans. They were flying back tonight, working tomorrow. It was their first time in New York, and they were eager to compare it to their native city. They talked about the gay scene in New Orleans, the secrecy of their clubs and the danger of being bashed. The tall woman made a comment about the political maturity of the New York lesbian scene, and Bonita laughed out loud. Lee leaned against her and signaled for two more beers. Kathy talked about a trip she'd taken to New Orleans in the nineties, and though Kathy rarely exaggerated her tales of sexual conquest, the New Orleanois' eyes widened.

Lee felt a kinship with Kathy that was hard to explain. Kathy's promiscuity was so profound and casual that Lee was certain she understood the aesthetic of anonymity. Kathy was so lax, so easy in her sexual friendships that there was something polymorphous about her. Kathy never *changed*, of course, but her oblivious forgetfulness seemed constantly to reinvent the world for her. The New Orleanois were being won over quickly. The tall woman bought Kathy another White Russian and started calling her *cher* with a softly southern lilt. Kathy's tale continued, and intensified. Lee exchanged a smiling glance with Bonita.

They went back to the dance floor together.

The pool had grown crowded. Blake was in, looking wet and uncomfortable. Lee pointed him out to Bonita, who laughed. They danced.

After a few minutes, Bonita's eyes took on an intent look. She reached out and brushed Lee's stomach with her fingers. The touch was feather-light, barely felt through the rough fabric of the baseball shirt, but it felt strangely sharp and distinct. A shudder traveled up Lee's spine and down to her loins, her sexual reaction somehow tinged with warning. A seriousness overshadowed Bonita's easy advances, an intensity unfamiliar in the languid protocols of the Glory Hole. Lee backed up a few feet, into a corner formed by the wall and a stack of speakers. Bonita followed.

Lee set her beer on the top speaker and took Bonita's hand in both of hers. Holding it lightly, she guided the hand under her own shirt, so that Bonita's fingers brushed bare skin. Lee's stomach was slick with sweat, and Bonita's hand slid smoothly across the wet expanse. The lush feeling between Lee's legs became deep and sovereign, like the precursor to a change. She leaned back against the wall. Bonita drew closer and her hand went farther up Lee's shirt, pressing hard into her sternum, holding her against the wall. Then she took the beer bottle in her other hand, freezing cold and sparkling with condensation, and rolled it slowly across Lee's stomach. Lee gasped. As the cold cylinder spanned her stomach, white freezing sparks shot out of it and into every nerve.

There by the speakers, the short encounter seemed almost private. The intense volume of the music shut them off from the rest of the room.

When Bonita released her, Lee took a long drink from the beer. She leaned against Bonita, who took her weight easily. Her head was reeling. She tried to organize her body's resources to stave off the effects of the alcohol in her system, but she was too tired from the night before. She felt she had spent the day in only a half-sleep. She wondered if she'd picked up any speed from Freddie's body. It didn't make much sense, but it felt that way. She leaned against Bonita for a few minutes.

Kathy reappeared, the New Orleans people in tow. The five of them danced, waving for Lee and Bonita to join them. Bonita stroked Lee's neck absentmindedly as they rested against the wall. Kathy put her half-empty drink down as she danced, and someone took it away. The tall woman took her to the bar to buy her another White Russian.

Lee finished her beer and pushed Bonita toward the remaining New Orleanois. She needed to find a bathroom.

She worked her way up the narrow stairs. The crowd upstairs had grown thicker and more butch. Lee noted a number of dark green army coats with cutoff sleeves. It had originally been a separatist uniform, but a lot of women were wearing it now. There were a few shaved heads, one of which had a swastika tattoo. The women's room had a long line. She waited sullenly for a minute, then rapped once on the men's room door. There was no answer, and she slipped in.

It was huge and empty, cool and dry, a luxuriant waste of space. The floor and walls were decorated with the same mosaic tiles as the floor upstairs. The trickle of her urine echoed thinly, and the toilet flushed with a hollow roar. When it subsided, she paused for a moment in the huge quiet. More than just empty, the place felt unused. Even with the paper towel dispenser neatly filled, there was a sense of ruin. A men's room after there were no more men. She ruminated for a few precious moments.

Of course, the club was for lesbians only Sunday through Tuesday. It was gay men on Wednesday, bi-night on Thursday, and het on the weekend. For the moment, however, the silence was holy.

Before she left, she thirstily drank tap water from her hands. The water pooled in her palms with strange efficiency, the webbing a useful adaptation. At the bottom of the stairs, Kathy, another White Russian in hand, amorously kissed the tall woman from New Orleans. Bonita had disappeared. Lee made her way down the hall toward the downstairs bar, which had grown even more crowded. Bonita wasn't there either. Lee bought a beer with the last of her cash. The other New Orleanois appeared, and one angrily announced that Wendy was sleeping alone tonight. Lee assumed that Wendy was the tall one with Kathy. Lee doubted Wendy was sleeping alone tonight. She also doubted Wendy was getting back to New Orleans tonight. She headed toward the dance floor.

Kathy was in the pool. She saw Lee and yelled, "Come on!"

The pool was less crowded than the dance floor. Lee slipped out of her sneakers and put her smartcard and last dollar coin in one and her beer in the other. She left the brace on. She went in ankle-

and then hip-deep. The water was warm and lush and licentious. She turned around and fell backward into Kathy's arms. Kathy laughed and pulled her across the pool. In the middle, Kathy let go, and Lee submerged into sudden and total quiet.

She stood up, and everyone was dancing.

One woman, whose pupils were huge, danced with a chemical light stick, green tracers arcing around her. A petite and beautiful woman in suspenders dragged her protesting girlfriend into the pool. The girlfriend handed a silk jacket back over the rail. Her chest was bare underneath, and she was wearing bright nipple makeup, probably the flavored kind. Most of the women in the pool were in their underwear. One in suspenders was otherwise bare above the waist.

The sex was clean. It was innocent and unintrusive. Like the half-submerged dancing, it was all above the waist. Lee went down on her knees and shot across to Kathy, and was struck by the chemical light stick midway.

Kathy said, "Isn't this great? Isn't this fun?"

"Fun until someone loses an eye," she answered.

Her shoulder hurt from the blow. Lee looked back at the woman with the lightstick. Oblivious. Beautiful to watch.

Kathy laughed at Lee's joke. Lee pushed her down into the shallow water and gave her a watery kiss on the shoulder. Kathy fought back with a shove of water, scattering the dry women at the pool's edge. Lee suddenly noticed how many people were watching them; the pool was bathed in track lights that flashed in time to the incessant, unchanging beat. The sudden realization that she was on display made her feel strangely faint.

She pulled herself onto the poolside. Her pinstripe pants were tight around the ankles, and ballooned with trapped water. When she stood, the water deluged onto the floor. It was embarrassing. She tried to strip to her underwear, but the pants' zipper was soaked and unwieldy. The air felt cold, and her beer was missing. She checked, and the card and dollar were still there. She shrugged and returned to the warmth of the pool.

Wendy and Kathy embraced each other in a slow dance that bore no relation to the music. Lee slid down, kneeling until her nose was just above the water, and watched them. Kathy's shoulders were beautifully wet, muscular, and tensed. Her olive tank top had turned black from the water. She stood a head shorter than Wendy, who had curly hair. Their kisses fell indiscriminately on neck, shoulders, forehead, mouth. Lee felt suddenly tired. Her wrist hurt, and it felt like something had been sucked out of her palm. She closed her eyes, like a child hiding her face to disappear. Kathy's and Wendy's embrace, the scene, the music, and the night . . . scattered. She took a tiny measure of control, making herself shed a few tears to get the clean rush that follows a good cry. The tears mixed indifferently with the overchlorinated water. She felt clarity returning.

When Bonita had touched her by the wall, something had rung a strange alarm in her. In her drunken randiness, it had excited her and overwhelmed her, but her initial response had been a warning from deep inside. She searched her memory for a similar feeling, but there was none. In this bar, she'd had dozens of encounters—casual, fleeting, and very safe. They had always left her with a sense of sisterhood, with rushes of delight, with the unfamiliar warmth of belonging. But there was something wrong.

When she opened her eyes, Bonita was in the pool across from her, also submerged to the chin. Her hair was wet, and clung tightly to her head. She looked different. There was no way to place the change;

cheekbones, neck muscles, eyes all were slightly adjusted. It was so subtle only Lee's sharp eye for physiognomy could have noticed. Bonita's eyes registered as Lee's stare became aware. The shock of recognition passed between them.

A long time before, Lee had gone to Florida with a rich man she had known for a few weeks. The six days out of state had been awful. The sterile hotel, the insipid tourist nightlife, the plodding boredom of a single identity and a single lover had left her desperate to return to New York. There had been an ugly scene at the airport. She arrived home in the middle of the night. As she pulled her bag from the taxi's trunk, she recognized a passerby, and shouted to him. She had trained herself never to show recognition, but the familiar face brought tears to her eyes. She couldn't really remember who he was (just a local bartender) but the sense of being home was as overwhelming as if he had been a long, lost friend.

Now, meeting Bonita's eyes, she had the same feeling. There was the shock of seeing someone whom she felt she knew intimately. But it wasn't the moment of playful sex beside the speakers that bound her to Bonita, it was something deeper. There was the excitement of a new friend but also an overwhelming sense of being home. Then Bonita smiled, half friendly and half evil, and she was positive.

Bonita was another polymorph.

There was someone else like her.

Lee's vision clouded, and she thought for a moment that she had slipped underwater. The fumes of the chlorine burned like sulfur in her lungs. The music lost its volume as blood rushed to her head. The bright reflections of track lights on the water's tempest surface turned red. A thousand lives, spent alone, fell away.

When her vision cleared, Bonita was approaching

slowly, gliding forward, only her head above the water. Their eyes were locked. There was no doubt that she also knew. Bonita took Lee under the arms and lifted her from the pool. She was very strong. She remained on her knees in the water and reached up to Lee's face. As Bonita's hand brushed her cheek, Lee felt a kiss from the palm, small moist lips surrounding the nip of a tiny set of teeth. She jerked her head back and saw the mouth resolve itself back into Bonita's palm. Bonita smiled up with her half-evil smile. She lay her head on Lee's lap.

In the relative cold outside the pool, in her fear (of Bonita's too-sudden morph, of having been seen for what she herself was), and in her sudden relief at being unique no longer, Lee shuddered. She leaned forward, cradling Bonita's head. She stroked Bonita's shoulders, wet and naked, and looked for the first time at another authored body. The ribs of Bonita's thin, arched back showed clearly, as did the sharp sternal muscles. The shoulders were as broad as a man's, and Lee saw how Bonita had arranged the leverage in her thin body to maximize its strength. Bonita leaned back, her arms still around the small of Lee's back. Lee saw how small Bonita's breasts were, as sharp and taut as tensed muscles. Her jaw seemed too wide and firm for her narrow neck, and it threw off her feminine, Italian beauty. In the bright track lights, the uncanny green eyes were stunning.

Bonita stood. In the shallow pool, her face was level with Lee's. Her forearms rested on Lee's shoulders. Her knowing smile hadn't wavered. Lee felt exhausted, but Bonita seemed sure of herself, almost casual. Their faces, their lips, were very close.

"I've been looking for you," said Bonita.

The possible meanings of the statement swirled in Lee's head. All she could muster was a questioning look. She wanted to say *Please explain this. Explain everything. Explain who we are.* But she knew instinctively that to do so would put her at Bonita's mercy. As overwhelmed as she was, Lee still held back her trust. Lodged fast in her throat was a kernel of fear, sustained by the mental image of the mouth she had seen disappear into Bonita's palm. She didn't trust the imagination that had formed that apparition just for the sake of a gesture. And there was another caveat, hovering at the edge of awareness. Lee had spent her whole life hidden. She couldn't bring herself to trust anyone who could see her for what she was. Not yet.

Bonita tilted her head, leaned forward so that her lips were inches from Lee's ear. "You're alone. Am I right?"

Slowly but surely, it dawned on Lee. The question had been quietly rising in her from the first second she had realized Bonita was a polymorph. In her initial confusion, it had been impossible to think about the question clearly. But it was inherent in the existence of another body-changer: Were there still more? Now Bonita had given her the answer. It was the source of Bonita's confidence, her surety. She had used the word *alone* to describe Lee because she, Bonita, was not alone.

There was no hiding that Bonita had the advantage. She leaned her head to Bonita's ear and spoke just above the music.

"There are more of us, aren't there?"

Bonita smiled her evil smile and said nothing. Lee despaired of simple answers.

Bonita's dropped an arm from Lee's shoulder and stroked her half-submerged calf. "Didn't you ever consider that you might not be the only one?"

Lee considered this. There was a mass of unarticulated memories to be negotiated. She had never spoken to anyone of this.

"At first," she said, "I thought everyone could change. Even before I found out what changing was,

I knew there was something that no one was telling me about. There was some force all around us that was powerful and frightening, and you could joke about it, or halfway suppress it, or fall into it with a vengeance and never crawl back out. When I found myself controlling where my muscles and bones went, I assumed that changing was the *something* that adults wouldn't talk about in front of us children."

Bonita looked at her quizzically.

"Turned out I was wrong. My parents were Reform Catholic. *Sex* was the hidden thing. It took me a couple of years to sort out that sex and changing were even different. Maybe I never really did learn to distinguish the two. So anyway, I spent my childhood thinking that changing was something only adults did, that it was part of experimenting with your body, like fucking or drinking or smoking, that kids weren't supposed to do, or even know about.

"The big surprise was when I started experimenting with other kids. One by one the hidden things became unhidden. I smoked a joint, drank a six-pack and puked, blew a guy off, felt up another girl. But those experiments somehow never led to talk about changing. I kept waiting for some older kid to say, 'So, can you turn your cunt into a dick?' "

Bonita laughed, leaned in a little closer. Her hands were warm on Lee's wet back. Lee's throat was a little hoarse from talking over the music, but she continued.

"Then I made friends with a kid called José. He was a pretty boy, and all the girls liked him. I thought I was in love with him. He was one of those kids who likes to play with his body. You know: burns his own skin with a lighter, puts a straight pin through the webs between his fingers, likes to show you his dick. He liked me because I could outdo all the other kids at the things close to his heart. I had double-jointed elbows, I could bend my fingers all the way back, and could curl my tongue like the devil, literally. So one day he came over and we spent an hour in the closet, trading secret knowledge by flashlight. I guess I went a little too far. I showed him one of my scariest face changes, which I used to practice in the mirror. He screamed bloody murder, ran like hell, and never came over again.''

Lee stopped. She had wanted Bonita to do the telling. It was new and strange to say all this out loud. As she spoke, the memories came to her as fresh as yesterday's. She had never spoken them, had even been afraid to write them down. Never before articulated, they came forward in whole cloth, pure and unretouched.

Bonita jumped into the pause. ''So, you finally figured out that you were a freak.''

''I wasn't sure right away. But I started to get the general picture. I figured that José would tell his parents, or the police, or someone, and that I was in deep shit. When no one came to haul my freak ass away, I vowed to keep my power under my hat. Having made a fool of myself, I went totally underground.''

''How very *human*,'' said Bonita. ''You made a mistake, so you adopted a position on the opposite extreme. Since *everyone* else was not a changer, no one else was. You went from Condom Catholic to existentialist.'' She laughed.

Lee didn't like the way Bonita italicized words at her. She realized she had said too much. She wanted to make Bonita talk. She decided to go on the offensive.

''How did you know me?'' she asked. If she was going to find more polymorphs, that was the key.

Bonita smiled and grasped Lee's ankle firmly, pulling her leg from the water. She felt the sole of Lee's foot for a few seconds, concentrating.

''As I thought. The hands give you away, of

course. Mother Nature did *not* come up with those mutations. But I wasn't sure. The brace was a good idea. I almost bought it: poor crippled girl. But you didn't hide them, like a cripple would. You seem to enjoy the shock effect your hands have. Even in this rather . . ." Bonita looked around at the revelry with cool eyes, ". . . accepting crowd, there's always the childhood imperative in the back of a disabled person's mind telling her that she's bad and should hide. You didn't grow up with those hands, and you sure wouldn't have paid a surgeon for them. So I watched you. When you got into the pool, you took off your shoes. I looked hard, and your feet didn't have any calluses. Surprise, surprise. It's a typical mistake, one I've made myself. I was doppelgänging this guy's wife, and I thought I had her perfect. But then he noticed that I was way too smooth; no writer's hump on my middle finger, no calluses on my heel, no cuticles—"

"You were what?" Lee strained to replay in her mind what Bonita had said. The music, her confusion, and the alcohol in her system made the last words too hard to process.

Bonita had stopped suddenly, seeming to realize she'd revealed too much. She smiled and kissed Lee's ear. With the license still heavy around them, it was exciting enough to be distracting. Lee pulled away to clear her head.

"When you watched me getting into the pool, I didn't see you," Lee said.

"You just didn't recognize me."

Shit, Lee thought. Bonita had made herself invisible by changing, almost as if it were as easy as combing her hair. Lee had felt the word "cripple" as Bonita had said it. It was directed at her. Compared to Bonita, her changing was slow and faulty. She shook her head.

She was tired as hell, and her beer drunk was turning sloppy. Having discovered another of her kind, she felt more alienated than ever. Her underlying fear of Bonita had settled into a measured dislike. There was something about Bonita that was too sharp and mean, especially in the warm and free environment of the Glory Hole. Bonita kissed her ear again. The advances were still enticing amid the newness of discovery, but there was something odd about them. Lee held Bonita close and gave in to them, trying to place it.

Around them, the pool had turned orgiastic. There were hands in pants, and pants that were off. The few boys had retreated out of sight. In the corner of the pool bounded by the club's walls, Kathy was going down on Wendy, dental dam gone to hell in the struggle to stay above water. Bonita's hands reached under Lee's shirt, and the lush feeling between her legs, which had never really gone away, expanded again. Lee relaxed. She had gone home with worse bitches than Bonita. She let herself sink down into the pool.

As her thoughts unwound from the tight knot of questions she wanted answered, they were reshuffled by the inane logic of her subconscious. Images from the past two days flew up in synch with her body's sexual response. Bonita penetrated her with a pair of fingers that gradually fused and smoothened, fingernails replaced by a cartilaginous ridge of bumps around the head of the new digit. Lee held on to Bonita's muscular shoulders and leaned back. She locked the muscles in her hands, so that her weight hung from Bonita without effort. Bonita's fused fingers splintered into a complex flower that probed Lee purposefully. Each offshoot inside her seemed self-directed, each wonderfully aware of her responses to its explorations. She drew in breath, expanding her vagina, and felt Bonita add another finger.

Her specific awareness of what Bonita was doing

to her fell away. Someone behind her, outside the pool, lent knees to lean against. An anonymous pair of hands massaged her shoulders. The slow internal progression toward orgasm began.

As waves of sensation cleared her mind, the dull-wittedness of beer and confusion lifted. Against the blank slate of the pleasure that engulfed her, she saw projected a faint shadow of Freddie's buzz, still inside her. Then it was replaced by a new connection; Bonita was linking herself subtly with nerves in the walls of Lee's vagina. It was not as extreme as her connection with Freddie had been, but it was still deeply intimate, and the approach of orgasm quickened. As the connection widened and intensified, the character of Bonita's imprint became apparent. She compared the flat, sharp texture of Bonita's nervous pattern with Freddie's more sudden, unpredictable buzz. As her body began to stiffen and pulsate, her mind remained strangely detached and observant. She started to gasp, and a wash of thoughts flooded her. She saw, with a finality as sudden and unexpected as any orgasm, what made Bonita and Freddie alike; what made them different from her.

The realization interrupted her orgasm, and she was only half-spent when she straightened and grasped Bonita's shoulders again. She had to know. She pulled herself to Bonita's ear and said in a firm voice, "You were born a man, weren't you?"

Bonita opened her eyes, a look of surprise in them. Inside her, Bonita's fingers re-formed. For the first time, Lee felt that she had gained the upper hand. It lasted for only a few seconds.

Then Bonita smiled her devil smile. She took Lee's hand from her shoulder and pulled it down into the water. Through the rough fabric of Bonita's jeans, Lee felt the unmistakable hard form of a large, engorged cock.

Lee's voice was dry. "You've had this goddamn thing all along, haven't you?"

"I wouldn't leave home without it," he said, smug as hell.

"You son of a bitch!"

"What's your problem? Don't tell me you've never had a cock."

"I have," she said. She leaned closer, her grasp sharp on the back of his neck. "But this is not a place for *pricks*."

He pushed her away with one finger on the center of her chest, and spoke sharply above the music.

"That doesn't make any difference to us. Gender is a *human* thing." She realized that, as once before, he had used the word pejoratively. "Besides," he said, "what's it hurt these dykes? Their mothers'd probably be glad they're in the pool with a man."

He didn't see it coming. Lee gave no warning, because she didn't realize what she was doing. The blow hit him solidly, open-palmed and flat, the heel of her hand right at the edge of his jaw. His face shifted briefly at its impact into a strange comic mask of befuddlement. He pulled it back together, but it still held a look of shock. One cheek was red, his lower lip split on one side.

Then he regained control. "You dyke bitch!" His voice was deeper now. He moved suddenly, and she instinctively raised an arm to ward off a blow. But he was out of the pool. He strode to the stair and turned back toward her, and his face shifted again. For a sudden, insubstantial second, he glared at her through a bizarre mask. His mouth lipless and suddenly too large, eyebrows devilishly arched, eyes reduced to slits, skin taut as a corpse's over his skull. The look was literally monstrous. It passed so quickly she doubted anyone else could have seen it. If they had, they would have fainted.

He turned and disappeared up the stairs.

She realized she had to follow him. How could she ever find her kind again? As she ran to the stairs, women parted quickly, alert with the embarrassment with which people react to a lovers' quarrel. The stairs were still wet where Bonita had passed.

The crowd upstairs slowed her progress toward the door. It had become still more crowded and butch, the women standing firm as she tried to press through them. She reached the door and stepped into the warm, fresh night air. There was no one in sight. She spoke to the doorwoman. "Did a woman just leave?"

"No. Some guy with no shirt on did, though. Looked mad, too. Somebody cut his dick off?" The woman laughed a low throaty laugh to herself.

Lee looked up and down Sixth Avenue. Bonita was gone.

There was a hand on her shoulder. Her heart sank. She would catch hell for hitting another woman in the club. She turned. It was Kathy, wet and flushed, but cheery.

"Girl, you *bopped* that bitch!"

Lee opened her mouth to explain but found herself speechless.

"I don't know what she said to you, but I never liked her one bit." Kathy paused, uncharacteristically thoughtful. "There was something about her that just pissed me off."

Lee couldn't help grinning. "You don't know how glad I am to hear you say that, Kathy."

A cool wind came up, chilling them in their soaked clothes.

Together, they went back inside.

A few women downstairs looked at her coolly. They had seen the blow. By the pool, there was a discarded black T-shirt. Lee frisked it quickly. Kathy, a concerned look on her face, put a hand on her shoulder. In a shallow zippered pocket sewn into the left sleeve was a single faded receipt, a phone number scribbled on the back. Lee blew the edges dry where her fingers had dampened them and tucked the receipt into her shoe.

Kathy offered to buy her a drink. Wendy and the other New Orleanois had left. They were catching the red-eye flight back home after all. Lee accepted. Her daze of confusion and alcohol had been broken by the adrenaline rushes of the last few minutes. But another sensation, quite unfamiliar, had replaced the bewilderment—a vast feeling, empty and reverberant, with a thin line of panic in it. She squeezed Kathy's hand harder and harder as they waited at the bar.

Somewhere in this massive city, there were other people who could change. Like her, they were hiding. No one could hide better. She had, for a moment, grasped a chance to join them, her own tribe. Now the chance was gone.

She looked down at the floor, a million kilometers below. For the first time in a long time, she felt alone.

Their beers in hand, Kathy led Lee to one of the back rooms in the hall and wound a few dollar coins into the lock.

CHAPTER 3

Candy

The next morning, she discovered that she had made it home.

Her brain was parched and beaten. She felt like something that had crawled out of the Bronx Free Enterprise Zone. A glass of water sat by her bed untouched. She swore. Her voice sounded like sandpaper trying to talk.

She popped four aspirol, and managed to drink about a third of the water before puking.

Hours later, the afternoon sun hitting her windows straight on, she woke up again. Her stomachs were on fire from the aspirol, but her head was steady. The puke by the bed was dried and thin. It reeked of alcohol. Her hands and the pillow smelled like chlorine.

In the shower, the water swung wildly between cold and hot, but she hardly noticed. Drying herself, she realized vaguely that her wrist was better. The muscles were still tender from disuse, but for the first time since curing Freddie the wrist felt whole again. She took the brace off and pitched it into the closet room.

She sat before the mirror. The vaguely familiar person that stared back at her looked pathetic. The muscles in her face were slack from the hangover. Her eyes were as bloodshot as a junkie's. The scar on her cheek was starting to scab, and her ass was sore with a fingertip-sized bruise. This last was Kathy's doing, she guessed.

She stood and bent at the waist until the top of her head touched the floor. She stayed that way, thankful that the aspirol had removed all dizziness. Vertigo was the part of a hangover she couldn't stand. Her arms rotated slowly through a full windmill, one way and then the other, and she straightened. Her hair looked like shit. She swore. It was time to deal with the hair once and for all.

She uncased the dog trimmer, and yanked open a spot on the power strip nearest the mirror. Plugging the trimmer in, she fumbled to set the blade into its carrier. She decided two centimeters was fine.

The operation was painless. The little motor buzzed against her head in a distant, benign sort of way. Dark locks fell around her like autumn leaves, only a straight, even burr remaining.

When she was done, she touched her own head with fascination. More than the way it looked, the feel of the buzzed, stiffly erect hair intrigued her. Her palm was tickled by its touch. She explored every square centimeter of her scalp. Looking at herself, she almost managed to smile. Between the red eyes, her scar, and the buzz, she looked like one mean bitch.

She sprayed down the puke with ammonia, and scraped it up with a handful of paper towels. She swept the pile of hair clippings into the biodegradable plastic bag she'd brought her last groceries home in and threw it all into the compost can down on the ninth floor.

On the way back up, she scratched her head. There was something she had to do today. Then she remembered. Track down the invisible. Find Bonita.

In her shoe was the receipt she had found in Bonita's pocket. It seemed to be from a restaurant. The name of the place wasn't on the receipt, just items and prices. On the back was a scribbled phone number and a name: Candy.

She didn't have a phone.

She dressed, moving cautiously in the fog of hangover. It was daylight, so she opted for the anonymity of all black. She found a mesh shirt that was fine enough to obscure her breasts and loose enough to keep her cool. The shorts she chose were a man's size, but their tight elastic waist held them on. They went down almost to her knees. She put on her fullerine sunglasses, which remained transparent in the dark apartment. The ashtray by the door was out of change, but there were three twenties under it. Between that and the $400 or so in her smart account, she wasn't doing badly; her next welfare direct deposit was tomorrow.

New York State gave her use of the apartment, subsidized by the Feds with FDPRA money. She rated Displaced Person status because of her welfare identity: Milica Raznakovic, a Serb refugee severely wounded in the vengeance bombardments after the Macedonian revolt. She had slipped in among a planeload of DPs at Kennedy, changed to an anthropologically generic Serbian body type with a horribly crushed leg and arm. She'd learned a few words of the most obscure Macedonian dialect she could find and claimed to know no Serbo-Croatian or Greek, just a half-fluent English. The overworked INS officials at JFK were happy with this unlikely identity. At the time, a lot of Eastern Europeans were showing up without their papers intact. She was given asylum, and eventually citizenship.

A few X-rays of her shattered limbs and she had been rated A-2 in the Cuomo hierarchy: set for life. On top of her $720 a week, she received a medical dispensation for prosthetics once a year. Her income wasn't much, but her needs were simple. If she ever wanted more money, she figured she could use her talent to get it, one way or another.

The prosthetics bonus had covered anatomy classes at Hunter College for two years. In that time, she'd learned everything relevant that the monomorph professors could teach her. The next bonus went to a computer. She poached various City University libraries for anatomy disks before her Hunter ID expired. Her true curricula, however, were the live bodies she picked up in bars. Anatomy classes were limited. The professors' understanding of the body was based on the static bulk of a cadaver, but her interest lay in the vital form. The bodies of her lovers, extended to their limits in the exhausting work of passion, were better textbooks than any disk she'd booted at Hunter.

The hall was hot and smelled of Spanish cooking. The elevator seemed to be working, but it passed her floor several times without stopping. She took the stairs philosophically; if the city were any more efficient, maintaining her welfare identity wouldn't have been so easy.

She changed two dollar coins into quarters at the corner bodega and fed its pay phone. Without any idea of what to say, she dialed the number. A digitized voice asked for two more quarters. She looked at the receipt, and realized that the number was a 9900- exchange, a pay call. Great, Bonita was a phone sex fan. No doubt Candy was his favorite. This was probably a waste of time.

She dropped in the money. Another digitized voice came on:

You have reached the Second Federal Guaranty money line. The charge will be 86 cents per minute. Hang up now if you do not want to be billed.

A resigned curiosity kept her on the line. She had more quarters.

Enter the PIN code for the account you wish to access . . . now.

It took a few moments for her to realize what was going on. When the voice asked her to, she pressed the # key for more time and dropped more quarters. Then she input 2-2-6-3-9: *Candy*. There were the obligatory pops and clicks of access. The voice came back, all business now.

Main Menu:
Touch 1 for account balance;
Touch 2 for last five transactions;
Touch 3 for the current rate;
Touch 4 to transfer money between working and high
     interest funds.
Touch 9 for an account specialist.

She pressed the 1 key. The emotionless digital voice named a staggering amount. When prompted, she touched * for the main menu again and listened intently. There was no way to transfer or withdraw the money.

Bonito, apparently, had figured out how to turn his soft flesh into hard millions.

The question was how to follow the money back to Bonita. She doubted that an account specialist was going to give her his name and address. Guaranties that handled accounts of this magnitude fought subpoenas to maintain their clients' privacy. She hung up.

She turned the receipt over and studied the bill. It looked pricey. Not much help. There were a lot of pricey restaurants in New York.

She got a seat at the bar of the Paradise Lounge.

The coffee was strong here. She focused the caffeine, forcing the hangover to retreat a little further. Her brain came slowly back to life. The receipt was printed on heat-sensitive paper. It showed prices and abbreviated names of dishes: *1specdujour, 1swdfsh, 2vchysois, 2cappno.* She remembered seeing a book on someone's coffee table once, *Menus of New York's 100 Finest Restaurants.* It had been oversized, with full color on every page; a coffee table book. She wondered if this restaurant was in it somewhere. The prices would probably be out-of-date by now, though. And what would she do if she found the restaurant?

From the Paradise house phone, she called the Main Branch Library in midtown. After navigating several levels of touch-tone branching, she finally accessed a human being. He told her that the tourist kiosk on the library network had access to on-line menus for all the expensive restaurants in town. He explained that she couldn't log on to it, though. It was direct-lined to terminals in hotel lobbies. When Lee asked specific questions about how the database worked, she was transferred. The next person to pick up had no idea what she was talking about. Transferred again, she found herself back to a touch-tone branch that she'd navigated before. She hung up. She needed help from someone who could log on to the NYPL service and hack the menu database.

She smiled. Freddie was her man.

AcNet was in the 411 directory. She called, and a digitized voice asked for the extension she wanted. She pressed 0 for a human and waited five minutes and two more quarters. The human came on and said that Freddie wasn't there.

She went one block west to the F train at First Avenue. The station reeked of the Transit Authority's new disinfectant, which smelled worse than urine. It felt like a hundred degrees on the platform. The only other person waiting with her was a woman on crutches, who swayed listlessly in the heat. She thought the woman might topple onto the tracks at any moment. She tried to remain very calm and still, and with great control managed not to break a sweat.

This close to the start of evening rush hour, the wait was short. Since she was headed uptown, the train wasn't crowded. The shock of air conditioning was brutal but welcome.

She wasn't sure exactly where Freddie lived but trusted herself to retrace her steps on foot. She exited at 23rd Street, squinting for the second it took the fullerine sunglasses to adjust. They were made out of the same fancy carbon as HARD plastic, virtually unbreakable. Rather than filtering light, they let a fixed amount through and completely shut out any light beyond that. When she washed them, water ran off the lenses frictionlessly, so they didn't need to be dried. They were good glasses.

She found Freddie's building downtown of the subway station. It was closer to the Glory Hole than she had realized. At the door, she remembered that the buzzers were broken. After counting windows, she started throwing change. He came to the window after the first direct hit, a loud flat smack against the double safety panes.

He waved, a qwerty bracelet on his hand, and disappeared. He looked glad to see her.

Freddie was out of breath when he reached the door, which she took as a compliment. They climbed the dark stairs wordlessly. His door was ajar. The sink was full of dishes, two qwerty bracelets thrown onto the kitchen table. He offered her a mug of the iced coffee drink they had shared thirty-six hours before. She accepted gratefully. In the study, his Sony was booted up, his VTV running the familiar screen saver program. She'd learned over the years that people's software, like their pencils, were usually stolen from the office. The bedroom was dark except for punctuated flares of light from the VTV in the next room.

They sat on the futon. There was a comfortable pause.

"So," he said, "*you're* a hell of a lover."

She laughed and waited, happily disarmed.

"I mean, next time leave a note or something." He ran his fingers through his hair. "I'm glad you showed up. I was gonna write you off as a dream. Nice dream." He paused. "Nice haircut."

"Thanks." The coffee was brutal on her empty stomachs, but worth it.

He repeated himself in a softer voice: "I'm glad you showed up."

"I'm glad I found you. I didn't have your number, and your damn buzzers don't work. It's lucky I hit the right window."

"My number's in the book."

"So what's your last name?"

He laughed, and said, "Smith." When she laughed back, he added quickly, "I'm serious, by the way. Smith."

"Okay, okay. Freddie Smith."

His eyes darkened.

"Where'd you get that scar?"

She realized she had been fingering it unconsciously and dropped her hand. "I cut myself."

He reached out and touched the scar. Another pause, that was more uncomfortable, and then he said haltingly, "You *are* a hell of a lover, you know." He almost seemed to blush.

"I'm glad you liked it."

"It's hard to think of anything else. Now I know why they . . . you know, everyone in charge . . . doesn't want you to enjoy sex too much. Why orgies are discouraged."

She smiled. For the last few weeks, the election

had settled into the usual round of moralistic mud-slinging. "It reduces their power over you," she said.

"And it makes it hard to get any work done! I have been the worst employee the last two days."

"That's what I mean."

He laughed and took her hand. "Oh, yeah. But I also mean, it makes it hard to concentrate. And to qwert . . ." He looked at her, an idea in his eyes. She could see him discard his thought as irrational. He had come close to asking a question.

It was time to distract him. "I have a favor to ask you."

His eyes lit up. "Sure."

She decided to put it as simply as possible. "I have a receipt, from a restaurant, I think. I want to find the restaurant." She showed him the scrap of paper.

He looked at it and turned it over. "Did you try this number?"

"Yes. It's a bank access number. 'Candy' is the PIN code. But that doesn't help me. I need to find the restaurant. The Library has a database with restaurant menus, but I can't get anyone up there to help me."

"You have interesting problems," he said.

He stood, looked around for a confused moment.

"They're in the kitchen," she offered. He left to retrieve the qwerty bracelets, returning with them on. Sitting, he flexed his fingers, and the monitor on the desk cleared. She stood behind him.

A series of overlapping windows retreated as he backed out of whatever he'd been doing. When the screen was clear, she saw that his system was bifurcated into a Delicious desktop and a Win6 domain. Her computer literacy was minimal, but she knew this configuration was impressive. She had assumed Freddie could hack, and was glad to see that she'd been right. He qwerted open a telephone icon on the desktop, and the white noise of disk access changed to the near silence of fiber traffic. The AcNet logo appeared.

"Aren't you going into the library service?" she asked.

"Yeah," he said, his words measured as he split his concentration between speaking and qwerting. "But we're going in through AcNet. NYPL responds faster if it thinks you're a network. Besides, city databases cost money, and this could take a while. I'd rather my employers pick up the tab."

A hacker's smugness tinged his voice.

She watched. In seconds, the New York Public Library seal appeared, and Freddie's fingers began to qwert in short, sudden bursts. The images on the high-resolution VTV shifted quickly. A flurry of windows opened, each from inside the previous one like Chinese dolls, then the screen froze and cleared. After a few still moments of fiber activity, the cycle started again. She strained to follow Freddie's course through the layers of access. The basic desktop background changed every few cycles as Freddie moved among the different systems installed over the years. He was searching for the tourist kiosk in the Main Branch, sifting through the various obsolete, up-to-date, and hypermodern machines that were kluged together to form the unruly cyberspace of the New York Public Library. She saw Freddie's two operating systems joined by a third as his Sony tried to compensate for the wildly incompatible generations of computers spread across the city.

He spoke in a distracted voice, just above a murmur. "Some of the older terminals at the Main Branch are pretty archaic, even compared to the primary system there, and they aren't directly connected to it. But they still maintain contact with their counterparts at other branches. If you build a UOS daisy chain of terminals out of and back into the Main

Branch, you can through-put connections between unconnected machines."

"Whatever you say," she said. As she watched the shifting images on the screen, though, some of what he said made sense. Windows opened and shut, some sharp, colorful, sophisticated, some with the tatty look of an old TV show. They offered glimpses into libraries across the city. The slow, monochrome text fields of a South Bronx database. The crisp, full-motion graphic domain of the new branch in East Chelsea. Different virtual worlds.

One of the older databases they encountered was dedicated to a Shakespeare concordance. The output was text-only. It probably had less memory than her portable. He paused at a few phrases: "tomorrow and tomorrow," "yonder window," "forever and a day." Whether it was literary interest or to check the machine's performance she couldn't tell.

As Freddie finally reached the higher-end computers at the Main Branch, one of the new prototypes caused the Manhattan Cable monitor to bleed with strange double images. Freddie explained that the Main Branch graphic environment was formatted for viewing with a VR visor. The uncanny landscape on the screen was studded with hypertext narrabases, *New York Times Book Review* kudos hovering over them unsteadily. Freddie showed how he could pick up the narrabase icons on the screen with mime-like motions of his qwerty-braceleted hands. But when he tried to open one, it shattered into fractile glitter.

He shrugged and murmured, "Not fully compatible, I guess."

The interleaved generations of computers in the NYPL system reminded Lee of something Freddie had said two nights before. The chaos of the library service resembled the kluges that held together the plumbing, heating, and communication systems of the real city. For that matter, it reminded her of the

complex legal maze of the welfare system. The lay-
ering of incompatible technologies in the library system created the same undependable, broken terrain.
She guessed that most computer networks suffered
from this generational incompatibility, that this was
the model from which Freddie had developed his
theory about the coming collapse of New York. Freddie's intuitions about the physical city's future were
inspired by the disrepair of the virtual worlds in
which he worked and played.

There was something to be said for starting from
scratch.

Still, he was enjoying himself, even if the network
was a mess. Behind him, she smiled. He enjoyed it
the way children enjoy playing in half-constructed
buildings and abandoned houses. He moved through
the broken terrain of the system as through a playground obstacle course.

As his search narrowed, his qwerting became faster
and faster, his breathing more and more shallow. It
reminded her of his passion two nights before. She
wondered if his qwerting speed had increased since
her surgery.

"Got it!" he cried, raising a hand in the air. A
handful of pulldowns crowded the screen as his fist
clenched in triumph. He opened his fingers slowly,
careful not to select anything.

They were inside the tourist kiosk. From here, se-
lecting the on-line menu service was simple. A few
copyrights and disclaimers appeared, and then the
title screen of the application. Freddie laughed. The
rococo screen was decked out with useless eigh-
teenth-century decoration. The interface was simple
and loud, with large buttons suited for fat-fingered
tourists using touch screens in their hotel lobbies.
After the morass of technological entropy they had
negotiated to find it, the user-friendly program itself

was comic relief. It had copious Help, it talked, and there were four languages to choose from.

Freddie started by probing its limits. He slipped into and out of a few of the restaurants' menus, ducking into sidebars, utilities, and small dialogue boxes crowded with credit card and reservation information. There wasn't much to it. In a search utility, he cross-indexed characteristics to generate a few arbitrary subsets: all vegetarian restaurants below Houston, all the places on Broadway that took Amex, and so forth. He began to look concerned.

"There's not a lot of power here. I don't think it'll search for item prices, which is all we've got to go on."

"What's under that dollar sign?" she asked, pointing to a pulldown icon.

"That just gives a general range, from 'affordable' to 'very expensive.' We need to search based on specific prices of specific items." He paused a second. "By the way, check this out." He momentarily switched the text language to Romanized Japanese, and the dollar sign morphed into a New Yen sign. He chuckled and switched back.

"Very cute," she said. "But back to our problem. Couldn't we just search them all?"

"Manually? Are you serious? There's thousands of menus in here. By the time we hit the right restaurant they'll have changed the prices."

"Shit," was all she could say.

"Well," he said, his energy a little faded, "when all else fails, read the paperware."

They looked again at the receipt. It was dated June 4. The meal was for two people: two soups, two entrées, and two coffees. Judging by the soups, the restaurant could have been French. But vichyssoise was a standard of expensive world cuisine, generic enough to be served at almost any fancy restaurant.

She looked at the mysterious numbers between the

subtotals and the final amount. One was probably the waitperson's designation, another, clearly the sales tax. The tip was also there, printed in the same dot matrix font as the other numbers. It was not a round amount. She tried some mental arithmetic, but soon gave up.

"Freddie, do you have a calculator around?"

He looked at her, slightly indignant, as one appeared on screen, overlaying the menu.

"Sorry. I should have known better. Listen, what's the relationship between the total bill and the tip? I bet it's a round number."

Freddie qwerted, and the amounts appeared on the calculator's readout. "Eighteen point one-eight repeating percent."

"Shit. Hardly round."

"But it's an *interesting* number," Freddie said. He was silent for a second, then his eyes sparked. "Right! You didn't mean the total amount, you meant the total amount before the tip. Look." He qwerted quickly, and numbers began to stack up on the calculator's extended readout. "When restaurants calculate the tip themselves, they don't include the tax before they multiply. So, without the ten percent sales tax, the tip is exactly twenty percent of the total. You were right. The tip was charged automatically."

"So, not many restaurants charge gratuity automatically, do they?"

"I've been to fancy ones that do," he said.

"Not for a party of two," she answered. "Listen, try to subset the restaurants that figure the tip for you."

"There's a field for that, but it's an exception field. I can't search it automatically. Whoever designed this interface didn't think anyone would care that much."

But he was already working. The calculator had been replaced by one of the menu program's utilities. A long table scrolled by, an alphabetical list of restaurants in its rightmost column. In the other columns of the table were various characteristics: credit card logos, the handicapped symbol, the green V for vegans, the cellular phone symbol with bar sinister. Freddie had highlighted one column, headed with the word "Special." As restaurants flew by, she saw that a few had superscript numbers in the Special column. Freddie's fingers moved like lightning. As each restaurant flew by, his left ring finger would flicker, and the restaurant name would carry a small black check as it filed up off the screen. He was manually marking all the fields containing a 5. In the fine print that was constant at the bottom of the window, she found the reference: "5: gratuities automatically included."

"We're on our way," he said.

It was manual labor, like some particularly grueling video game, but Freddie's speed never flagged. He punctuated his qwerting with curses. The process went on for twenty solid minutes.

When it was done, he sighed and said, "Damn, that was crude. Computers are supposed to do this stuff, not people. Man, I hate this town."

Freddie compiled the list of restaurants he had marked. There were 124 in all.

"Great," she said. "Now we can just check them all."

"Please," said Freddie. "Let's do this the civilized way."

He began qwerting. "I've been thinking. First of all, June 4 was a Monday. So, which of these places are closed on Monday?" In a few seconds, the list shrank noticeably.

She laughed, and clapped him on the back. The list was down to a few dozen restaurants. "Great. You're a genius. Now check to see which one of these damn places charges $17.95 for vichyssoise."

But Freddie was staring, openmouthed. He took

the receipt from her and stared at it. Then he shook his head. "We don't have to." He called up the menu for one of the restaurants and pointed. Vichyssoise was $17.95.

"But how did you know?"

He pointed at the restaurant's name, emblazoned large at the top of the menu. It was called "Candy." He handed her the receipt. Of course. Candy.

She groaned. The name wasn't just a bank access number. Like most people, when Bonito chose the PIN numbers and other codes that identified him, he picked words and names that meant something personal. Candy was a PIN number and a restaurant.

Lee considered this. She had glimpsed narrowly into Bonito's life. The information, even if it was basically insignificant, gave her confidence. Lee was willing to bet that Candy was Bonito's favorite restaurant. It was, in any case, a place to start.

Freddie leaned back and sighed deeply. "I may never eat out again."

She wanted to laugh but held her hands to her mouth. Freddie's hands hung slackly, his eyes were red-rimmed. She took his wrist and looked at the clock on his qwerty bracelet. They had been at it for more than an hour.

"Listen, thanks a lot. You're amazing."

He looked at her with a weary smile. Then he held his wrist where she had touched him. It was the wrist he had worn his brace on.

"There's something I've been meaning to ask you," he began.

"When does Candy open?" she interrupted.

He looked wearily at the monitor. "Six."

"Shit, I've got to go. Listen, I owe you a big favor. I'll call." She backed toward the kitchen and the door.

"Don't you have a phone number?" he asked.

"No. No phone. Honest. But you're Freddie Smith, right?"

"Right. In the book."

She paused, her hand on the door. He had not gotten out of the chair. "Are you the only one?" she called.

"The only what?"

"The only Freddie Smith. In the book."

He considered briefly. "I don't know. I doubt it."

"I'll try them all."

"It serves you right," he said, managing to grin.

"Good-bye, and thanks again." She came back into the bedroom and bent over him. They kissed deeply.

"I hope you find this guy," he said. "But call anyway."

"I will," she said.

She took an old Japanese cab home. The ethanol-burning engine accelerated the low, saucer-shaped car like a bolt of lightning. At her projects, she threw the driver a twenty and didn't wait for change. Candy was opening in thirty minutes. She wanted to get there as soon as possible. She dropped fifty cents into the phone on the corner and made a reservation for six-thirty.

The elevator wasn't working. She cursed as she took the stairs, two at a time.

She felt faint by the time she reached her door. Fumbling her card through the door's reader, she realized that she hadn't eaten much today. At least she would be hungry for a long dinner at Candy.

The windows had been closed all day, and the closet was stuffy with the smell of old clothes. She stripped and searched quickly among the few suits that hung tightly packed on the wire. Most of her formal wear was out-of-date, suitable for the funky aesthetic of a downtown club but not for an expensive restaurant. She found one suit, less threadbare than the rest, that might pass inspection. If she kept herself young, the antique-blue suit would look affected rather than simply old. Spreading it out on the bed and unrolling the sleeves, she measured its cut with her eyes. With the body just right, the suit could seem well-tailored.

She found her whitest shirt. The suit was double-breasted, so the stains on the shirt front wouldn't show. The closet held a lot of ties—they were easy to steal—and she chose black silk. As always, the shoes were the hardest choice. She wasn't quite happy with the black, tasseled, fake-leather ones she decided on, but they were the best she could find.

When the clothes were all laid out, she sat before them and considered the shape that was to fill them. If Bonita was at the restaurant, she needed to be as anonymous as possible. Her usual goal, to create an odd and striking juxtaposition of features, would have to be discarded. Bonita's eye was too sharp. She left the clothes on the bed when she went before the mirror. The apartment was much too hot to perform a change in the heavy suit. She stared at her wonderful, alien hands once more, trying to memorize them. She sighed. Once gone, she doubted the hands would be easy to re-create.

As she stared, she felt the chemical triggers in her body build slowly toward change. Her stomachs churned, and her breath became ragged and harsh. A sweat broke across her back and inside her thighs. Her eyes closed, and her mind concentrated on the image she had designed to fill the suit. The upset in her gut became harsh pain, expanding and then rushing into her head and hands. It pressed relentlessly against her soft organs, pushing them into small neutral holding shapes, out of the way while around them the structure of bone and flesh shifted grossly. Panting, she rolled onto her back.

Her body stretched in length, the pain pulled into

taut, bright strings of fire up and down her nervous system. Her bones grew thinner and more porous as they stretched into the larger frame, skin sliding slowly off breasts and buttocks to cover the increased surface area. Her breathing had almost stopped.

There were sharp jabs as her pelvis broke and rejoined, thinning and elongating. The change was taking longer than it had two days before. In her haste, it was more brutal. She paused to take a few breaths. Her half-formed lungs protested and seemed full of fluid. Then she started the hardest part of all.

The fiery pain gathered and concentrated itself in her genitals. With a conscious effort, she pushed the sensitive walls of her vagina outward. Nerves screamed as they hit the hot air of the room, the soft tissues folding inside out to form a long, soft member. He shaped it slowly. To cover it, he drew skin from where folds of flesh hung loosely around his narrowed hips. He relaxed again. The newly arranged muscles in his lower back were sore from the contractions that had formed the penis. He wondered if this raw, exhausting pain were like that of giving birth. As the tiny tubes and nerve bundles wove themselves inside the penis, he wondered briefly if he would ever dare the wrenching, uncontrolled experience of making a child.

Usually, he changed the fragile vocal cords as little as possible; keeping his voice low for a woman's, high for a man's. Now, however, he lengthened and reinforced the chords, deepening his voice to disguise it thoroughly. He sighed half-vocalized *aaahs* as he tuned the larynx to a chesty bass.

He was tired, and the balance of hormones in the new body dizzied him. But he wasn't done yet. He relaxed more deeply.

When he had quieted his body enough, a set of newly-made glands opened to release a rush of chemicals. The hormones spread across his skin like oil on water. The warm, heady glow of melanin played upon the flesh of his limbs, trunk, and face, breaking onto the surface like a light sweat. He let the process go forward, intervening only occasionally to even the melanin across his skin. He made sure that his palms and soles remained a dark pink.

There was more. Woven through with a thin and flexible cartilage, the texture of his cheeks and chin hardened and roughened. This subtle change gave his face the scratchy feel of a five o'clock shadow. (Once, he had increased his testosterone level until hair grew on his face naturally, but it had been hell to get rid of.) He was also sure to callous his hands and feet. This time he wasn't giving Bonita's sharp eyes any clues.

When it was done, his breathing slowed. He turned over and looked into the mirror.

The body was tall and lean, the muscles standing out sharply under taut skin. He rotated his legs, arms, and digits socket by socket. The joints between limbs and trunk moved with a loose and agile flex, and the muscles felt too strong for the slight frame. He had never been this tall or this thin before.

The face was unremarkable. He had summoned it from the blurry images of half-remembered faces on the subway, and had shaped it with less attention than he usually employed. The nose seemed a little broad to him. He narrowed it with a rough massage, chastening himself for this stereotypical touch. His high forehead was emphasized by the buzzed haircut, but that was the only feature that stood out. This would be a good face for a spy or an undercover cop, fading into the crowd as he trailed a suspect. The only thing in the mirror that struck him was the intent gaze on his face as he inspected the new body.

The long fingers touched his member carefully. It was still tender. Usually, the transition from male to female left a deep and resounding horniness behind.

The change from a vagina to the exposed and fragile male genitalia, however, just left him vaguely sore.

When he slowly licked his lips, luxuriating in their fullness, he wondered if his tongue were too red. He stuck it out inhumanly far and looked at it top and bottom, but remained unsure. A few minutes with the anatomy disks assured him that African tongues were no darker than Asian or European ones. He smiled at himself. As usual, he felt a little uncomfortable with this transition. It was a glimpse into a world that went further than skin deep.

He showered cold and dressed slowly. His metabolism was still running high from the change, and he didn't want to overheat. The suit fit perfectly. Perhaps it was easier to fit a body to clothing than vice versa, or perhaps it was simply that any suit would look good on this thin model's body. He struggled with a pair of cufflinks from the ashtray by the door, ultimately succeeding only with help from his teeth. He spent too little of his time as a man to negotiate male formal wear easily.

He took the stairs at an even pace, the address of Candy firmly memorized.

On the street, he remembered how hard it could be to get a taxi. A few went by, empty and with their duty lights on, while he stood with arm outstretched. It was a petty humiliation that brought back memories. He (then she) had spent a winter semester at Columbia as a woman of color. She had clung to the form longer than any of her others, trying to pin down the difference in her professors' and fellow students' attitudes toward her. Of course, sometimes the difference was plain. But when it was latent, it hovered like a smear at the edge of vision. It slid sideways when looked for, retreated when confronted. It was deeply buried there in the well-educated environment of medical school, but it was present. In that cold, depressing time she had discovered the Glory

Hole. Among the sexually marginalized, her difference was, if anything, overcompensated for. She welcomed the warm acceptance she felt in that small, hot fortress of sophistry, as inclusive and definite as the sexual action in the pool.

He walked half a block to Houston, where cabs came by more frequently. Eventually, one stopped. The driver was a white-haired woman from Queens. She bitched about the election, which had already begun to snarl traffic in Midtown. Both nominees-apparent had addressed the UN for the anniversary of the climate treaty, and it had been a long time since either party had held a convention far from the compressed national media market of New York. Gridlock seemed to paralyze the city on a daily basis.

Candy was in the East Thirties. The driver shot up First Avenue until forced westward to the brief and crowded two-way stretch of Second Avenue that skirted the Fire Reconstruction Zone. The '02 Fires had taken down a solid stretch of Chelsea East; mostly hospitals and the Stuyvesant projects. A plan to replace the burned tenements with the city's primary light rail station had raised hackles, and the reconstruction of the entire neighborhood was mired in protests and court actions.

By the time they had cut back to First Avenue, Candy was only a few blocks farther up. The restaurant was situated in a grand old building that had stretched along a quarter mile of the East River. The giant, turreted redbrick castle had been a psychological hospital until the city's bankruptcy scare at the turn of the century. Now it was an odd melange of residential, office, and retail space, neon and halogen lights gleaming harshly through the scant openings in the dark old stone.

They turned up a grass-lined drive, and the driver strained to read the copper signs mounted discretely by the roadside. She wound her way to the north-most tower of the old structure.

"This looks like it." He paid silently. He felt compelled to tip well, having arrived at such an auspicious address.

Past a uniformed doorperson, the holographic sign in the lobby read, BELLEVUE TOWERS #2. Candy had its own elevator. He fingered his smart card half-consciously in his pocket. This was going to be expensive.

A young white woman in strange livery trimmed with red mylar pushed the Up button for him as he approached the elevator. The button glowed a bright laser red in the dim lobby. The elevator arrived without a sound, and the inside door slid open. The woman pulled open the copper-colored outside gate of the elevator. He entered the spacious car, and she reached in to push the largest of the few buttons on the control panel. She pushed the gate back across the entrance, and the inside door slid closed quietly. The elevator was floored with bright-green carpet and as dimly lit as the lobby. Soft music played as the car ascended.

The walls were mirrored. Being imitated by his new reflection was momentarily disconcerting. Usually he spent a few minutes in front of the mirror at home before venturing out in a new body. He straightened his tie and regarded his nose critically. Suddenly it looked too thin.

The door opened. A young woman, who wore the same livery as the woman downstairs, said, "Welcome to Candy." He was speechless for a moment, then he got the joke. The women were identical twins. For a second, he'd felt like the elevator hadn't moved at all.

But this was Candy.

The elevator faced a long room, about ten meters wide. One side was walled in dark, red brick. The row of giant industrial windows, filled with reddening sky and the East River, comprised the other. Small tables lined the walls, most of them empty except for the flicker of a single candle. The music in the restaurant matched that in the elevator seamlessly, not missing a beat as he stepped out.

An old white man with wild gray hair, who looked like he could have been left over from when the place was an asylum, asked if he had a reservation.

"Mr. Milica Raznakovic. For one."

The maître d' looked at him a little strangely, probably thinking the name didn't fit the skin. He accepted it, though. The good thing about the Serbian name on his smartcard was that, as unusual as it was, it could pass for male or female, Eastern European or simply Other.

He followed the maître d', who led him along the tables against the wall. In the nearly empty restaurant with such extravagant windows, this was something of a snub. He charitably assumed that his rumpled suit was the cause. He steered the old man to a table in the back corner, by the kitchen door. The view from the windows was splendid, but the corner was a better position from which to observe. The long, thin room allowed an unobstructed view of the rest of the restaurant.

From behind a menu, he surveyed the other diners. Across the central aisle, a pair of women with empty wineglasses spoke to each other earnestly. One wore a white dress that was plagued with huge black polka dots. Her hat matched it. The other woman wore a coral-red jumpsuit under a white fox wrap. He cringed. A large MOMA bag was stuffed under their table. They were rich tourists.

Farther away, two Asian men in business suits studied their menus silently. They were Japanese; the *Shimbun Romanji* lay neatly folded on the table. They were dressed in muted, conservative colors. Somehow they didn't seem like Bonita's style.

A young Anglo woman sat with her back to the window, reading by the ruddy, polluted light of sunset. A glass of champagne fizzed, untouched, at her elbow. She was absorbed in the book, concentrating serenely. Occasionally a smile would flicker at one side of her mouth. A cigarette dangled, its ash precariously long, from her lips. He studied the petite, round face for future use. Her nose was small and upturned, leading back to a strong brow. The center of her forehead was marked by a vertical frown line. Her bare shoulders and upper arms indicated a body that tended toward chubbiness. Her lips were very red, as was her hair.

She was wearing a green strapless dress, formal enough to get into Candy, at least at this early hour, but funky enough for a downtown club. Her body was small, well-rounded, and sensuous. The calf of one crossed leg was tattooed, but fishnet stockings hid any detail from his eyes. He instinctively liked the woman, and found it hard to believe she was Bonita.

A waitperson appeared. Knowing that he might be here for hours, he ordered a small glass of sherry, saying he hadn't finished with the menu yet. He hadn't.

The only other table in use was occupied by a pair of couples in evening wear. The men were dressed in black tie and the women in long silk dresses, probably to catch an eight-o'clock curtain. A gunmetal champagne bucket rested on three ornate legs by their table, and their voices carried to his ears over the soft music.

He began to realize the hopelessness of his mission. Any of the four might be Bonita. For that matter, so could one of the other five patrons. He didn't know the extent of Bonita's powers; she might be able to change her mass, her hair color, her eyes. His own limitations precluded certain shifts, but Bonita's abilities were an unknown quantity.

There was another problem on top of all this. He reluctantly let form the thought that had been bugging him all day: Bonita might never come to this restaurant again.

More immediately, the place was expensive as hell. The *prix fixe* dinner he was considering, marked with a warning that extra preparation time was required, was priced at over three hundred dollars. He would need several slow courses if he was going to sit here for the whole night, but it would be a costly night indeed. He leaned back and pondered.

Bonita's existence was a piece of information that would not, no matter what Milica did, go away. From now on, he would feel his aloneness. His innocence was irrecoverable. Until he found other polymorphs, his solitude was as desolate as a shipwrecked alien's. As he considered this, some resolve returned. In some ways, this new knowledge took his reality to a higher resolution. It was as if the long, unfocused twilight of his adolescence were breaking into clarity. The day before, the world had been peopled by a featureless mass, beings distinguished only by their sexual roles and the features of their bodies that he could arrogate. Now, reality had become defined by that most distinct arrangement; it was divided into *them* and *us*. *They* had always been there, but now *we* had taken form. And Bonita was one of *us*.

The waitperson returned with the sherry and lingered to complete the order. Milica smiled at her, folded his menu, and put off dinner with an old and expensive bottle of red wine. After all, Bonita had proved that there was money in being a polymorph.

He drank the wine slowly, waiting until the bottle was half emptied before ordering his chosen prix fixe. Over the course of a long, varied, and excellent meal, the restaurant swelled with a host of faces and bodies. He kept his ears finely tuned. There were lawyers, tourists, commodity brokers, currency traders, diplomats and emission rights dealers from the UN, junk bond salesmen, prostitutes, software engineers, drug dealers, politicians—all the varied flotsam of late capitalism. Through the various stages of melancholy, elation, and profundity that are the inevitable result of eating (and drinking) alone, he searched for a sign that one of them might be Bonita.

Through it all, the woman in the green dress remained a strangely constant presence. First by the waning sunset, and then shifting in her chair to catch the candlelight, she silently read her book. She looked up occasionally for brief, annoyed instants, but otherwise seemed unaware of the passing time. The staff made no move to ask for her order, and twice refilled her champagne glass without asking. As the crowd swelled and subsided around her, she was curiously self-contained and alone.

Milica's long-delayed main course, wok-scorched albacore with pineapple salsa, had just arrived when the woman was joined by an angular young man. He was underdressed, wearing a blue blazer and white pants. Milica detected a slight hush in the crowd as the young man crossed the restaurant. It was the hush of celebrity. The society women at the next table exchanged knowing glances. The maître d' shuffled over to pull his chair back for him, and they shook hands after he was seated. The woman in the green dress closed her book and offered her hand across the table. He kissed it, and they laughed together.

Other people arrived and left, but Milica watched the two of them. The young man was animated, garrulous, and intense. He spoke in long torrents of words, punctuated with broad sweeps of his arm.

Each time their waitperson would refill a glass or
retrieve a dish, the young man would include her in
a few minutes of his frantic conversation before letting her withdraw. He drank champagne like water.
The woman remained steady, as unflappable as when
she'd been waiting for him. She chainsmoked her
long cigarettes, coolly regarding him with large eyes,
sometimes interrupting his stories with a wave of her
hand and a single, precise comment. Whatever she
said seemed to keep him off balance, kept him rolling
from one torrent of words to another. The two were
perfectly matched. They were pure theater. Instinctively, and from clues in the eyes of the other patrons,
Milica understood that tonight Candy revolved
around these two.

He returned his gaze to the rest of the crowd.
Again he counted bankers, lawyers, actors, the idle
rich. It seemed an easy thing to categorize these people, who gave no thought to subtlety. But no matter
how he tried, he could not see Bonita.

It was easy to survey the room unobserved. Most
eyes were on the young couple. One woman, who
sat alone at a wall table by the front door, seemed
particularly interested. She was watching intently,
surreptitiously taking notes on a small palmtop. She
looked like a reporter. Milica took it as evidence that
he had been right about the young couple's celebrity.

Then he noticed a peculiar thing. The reporter's
dress was cut identically to that of the young woman.
It was the same shade of green. After a moment of
considering what this might mean, he realized that
the two women shared the same haircut. Suddenly,
the woman put down her palmtop. The look in her
eye had changed. Milica shifted his gaze to the
couple.

The young woman had produced a tiny telephone,
was telescoping its mouthpiece. She spoke into it for
a moment, then covered the receiver and spoke to

the young man. He frowned. She stood, leaned over the table to kiss him, and then went toward the elevator. Phone in hand, she disappeared through an archway marked with the international symbol for bathrooms.

The other woman stood, a determined look on her face.

She walked toward their table. As she strode, her face rippled, the brow jutting a little forward, the cheeks fattening, the nose shrinking. Milica realized how close the two faces had been in structure, though the resemblance had been invisible until now. He was again awed by Bonita's ability. Milica looked quickly around. No one else seemed to have registered the change.

She reached the table. Approaching the young man from behind, she took his shoulders. He turned, perhaps a little surprised. She remained standing and spoke to him quietly, their heads close. Then, suddenly, she kissed him. The kiss was hard and intimate, her hand behind his head, her feet planted a little apart. Milica wiped his brow and looked toward the bathrooms. There was no sign of the real girlfriend.

Bonita lingered with the young man, toying with his hair and shirt, whispering into his ear. She stayed just behind him, intimate but ready to move.

Milica waited, glancing from the couple to the archway. Bonita's confidence was maddening. Milica found himself more and more anxious. It was like watching a thriller, wanting to scream, *Watch out, she's coming back!* But he realized that the monster was Bonita.

After a few minutes, she surely disengaged herself, patting the young man on the shoulder and striding away toward the bathroom. Milica watched in fascination as the real girlfriend emerged, as if on cue, and the two passed each other without apparent rec-

ognition. Bonita must have shifted as soon as her
back was turned, subtly enough to escape detection,
completely enough for the other woman to ignore
her as they passed. Not for the first time, he was
amazed at the blindness of monomorphs. Of everyone in the crowded restaurant, no one else seemed
to have noticed the artfully choreographed exchange.

On the other hand, it had been too neat. Someone
must have cued Bonita that the woman was returning. Perhaps someone had arranged the phone
call as well. He searched the crowd again. The faces
were disinterested, gay, and unalert. He wished for
more powerful eyes. If Bonita had accomplices, they
were as smooth as she.

The woman, the real woman, rejoined the young
man, and immediately started to talk frantically. She
had been upset by the call. The young man seemed
confused for a moment but remained quiet. From his
perspective, she hadn't been gone long enough. Milica saw questions rise in him a few times, but as
with Freddie, they never materialized. Milica smiled,
having seen it before. Life was built of small inconsistencies, and people rarely bothered to sort them out.
If they did, Milica himself would have been found
out long before.

Then he saw Bonita across the room, paying. He
rose and fumbled for his smartcard, looked for his
waitperson. She was nowhere.

He walked quickly toward the elevator, a little
wobbly from the wine and long meal. A foot was
asleep, and he bombarded it with oxygen-rich blood.
As he drew closer to Bonita, he became wary and
slowed. He stopped at the maître d's podium, only
a few feet from her. She glanced at him, and his
spine iced over, but her eyes passed over him without change. Milica felt himself cloaked by an anonymity four hundred years old. He had felt this
invisibility before—at taxi queues, in medical classes,

at uptown bars. He realized that he had chosen this disguise instinctively, subconsciously sure that Bonita was the sort of person who would look straight through a black man.

The maître d' appeared, and Milica asked for his check. The old man nodded and spoke into a handphone. The elevator arrived, and the liveried twin ushered a few drunk and underdressed teenagers off. Bonita stepped inside.

Milica waved his card at the maître d', who shrugged his shoulders. No check had arrived. The copper gates slid closed. Milica's heart sank as the car slipped away.

The next elevator came up empty, and he left the slightly baffled staff of Candy behind with a vague and hasty apology for being in a rush.

On the street there was no Bonita, just a line of taxis and limousines. She had melted into the night again.

He was no closer, but much poorer.

CHAPTER 4

Sean

Outside Bellevue Towers, the night squatted, a wall of humidity and heat. The door worker offered him a taxi, but he declined. He still had a slender line of connection to Bonita: the couple, still upstairs at Candy. He would wait.

He told the door worker that a friend was picking him up. The man offered a small elegant house phone. He pretended to dial and made a "no answer" face at the door worker.

"I'll wait," he volunteered. The door worker frowned slightly.

He was soon sweating. He tried to concentrate on negotiating the passage of the complex and heavy meal through his system, but he was drunk and very tired. The wine was too far metabolized to be neutralized. The drunk was a vague and listless one, which the heat turned to a kind of sleepy torture. He wanted to sit, but the edges of the sedate fountain beside the Tower's entrance were toothed with loiter spikes. He looked for stray stars in the mercury-vapor sky. In ten minutes he counted only seven.

He heard their voices behind him.

As the couple emerged from the lobby, a stretch limousine rolled out of the darkness. The long black car moved almost silently on tires that had the deep-cut treads of solid fullerine Pirellis. The plates were New Jersey. Across the limo's back window, the re-

flective matrix of a microwave antenna glimmered.
The engine was fully gas-burning, raising a ghostly
curtain of exhaust in the bright white fountain lights.

The chauffeur got out and opened the rear door.
He wore a wire-thin headset, the bead in front of his
mouth smaller than a teardrop. He was a large man,
his uniform creased with the rigid bulk of kevlar.
The flickering glow of a monitor showed within the
car. There were already people inside. The driver
fixed Milica with a suspicious stare as the couple
approached.

The two had a short conversation in front of the
limo door and then embraced. Milica realized that
they weren't leaving together. He sighed with relief.
The thought of pursuing the limousine and its impos-
ing chauffeur had scared the hell out of him.

He strolled slowly to the taxi queue and took the
second one in line. As the driver ran Milica's
smartcard through the cab's reader, the young
woman took the cab just in front, as he had hoped.
Milica's driver, a man of color with a patois name
and accent, handed the card back and said, "Where
to?"

"Follow the cab in front of us." He felt a little
ridiculous saying it.

"You mean it?" the driver said. "You a reporter,
right?" The woman's cab pulled away, and they
followed.

"Why do you ask?"

"Come on, man! You want me to follow the girlfriend of the King of America, and you are not a
reporter? Who you think you fooling?"

"The King of America?"

The cabbie laughed and said, "Don't you know the
King, man?"

"I didn't know we had a king. In fact, I didn't
know we had much of a government at all right now.
The election seems to have paralyzed everything."

The driver struck his head with an open palm and made a grunt so strange that Milica considered briefly that he might be insane. "Ah! You may not know it. He's much more important than the President. He's the one with the big power. *Enter, Accept, Confirm.* The King."

Milica leaned back into his seat and waited in silence. He hoped the driver would stop talking. Usually he enjoyed the occasional performance that went with a cab ride, but tonight he wasn't up to following the story.

"That's right! That's why he's come, to give us a king. Maybe it's not so good to have a king, but it's better than nothing at all." The man reached up and adjusted the rearview so that he caught Milica's eye. "Take it from a Haitian."

Milica reflected drunkenly on this.

They headed downtown for a mile, never more than a few meters from the woman's cab, then turned onto Delancey. As they followed it eastward, Milica became afraid that the woman might be headed for Williamsburg Bridge. The evening had been expensive enough without a cab ride to Brooklyn or Long Island or who-the-hell knew where. But then her cab turned up Pitt Street.

Pitt was the easternmost street but one in the Lower East Side proper. It was separated from the river by the Gompers projects, which had been half burned down in the Turn-of-the-Century Riots and were still under FEMA control.

Pitt Street itself was well named. To the east, the dark bulk of the jagged buildings loomed behind a tall razor-wire fence. The entrance to the shattered projects was through a narrow gate framed by a metal detector. Next to the gate was a long, one-story building stenciled with the Federal Emergency Management Agency seal and marked with illegible glyphs of hurried graffiti. The building sat on cinder blocks and had the shabby look of a once-temporary structure that has become permanent. The other side of Pitt was lined with four- and five-story residential brick buildings. Gates were down over the ground floor storefronts. Only one streetlight on the block worked.

The cab in front of them was slowing. Milica's driver stopped half a block behind it. They waited, and he said, "What you think, man?"

The interior light of the woman's cab turned on, and he could see her red hair as she leaned forward to pay.

"This is fine," Milica said.

"So, if you are not a reporter, you maybe just *like* this girl?" the cabbie asked.

"Actually," Milica said, "I think she's in danger."

"From you? You don't look like a dangerous man. And the King, he look like a nice man."

"No." He named a tip, and reached forward to authorize it. "From someone I met last night. A real mean son-of-a-bitch."

The driver whistled. "Well if I was you, I'd tell the King. He'll kick that son-of-a-bitch's ass. He'll kick your ass, too, you mess with his girlfriend. *Newsday* says they are in love." The driver nodded his head vigorously.

"In love, huh."

"It's a Cinderella story, man. She a local punk girl, and him a king!"

"Thanks for the advice," Milica said. "Bye."

"Take care," said the cabbie.

The woman had gotten out and taken a few steps down a basement doorway, disappeared. Milica's cab pulled silently away behind him.

As he walked, he discarded his tie. He wouldn't miss it. There were advantages to having a roomful of clothes. He rolled up the jacket's sleeves and opened his shirt, trying to look like he belonged in the neighborhood.

The building was an old church, decorated with a crude mural of Jesus, in whose chest an anatomically correct heart glowed bizarrely. Behind Jesus a cityscape had been painted that matched the view uptown. The painted city was alive with glowing headlights, windows, streetlights. Under Jesus, a scroll bore the words, "A Thousand Points of Light." The windows of the church were boarded over. The crucifix above the door was decorated with bits of broken mirror and safety glass. Shiny fragments had also been glued to the surrounding brick, as had a host of cherubic plaster faces. From the basement doorway into which the woman had disappeared came the muffled murmur of a crowd.

A color photocopy of a row of drummers on the door was captioned, TONIGHT: EMPIRE LOISAIDA SAMBA SCHOOL. Nailed to the door above it was a crudely painted sign:

LOISAIDA SOCIAL CLUB

Inside the door, two young Hispanic men checked him out. The cover was five dollars. A pall of smoke hung from the low ceiling. A hundred-or-so customers crowded the basement room, dancers occupying a good part of the floor. Behind them, a line of about a dozen drummers swayed as a short white woman shook out a compound rhythm on a beaded gourd, soloing while the rest of the drummers caught their breath. Beside her, an old Hispanic man listened intently, eyes shut, a metal whistle in his mouth.

Along the far side of the club a makeshift bar had been constructed, a row of sawhorses that held HARD plastic I-beams. The red-haired woman was there, sitting on a rickety stool, a can of beer beside her. He made his way toward her.

The gourd player's solo waned in energy, tapering off to a quiet but persistent shake. The old man raised one hand, and the drummers lifted their sticks. There were tambourines, small hand drums with bright tassels, a trio of snares, a whole family of larger drums, a concert bass that almost hid the Asian kid it was strapped to. The old man blew three sharp blasts, reestablishing the almost lost tempo. There was one silent fourth beat, filled by a gasp from the crowd. Then the sound of the massed drums exploded like a car bomb in the small club.

The concussion of sound struck Milica bodily, almost halting his progress. Around him, onlookers flowed like water onto the dance floor. The naked rhythm was furious, driving the dancers into a blind frenzy. Milica stumbled as he negotiated the maelstrom.

When he reached the bar, he stripped off his jacket. The length of the bar had been half-emptied by the music, but the red-haired woman remained. He slipped onto the stool next to her.

She gave him a sidelong look and seemed to recognize him.

The bartender brought an open beer and spread his fingers to indicate five dollars. Milica paid. The beer was a Brazilian import, the can warm in his hand. The empty case-boxes stacked behind the bar bore its logo. Evidently, it was the only drink the social club served, and to sit down was to order one.

It was thick as English bitter. For warm beer, it was good. In the hot, smoky club, logy with rich and exotic food, it was the last thing Milica needed.

The woman's legs were crossed, and from this distance he could see her tattoo through fishnet stockings. It was a trompe l'oeil, designed to look like the flesh of her leg was freshly torn. Inside the shadows of the faux wound, Milica glimpsed the metallic sheen of vaguely organic machine parts. It looked like the leg of a damaged cyborg; torn flesh and ruptured machinery wound together indistinguishably. He had seen the style before.

She caught him staring and shifted to give him a better look. "It's a Hunter."

"What?" he yelled above the din.

"A Hunter. A tattoo by Hunter, the tattoo artist. Wanna take a picture?" Her accent sounded like Brooklyn.

"Uh, no. Forgot my camera."

She shook her head in disbelief. "What kind of reporter are you?"

He frowned. "Not one."

"What?" It was her turn to yell.

"*Not* a reporter," he said.

"So why'd you follow me? Pervert?"

He laughed. She held his gaze. He leaned a little closer, lowered his voice.

"I live near here." Paused. "But yeah, I followed you."

She leaned back, satisfied. "Thought so. Saw you at Candy."

"Yeah, I was there."

They sat uncomfortably for a few moments. She reclined, a cigarette at a precarious angle in her mouth, and seemed to be waiting for an explanation. He searched for one, hopelessly.

"I'm a tattoo fiend."

The odd statement piqued her curiosity. She turned to face him better.

He talked, activating a small change, a churning of skin along the inside of his arms. "So when I saw your leg at Candy, I got excited. I couldn't stop myself from following you. I've got this thing about . . . body manipulation."

Her eyebrows raised.

"Well . . . you should have just come over."

He shrugged his shoulders. "Your boyfriend was there, and it looked like a romantic thing. I didn't want to walk up and say, 'Hey, can I look at that hole in your leg?' "

She smirked. "I'm used to it. So's my boyfriend." Then she frowned. "I'm surprised you haven't heard of Hunter. He's the big name right now."

"Don't know the scene, I guess."

"I see." She took a drink. "Got any yourself?"

There had been just enough time. Milica rolled up his left sleeve. From the inside of his elbow to the wrist, two parallel ridges of flesh ran, pink and raised. It was an imprecise job. The skin was strangely wrinkled between the keloids, a more frightening sight than he had intended.

Her eyes widened.

"Wow. That's not a laser process, is it?"

"No. Actually, it's all done with wooden tools." He rolled up the other sleeve. The pattern was the same, but the scars were wider. "I guess you wouldn't call them tattoos. Scarification."

"They're beautiful," she said. She didn't seem to be bullshitting him. Her eyes were still wide. "Are they tribal?"

"My mother was half Yoruba."

She nodded in a way that indicated the word meant nothing to her. Milica was relieved. He'd read an article—somewhere—about Yoruba scarification, but there hadn't been pictures.

"Did it hurt much?"

He smiled. "Like hell."

She shuddered. "I'll stick to lasers. Quick, clean, removable."

"Expensive."

"Got a rich boyfriend." She fluttered her eyes, unapologetic. He was starting to like her.

"So I saw. Nice limo."

"Yeah, he's into cars. Likes tattoos, too. On me, anyway. I don't know if he'd go for any scars, though. When we met I had a lip-ring. Didn't like that.''

She stubbed out her cigarette and pulled out a half-empty pack. She contemplated it for a moment before pulling one out. Then she tilted the pack toward him. "Want a gasper?''

He shook his head. The slang term pegged her as definitely Brooklyn or Queens.

"My name's Milica.''

She raised an eyebrow. Pronounced, the name sounded distinctly female. He spelled it out for her.

"That a Yoruba name?'' she asked.

"That's what Mom said.''

She nodded and said, "My name's Sean.''

"Well, Sean,'' he said, raising his beer, "here's to rich boyfriends.''

They toasted and drank. Then Sean licked her lips and said, "It has its ups and downs.''

Milica sensed an opening, decided to take a risk. "I once read that the very rich are very strange.''

She looked away, and he thought he had offended her. Then, out of the side of her mouth, she said, "In some ways, they aren't even remotely human.''

There was a pause. As it stretched out, he felt the connection they had established slowly unravelling. Her reactions were somehow distant. He caught an image of himself in a dirty mirror behind the bar, and remembered how plain and unremarkable he had made his face. It had been a long time since he had been anything but beautiful, or at least striking. He considered how different it was to be average-looking, how it affected even the most simple conversation. As practiced as he had become at facile repartee, he realized that most of his ease with people was bought with the superficial currency of appearance. It brought back memories of childhood. He had been plain faced as a little girl.

He tried to salvage the conversation.

"You thought I was a reporter. That because of your rich boyfriend?"

She turned to face him again. "Yeah. He gets a lot of press. Gets followed. He's made some enemies. Has a shitload of security."

"What's his name?" he asked.

She looked at him squarely. "Ed." There was an edge in her voice.

"Sorry. Didn't mean to intrude."

"I just don't know if I trust you."

He held her gaze. "I don't blame you. Why should you trust me? I mean, has it ever occurred to you that this guy might want to spy on you? Rich boyfriends do that, you know."

"Oh sure. His security people are around me all the time." She looked around the club. "Somewhere. Protection. But you aren't one."

"How do you know?"

"First of all, you're a lousy spy. I mean, you stumble in here five minutes after I do and sit next to me at the bar. And you don't fit the corporate type, anyway."

"Why not?"

"You're African." She made the last point with a wry, unapologetic grin, stubbing out another cigarette.

He grinned back at her. "Yoruba, to be specific."

"I'm from Brooklyn, myself." She looked around. "I hope you're really not a reporter. I don't think Ed would like it if some gossip columnist found me here."

"What's the matter? He doesn't like you mixing with low life?"

"No. It's just that—" she paused, looked at him intensely for a moment, and then shrugged. "I'm meeting someone."

He couldn't hide his surprise, and so he exaggerated it. "A secret lover?"

She laughed. "It's not a secret from Ed. He knows I'm an Amy-John. In fact, it turns him on. But we get enough press as it is."

He took a drink, trying to place the slang. "I just liked your tattoo."

She smiled and said, "Thanks."

He returned her smile, but an awful thought had occurred to him. He waited, silent.

The samba band let the barrage of sound fade again, instruments dropping out one by one until only a young African kid on a tight and tinny snare remained. The others musicians listened intently.

Milica realized that in these periods of relative quiet, an energy built slowly in the club. The solo drummer had the undivided attention of the band, and the dancers waited anxiously for the next assault. The old Hispanic man seemed to concentrate most during the solos, whistle at the ready, his eyes shut in a deep, ecstatic trance. As the sound of the single drum slowly faded, Milica found his anticipation building. In the dimming rhythm, the dancers were less frantic, but took on an intense, feral look. Their smaller movements became sudden and shifting, like big cats in small cages.

Then a face caught his eye. A woman strode through the dancers, undeterred by the moving bodies. She had a steady confidence that carried her untouched through the crowd. She was tall, beautiful, and Italian. The lines of the face were not much changed from the night before.

And the uncanny green eyes were on Sean.

She approached Sean from behind. When she put her hand on Sean's shoulder, Sean melted to the touch. Sean turned and kissed Bonita. Their hands came together. Bonita leaned her head close and spoke in Sean's ear, as she had with Milica the night before. A few words were exchanged, and Sean leaned back and indicated Milica with a small jerk

of her head. Milica's full stomachs suddenly felt vacant and sour as Bonita turned toward him. For a
moment, her expression was murderous. She turned
back to Sean, who seemed to explain something
quickly. A movement of her eye indicated his arms,
where the scars were still exposed. Bonita turned
back to Milica, looked him up and down. The familiar evil smile played on her lips.

And she offered her hand.

With a shudder inside, Milica took it. Bonita's
handshake was weak. The grip shifted slightly, one
way and then the other, feeling the surface of Milica's
palm. The shake lasted only a few seconds, but felt
like a lifetime of practice had gone into it. An almost
unconscious habit, to check for calluses or other
clues; to determine if the person touched was another
polymorph. A thought shook Milica: *Are there really
so many of us?*

He looked for a hint in Bonita's eyes that he had
been discovered. But that same vacancy was there,
the unveiled disregard that looked straight through
him. Bonita simply wouldn't suspect that she might
have turned herself into a black man. And Milica's
new hands were very callused.

Bonita put a hand on Milica's shoulder and leaned
forward confidentially. She drew very close, closer
than was necessary to speak above the all but inaudi-
ble samba beat. Almost at Milica's ear, her lips whispered, "I saw you at Candy, didn't I? If you're a
reporter, I'll kill you." She leaned away, smiling.

The voice had been almost as low as a man's. It
had been a subtle transformation in the complex
soundscape of the club, but distinct. Bonita knew
how to make a point.

A surge of the same helpless panic she had felt at
the Glory Hole overwhelmed Milica. Bonita was too
powerful not to mean what she said. Milica shud-

dered, wondering what Bonita would do if she discovered who he really was.

Then the whistle blew its three notes, and the drums of the Samba School exploded yet again. Sean and Bonita shared a wicked, childish glance into each other's eyes. Sean jumped up and ran to join the swelling mass on the dance floor. Bonita followed her, with a dark glance look at Milica.

The two danced.

There was a strange intensity about Bonita. Her attentive gaze never left Sean's face, hair, the energetic movements of her compact body. Bonita would often reach out to touch her arm or grasp her hand, as if the lack of contact in the frantic dancing was too much separation to bear. Milica allowed himself to think for a moment that Bonita was in love with Sean. Maybe it was simply a triangle: Sean in love with Ed, Bonita with Sean.

But as Milica watched, adjusting his vision to make up for the darkness and smoke, he concentrated on Bonita's face. It was attentive, but there was a cool and distant intelligence about it. Bonita collected every motion with her eyes, attended the shape of every muscle rippling beneath Sean's skin, caught each expression on her face. Bonita was not drinking in the sight of Sean with the vague appreciation of a lover; she was measuring her.

There was a kind of malevolence about it, an eerie acquisitiveness. Bonita's stare did not savor, it penetrated. Watching Bonita watch Sean, Milica realized that she was here for one reason only.

She was perfecting her impersonation.

Bonita had dared sustain her imitation at Candy for only a few seconds. A fleeting moment of conversation and a hasty retreat, a practice skirmish. But before the change, Bonita had been watching there, too, recording every detail as the couple interacted.

Milica could see it clearly on the hot dance floor,

Bonita absorbing, motion-by-motion, the woman she danced with. *Doppelgänging*, he had said in the Glory Hole.

"Doppelgänging some guy's wife."

As the drums began slowly to subside again, Bonita tugged Sean toward the door. Sean turned and waved at Milica as they left. He smiled back at her, feeling hollow inside. There was no following them. Bonita was too dangerous.

And home was very close.

Milica stayed at the bar until the chill in his spine subsided.

As he walked home, Milica looked into a few paper-only trash cans. In one he found a slightly crumpled copy of the day's *Newsday*. A telegraphic headline about pre-convention posturing filled the front page of the tabloid.

He stood under a streetlight and leafed through it. There was nothing about a king. The cab driver had clearly been insane.

But there were ways to track down the very rich.

At a pay phone, he punched 411. Phone numbers for various Freddie Smiths were listed, but at the word "Chelsea" the information voice narrowed it down to one. Milica reached for his smartcard to record the number. The card was gone.

He searched the jacket and pants pockets as the number repeated in his ear. The voice asked if he needed more help. His *yes* was sharp, annoyed, and the machine didn't understand. He hung up in disgust. He emptied the trash can he had salvaged the *Newsday* from, scattering newspapers, paperbacks, junk faxes. Finally, he retraced his path for a couple of blocks. Nothing.

Swearing, he stalked toward home. His apartment door was coded to the smartcard, and the superintendent wouldn't recognize him. The domino players would probably let him into the lobby, but the doors in the projects were strong. The best he could manage would be to sleep on the roof.

He kept a duplicate card in a safe-deposit box on Second Avenue. The upscale bank used a retina scanner, which so far had never failed to identify him. Thinking through the process calmed him, and he detoured toward a pay phone to report the card lost.

Then Milica stopped in midstride. The card wasn't lost. It had been stolen.

He heard Bonita's voice. *"If you're a reporter, I'll kill you."*

He imagined a slender tentacle formed from Bonita's left hand as she leaned close to deliver the threat, reaching into his jacket and lifting out the card. Bonita's words weren't empty. She wanted to know for sure whether Milica was a reporter. She left nothing to chance.

With a good hacker, Bonita could have his name, his address, his numbers within hours. Milica tried to calm himself. Probably, what Bonita found would make her happy. She would have little interest in a welfare recipient from the projects. But the invasion of anonymity was monstrous to Milica.

There was, of course, another possibility. Bonita might have recognized Milica from some clue that he wasn't aware of: his hair, a flaw in his eye, an eccentricity of bone structure. Bonita might have developed an organ able to identify a polymorph's characteristic pheromones, for all Milica knew. If Bonita had lifted his card to track him down, she might be at the projects within hours. Perhaps she was already there.

Milica sat down on the stoop of a bodega, his head heavy in his hands. His body still complained from the meal, and he realized how little he usually ate compared to other humans. His belly felt bloated. The beer and wine struggled in his bloodstream. A warm night breeze carried the scent of urine from the stains that ran down the metal storefront grates.

He realized he would never be safe in this identity again. It was time to disappear. He considered changing but was simply too tired.

He secured his last twenty-dollar bill and a handful of change and threw his jacket away. With the edge of a discarded aluminum can lid, he ripped the shirtsleeves and the cuffs of the already wrinkled pants. The shoes fit less perfectly after he had removed the socks. He replaced the belt with a length of extension cord he found protruding from a split garbage bag.

When he was done, he stumbled north toward Tompkins Square Park. The orange sky looked hours from dawn. First Avenue was empty except for a pair of guards sitting on upended milk crates outside a brightly lit Korean. They eyed him suspiciously as he passed the shelves of fruit on the street.

On the south side of the park, a FEMA cruiser lurked under the overhang of oaks. The big six-wheeled van had been parked there for a year. Its black fullerine windows and gun ports stared blankly into the night. Milica avoided it, slipping through a rip in the barbed wire on the park's east side. The park reeked of dog and human shit, and there were no anarchists here.

He made his way toward the old community center. The cinder blocks that had sealed its front door were broken down, but an old white man with a pentamidine inhaler stared vacantly back at him from the opening. Milica moved on.

He walked around the park for half an hour, finally settling under the lean-to of a collapsed chain-link fence. The fence protected the grass under it, where a riot of weeds and viny growth softened the ground. Exhaustion drained his consciousness within a few minutes.

*   *   *

Morning light woke him early. He was sore from sleeping on the hard dirt and was covered with a thin film of something worse than sweat. As fresh morning air blew over him, not yet hot, his head cleared quickly. There was a procession of the park's inhabitants toward the southwest corner, where the rattle of Hare Krishna drums signaled a free breakfast.

He wasn't hungry.

He was mad, violated in some way he'd never felt before. In stealing the smartcard, Bonita had not only compromised an identity, she had stolen a hiding place. In his long-cultivated niche in the margins of the city, Milica had been free from the dictates of tribe and social strata, unencumbered by the mechanics of the state and the imperatives of the monomorph economy. But now Bonita had breached the private and secure realm of his deception. Along with Milica's identity, Bonita had stolen his anonymity, the only thing that Milica had really cherished as a signifier of who he was.

Bonita was going to pay.

He shambled onto the street, looking for a place to change.

PART II

The Principle
of Mobility

CHAPTER 5

Self

She replaced the shoes with tied rags. The shirt hung like a tent over her. The pants had to be belted just below her breasts.

An oily mist hung in the morning air. More HARD plastic ash had fallen during the night. Its color was different, and it was finer than usual. She wondered how much of it she had inhaled.

The walk to Freddie's seemed longer than it had the day before.

Few homeless were fit young Asians, and there was a strange visibility in the shambling gate and strong smell of an indigent. Eyes turned away. The gaze of storefront security guards turned harder. Shoppers tried not to stare. A German tourist took her picture. She realized that homelessness was very public—a world defined by other people's vision.

At Freddie's door, the buzzers were fixed and the buttons labeled with bright metal nameplates. A security camera pointed at her from a corner of the vestibule. She leaned on Freddie's buzzer for a solid minute before he answered. He sounded sleepy, and his voice implied that seven-thirty was a hell of a time to drop by. At the door, he said, "Jesus Christ," and stood back as she entered, his eyes wide.

"Mind if I use your shower?"

He recovered a little. "Please do."

The water, extravagantly heated and pressured, restored her humanity.

Drying herself, she stared sullenly at the filthy pile of clothes she had discarded. She stepped out of the bathroom naked. Freddie was microwaving two mugs of his Japanese coffee drink. He looked at her body in a kind of unself-conscious daze.

"Mind if I borrow some clothes?"

He rubbed sleep from his eyes and managed to find his voice. "If you insist."

The microwave buzzed. He looked at it as if the sound were new to him.

She searched his closet with coffee mug in hand. The plastic was strangely hotter than the coffee. Freddie stood by, having rediscovered his self-consciousness, his eyes on the brick wall outside his bedroom window. It didn't take long for her to dress. Compared to her collection, Freddie's clothes were all woefully alike. She chose a black shirt with bright-red sleeves and a pair of huge-legged shorts like roller bladers wore. They came to just above her knees. As she pulled them up, he turned toward her. She looked into his still-sleepy eyes, and for the first time noticed they were flawed with tiny radial keratomy scars.

There was one of Freddie's usual pauses. He seemed in no hurry to speak. She realized she didn't know what to tell him. For once, the silence made her nervous.

"Your buzzers got fixed," she offered. It felt like an idiotic thing to say, but it roused him.

He smiled happily. "Yeah. Welcome to the People's Republic of 104 Sixth Avenue."

"Rent strike?"

"There's no one to pay rent *to*. No one has legal title on this place anymore. The first tenant group disincorporated, the managing agency went out of business, and the guaranty bank is under FDIC warrant. So we're all—most of us, anyway—paying five hundred a month to an escrow account. This month, we took some money out to fix the buzzers. Next month, the doors."

"Sounds like a good deal."

"The rent's cheap enough. And it's better than the street. Speaking of which." He made an expansive gesture with his mug. It seemed to refer to her, to the whole situation.

"Yeah," she paused. "You must be wondering. I'm, um, sort of underground right now." She had meant to be flip but sounded to herself as if she was on the edge of hysteria.

He didn't react, except to take a drink of coffee. They looked at each other.

She decided to say as much as she could.

"You know the guy I was trying to find yesterday?" she asked.

"No. But I remember you were looking for someone." Freddie was speaking carefully. He didn't sound completely friendly.

She went on. "Well, I found him. But he didn't want to be found. In fact, he said he'd kill me." She looked down at her hands.

"Who is this guy?" His reserve hadn't lifted.

"I don't really know that much about him. His name's Bonito. He's rich, powerful. And he knows something about me that . . . that I can't tell you, or anyone else."

"Ah," he said. The sound was completely noncommittal.

She already regretted her decision to tell anything of the truth, but barreled ahead. "Last night I tracked him down. He didn't know who I was, though. I was . . . in disguise. But he got hold of my smartcard. So now I figure he's got my numbers and I'm afraid to go home."

He considered this. The mention of the smartcard seemed to steady him, to put him on firmer ground.

He said, "You mean he found out . . . this thing about you that you can't tell me about . . . from your card?"

She shook her head. "He already knew it. He just didn't know my name, or where I live. But he's rich. By now he's probably had someone soak my card."

Freddie nodded. "Probably." There was a flicker in his eye, and he added, as if an afterthought, "Your scar is gone."

"My what?" she started, her mouth dropping open. Her hand went to her cheek. The knife wound she had opened two nights before was gone. It had been subsumed in her change to a male body, and she'd forgotten to replace it.

She tried to smile, as if letting him in on a joke. "It was fake. Scar Stuff, like Gothics started wearing a couple of years ago."

His voice was steady. "No, it wasn't. I touched it. It was real." He reached out, and she took an involuntary step backward. He waited, arm half outstretched, until she moved forward again.

He took her hand. Looked at it intently. Took the other. He splayed the two sets of fingers out. Inside her, a cycle of adrenaline and noradrenaline began, the sick feeling of panic being fought under control. It was made worse by the realization that she was not preparing for violence or action; there was no fighting or flight out of this situation. She was being violated again. Her citadel of privacy, of deception, was again under attack.

She knew that the deformed hands were not the same. Her transition, without a mirror, without enough sleep, without the X-rays and 3-D views on a nearby screen, had been faulty. She hadn't realized how perceptive he was, how exactly he had noted the deformity.

He raised his eyes to hers. She could not hide her panic.

"Your hands have changed." He put it simply. As if it were some interesting but unenlightening datum amid a host of clues. She had never seen anyone react to this discovery before, and she had no idea what to expect. Only Bonito, with his sick and knowing smile, had ever found her out; and Bonito was a polymorph himself. Freddie looked at her steadily, the impossibility and the truth of what he was suggesting dawning on him slowly and surely.

There was a long pause, in which her mind flailed for the radical act that would save her secret. The pressure in her head built, until the red mist of an incipient blackout gathered at the edges of her sight. She removed her hands from his grasp and sat down heavily on the carpeted floor.

He was instantly beside her, an arm around her shoulders.

"What's happening to you?" he asked, his voice soft for the first time.

"I'm—" she choked on the word. "I'm different."

She constricted into a fetal curl, tired and disoriented from too many changes, feeling a hundred times more naked than she had in front of Bonito. Freddie, a monomorph, had begun to see her for what she was.

The nervous energy building inside her finally found purchase: It triggered the chemical of a change. She submitted to it and held out her hand to Freddie. The fire formed in her abdomen, became a pulsating sphere. The muscles of her arm bulged as the ball of pain forced its way toward her hand. There were a dozen unrelated, unbidden transformations, spontaneous in the wake of the fire. Her right aureole flared, one shoulder dislocated, and she felt the warm rush of a swath of melanin breaking into a mottled birthmark on her forearm. When the fire

reached her hand, she set it to work savagely; breaking down the small bones before they were properly
limbered, threading the muscles strong and thick
through the lengthening digits, leaving nervous tissue screaming in the skin as she reshaped her hand
against his.

When she was done, she opened her eyes, blinking
away sweat. He sat, expressionless, staring at her
transformed hand on his lap. It looked a little swollen
and it ached badly, but it was basically normal. Next
to it, her other hand looked freakish.

She sat, raising herself a little tenderly on the new
hand. He was speechless.

She tried to smile. "There you have it."

"Your hands. They were fake. Like the scar." There
was no accusation in his voice; just a small distance,
someone speaking of something lost.

"You don't see, after all, do you?" she said tiredly.
"It's not just the scar and the hands." She rose to her
knees. Now that she had shown him the change, she
was pleading for him to understand. "It's the face,
the eyes, the body, the bones, the cunt, the voice, the
muscles, the skin. It's *all* fake. Or none of it's fake,
really. It's all whatever I want it to be."

His eyes came up from the spot where her hand
had changed. They were clear, penetrating.

"And the nerves . . . the nervous tissue," he added.
He rubbed one forearm against the other, frantically,
like a junkie. "You can change your own nervous
tissue. That's what happened to my carpal. You can
change other people, too. You came in and fixed me,
didn't you?"

As she nodded, he moved forward, grasping her
by the shoulders. The right one was sore, and she
cried out. He kissed her softly on the mouth. "Thank
you," he said.

He held her, and after a while the fear that had

sutured her to consciousness collapsed. Slowly, she passed out in his arms.

She awoke on the futon. He was watching her from the floor a few feet away. She came fully awake quickly. His gaze was too intent to doze under.

She was naked. Her hands, shoulders, nipples were uneven. The new birthmark was still there. She rubbed her normal hand with the alien one and sat up to lean against the coolness of the wall.

"Seen enough?" she asked. She tried to find terror or disgust in his gaze.

"I have a hundred thousand questions." He smiled. There was only amazement in his eyes. And something else. Affection.

"What's the first one?"

"Hungry?"

"Starving." The prosaic thought of food filled her with relief.

While he took a shower, she dressed and turned the VTV to cable mode, losing herself to the mind-numbing drama of the Housing Court Channel.

They ate Japanese at a restaurant next door. It was only two in the afternoon. Her imbalanced hands were far more embarrassing and annoying—than they had been when both were deformed. Her new hand was still swollen, and chopsticks proved impossible despite her ambidexterity. She was too mentally and physically exhausted to make any corrections yet, having changed more often in the last few days than she usually would have in a month.

She answered Freddie's questions as well as she could. It was hard to fight her instincts, which screamed for deception. But the slow unraveling of the truth brought an awesome feeling of release. As they had with Bonita two nights before, her memories unfolded pristine and urgent.

Her life's story was unrehearsed, unarticulated.

The telling was new territory to be traversed, unre-fined by the habits of a familiar narrative. She real-ized how strange it was to have such a strange story, yet never to have told it.

Because Freddie was from the Midwest, he was amazed even by the mundane: childhood in the proj-ects, a public school education in impoverished New York. He was as interested in these as in her slow realization of her ability and of its uniqueness. It made telling the story easier, to mix the prosaic fact of an absent father with her secret experimentation on skin, bone, and sinew. Judging from his reaction, her first venture out in a fully changed body as a teenager seemed no more strange to him than her everyday existence in welfare housing.

Instead of Bonita's knowing smirk, Freddie's reac-tion was unconcealed awe. His mind was quick to adapt, however, to see the inherent tensions and chal-lenges in her position. His questions were intelligent and teased out strands of continuity in her life that, having no interlocutor, she had never assembled before.

For five years her life as a polymorph, scattered among clubs and communities, sundry identities and sexualities, had shown her a host of difference. She had learned not to take sides and to accept any num-ber of roles. She looked on the monomorph concept of identity with contempt. It was founded on vio-lence and power. In a terrifying city, full of people who clung to their roles as a bulwark against its hor-ror, she had sought anonymity as a moral imperative. But as she spoke to Freddie, the flow of memory broadened and her past began to open to her. She began to rethink her isolation.

Bonita's appearance had triggered a need that had long been latent in her. She had assumed that the community of polymorphs was the answer to that need, the hunger for a tribe. But now the desire was changing in her, taking on a more concrete form. She wanted to organize her memories for a listener, to explain her life story. As she spoke, she realized that she had been living without a past. It had been a pleasant hedonism, timeless and anonymous, but it was utopian in both senses of the word: a good place and no place at all. She found herself tripping over words in her hurry to tell Freddie everything, to explain everything. There was a fierce need to draw together the many lives and make a life.

Across the small table from Freddie, she began to invent herself.

"Do you ever see your mother?" he had asked at one point. She was still trying to answer.

"I keep just one picture of myself—my original self." She saw him register the idea that she had an original self, an infant body. "I've stared at it for hours, trying to remember what it was like to be *that*: a short, ugly, Dominican girl from Loisaida. It's one memory I've worn out: The day my mother took the picture. She'd bought a disposable camera off a rack outside a Korean. For no particular reason, she went through the apartment taking pictures of everything. The furniture, the cats, the brick wall against the kitchen window, just as fast as the whining little rechargeable flash would let her.

"She seemed to need to secure these things, these objects, this house. And as I followed her around, half hoping she would take a picture of me, I saw something in the flash: that everything was frozen." Freddie's look questioned her. "You know, when the flash pops and there's an afterimage burned into your eyes. That was what my mother wanted—that freezing flash—to keep everything the way it was.

"As I realized that, I felt myself turning away. Because what I wanted was *out* of that apartment, out of those projects. Shit, I was fourteen and I could change myself into anyone I wanted. I'd have wanted out of any place. And, with a mother's instinct, she chose that moment to take a picture of me. When we got the pictures—that was back when you mailed them in—she made me a big present of my picture. It was horrible. It's *really* a bad picture." She laughed.

"That night I changed my body all the way for the first time. Made myself look twenty-five, went out to a bar about two blocks away, got shit-faced enough to be afraid I couldn't change back."

"Could you?" he asked, all amazement.

"Yeah. Back then I was like a rubber band. I tended toward my primary shape naturally; snapping back was easy. But now I'm pretty loose. The difficulty of any change depends on where I happen to be at the moment.

"But anyway, to answer your question, I don't see my mother anymore. After I moved out, I tried to, but it was such a drag changing back into that old body. She had my address, and she came by once looking for me. I told her to her face I didn't know who she was talking about. I was a man at the time."

There was a rush of moments in which she couldn't talk. Freddie was silent.

"I moved a week later," she continued, her voice small. "Since then, there's been no one. No one who knows who I am."

"So, I'm your only friend," Freddie said plainly.

She took his hand, but was distracted by a thought. "And Bonito my only enemy."

"Right, Bonito. So how the hell did he find out your dark secret? Did he catch you in the act?"

"No." She paused. Having told Freddie about herself, she was still reluctant to reveal that Bonito was also a polymorph. Not that she gave a damn about Bonito's privacy. It was just that Freddie would realize that if there were two polymorphs, there were probably many. As long as Freddie thought of her as unique, a mutant, the larger community of poly-morphs (wherever they were) was still a secret. "All I know is that he has a lot of money. I assume he somehow got hold of my data trail, or my welfare identity's data trail, and figured that something was weird about me. Since then he's seen me in two different bodies."

"I suppose that's probably it," said Freddie, in a voice that didn't confirm belief.

"In any case, he's got my numbers by now," she rushed to add. "He's had my card for almost a day."

"I think I can help you with that. That is, I've got a friend who can. If Bonito's been soaking your card, we might be able to double back on him. Even if he hasn't left any traces, you've got his PIN number, right?"

She groaned. "Shit! The receipt! It's at home."

"Can't your super let us in?"

She looked at him darkly.

He figured it out. "That's right. Your super doesn't know you. You're the invisible woman. But you must have a copy of your card somewhere."

"Yeah. Safe-deposit box."

"Of course! A bank with a retina scanner."

"Pretty smart, Freddie."

He looked nonplussed for a second. "Thanks. But at a bank? What a hassle. I just leave a copy of my card with my friend Sam."

"You trust him that much?"

"Leaving your smartcard with Sam is like giving your phone number to NYNEX. He doesn't need it, anyway. Sam's my friend. After we get your card and the receipt, we'll get his help."

"I'm not sure if I want to risk going home," she said.

"But you can disguise yourself as anyone! And he's never seen me. Who is this Bonito guy, anyway? Why are you so afraid of him?"

"He's the devil." She smiled, but to herself she sounded serious.

"Great. Thanks for telling me. Look, if I had the devil's bank account number, I'd risk going home to get it."

"Can't we do anything with the PIN code? CANDY, remember?"

"Not without the account number," he said with finality. "Account numbers are rule-governed and unique, passwords are self-chosen and therefore may be duplicated." He said it like a rule. There was more to Freddie's hacking than playing around in the New York Public Library system.

"If you say so. All right, we'll go." She paused for effect. "Got a gun?"

"Just an electric."

She snorted. They paid and left.

In a strongbox high in his closet, Freddie had a knife as well. A triangular-bladed trench knife, military issue and a lot more battle-worthy than her Canal Street switchblade. She slipped the knife into the enormous pockets of her shorts. It had just about enough blade to piss Bonito off. She also took a large black vinyl duffel bag that she had seen in the closet.

They taxied to the bank in an unair-conditioned electric Ford whose radio cheerily announced that it was over ninety degrees again. Freddie waited outside with the weapons. The metal detector at the bank's door offered a gravely digital *Thank you*. Downstairs, she leaned over an ancient and grimy retina scanner. Bright green flickered over her eye twice, and another synthesized voice assented. The guard, a short and compact black man, left her alone with the safe-deposit box in a cubicle with yellowing seven-foot walls. She would have traded him the box's entire contents for the pistol he wore, an old but formidable revolver with a wide, short barrel.

Inside the box was another smartcard, reassuringly identical to her last one. The picture her mother had taken was also there. After a painful glance, she left the picture. The dues on the box were paid up in cash for seven years. Some part of her might as well have a home. She was glad she hadn't charged the box to her smartcard. The safe-deposit box was the last inviolate corner of her life.

The sun was bright outside, and she made a mental note to collect her sunglasses at the apartment. She remembered to take the knife back from Freddie.

They ate at a Dominican-run Mexican restaurant called El Sombrero, taking their time, waiting for evening. She wanted to enter the projects after kids had gotten home from school and were playing in the hallways and stairwell. She figured that if Bonito turned into anything too monstrous, some kid might shoot him.

They waited. She was quiet. Freddie asked her what Bonito looked like. She described him roughly as he had appeared at Glory Hole, knowing it was useless. She warned Freddie that Bonito might have hired someone else.

"Just asking," he said.

Her nervousness began to rub off on Freddie, and he began talking about his childhood. They split one margarita and then another as the sunlight angled steeper and steeper. She fed the jukebox her last few dollar coins, stalling and trying to find a samba piece with only drums. There were none on the box's drive. Finally, Freddie paid and pulled her to the door. Her project was two blocks away.

As they entered the lobby, the old men looked up from their game of dominoes. She looked them over surreptitiously. All looked vaguely familiar. One or two of their glances lingered over her still-freakish hand. She wished that she had changed for this. If Bonito was waiting, she was making it easy for him.

Freddie pushed the Up button, but she nodded toward the stairs. He wasn't used to the climb, and outside the eleventh floor they waited in the stairwell as he caught his breath. He went out first, calling an all-clear after a few seconds. She controlled her adrenaline as it built and then let it rush through her system, drawing the knife as she carded open her door.

The bedroom was empty, untouched. She nodded Freddie toward the closet. He swung around the door frame with his stun gun at the ready, like a TV detective at a murder scene.

He lowered it and smiled nervously back at her. "Damn, you've got a lot of clothes."

She pushed past him, peering into the dark corners. No one was here. She paused to neutralize some of her adrenaline, pocketed the knife.

He stayed in the closet, still a little awed, while she went to work in the bedroom. First, she double-locked the door. The optical anatomy disks didn't take up much room in the duffel bag, nor did a hard copy of Milica Raznakovic's welfare records. At some point, she might want to reconstruct the identity. She went through the pockets of a few discarded pants and came up with three more dollars in change.

Standing with the third-full duffel bag, she was struck with how little there was to gather. No diaries, no notebooks, no flopticals backing up a desktop calendar, no friends' phone numbers, no business cards, no saved letters, no college papers. Almost nothing. There was a list in her head, assembled from observation, from conversations, from films about normal people. A list of things she knew she should have collected over twenty-three years but hadn't. Her college papers and the letters from her short attempts at relationships were gone, trashed. Most of the rest had never existed to begin with. Just Freddie was there.

She approached him from behind, put her hands on his shoulders. He turned around and they kissed. In the hot mustiness of the closet, she felt safe for a moment. Pressed against her shorts, Freddie was growing hard. His hands massaged the tightness in her shoulders, and she relaxed.

The clothes were her one collection, the one record of her life. As she looked with half-lidded eyes across his shoulder at them, they told stories from the last five years. She would bury a thousand lovers when she left this room.

She and Freddie kissed again, and she pushed him back against the soft mass of clothing hung on the wire. The coats, shirts, and dresses parted for them, swallowed them. She reached behind her to a stack of three wired-together milk cartons, tipped it over. A bed of scarves, socks, hats, T-shirts, and underwear scattered from the cartons. She knelt, holding his shoulders tight so that her weight brought him down.

His clothes were light, elastic-waisted, cotton—the insubstantial garments of summer. His body surrendered them easily. He watched her silently as she stripped herself, his gaze on the nipple that her earlier change had disrupted. She held her breasts with the dissimilar hands, squeezed them tightly for a second to sharpen the blood flow in them. She leaned over to kiss him, hard and long, until their lips swelled against each other.

She straightened and then arched her spine, missing the feeling of hair falling against her back. Freddie took a condom from his pocket and broke its package. She breathed in the bright smell of antiviral lubrication. The chemicals of change and sex were coursing strong enough to admit him easily inside.

She stroked him with a small rocking motion, letting herself gasp aloud at the pain in her knees, hard against the floor. The change built, until her vagina was articulated enough to undulate with its own muscles. On her toes, she lifted her knees off the floor, squatting down hard onto Freddie's pelvis. He groaned and grabbed her wrists. Her palms were pressed sweatily against his chest.

The compression waves inside her gradually changed to a slow constriction around his cock. She tightened the grasp of the vaginal muscles into a double twist, like two hands wringing a rag, and Freddie cried out so sharply she almost released him. But his panting steadied, remaining short and harsh. She wrung him again, in the opposite direction, and his groan was definitely pleasure. As the new muscles organized themselves inside her to optimize the hard and twisting constrictions, she gained purchase with her feet. She pushed up and forward, resuming the rocking stroke along the length of his cock. He cried out again as the coarse motion of their bodies compounded her internal manipulations.

The sex became fast and hard, frantic in the compromised security of her apartment. She led him quickly to orgasm, squeezing red hand marks into the skin of his chest as he came. His cry of pleasure trailed off a little painfully, and she stopped her motion against him. With his breath still gasping, she tightened herself around his cock and let herself come to orgasm in a slow, determined wave. Freddie felt the wave hit and cried out along with her. They shuddered together through a lingering series of aftershocks.

She leaned back, propping herself up with weak wrists. As they separated, the condom pulled off of Freddie's cock and remained half inside her. She sat back into a split and pulled it out. Freddie smiled at her, a little embarrassed. She leaned forward and went down on him. He protested feebly but unmistakably, and she desisted. His cock was hot and limp, a little worse for the wear.

"Too hard?" she asked.

"Just right," he answered in a ragged whisper. "But I think I rolled over on my stun gun by accident."

She laughed. Next time, they wouldn't be so rushed.

They dressed and she gathered a few favorite clothes, mostly female, filling the duffel bag. She figured she could use Freddie's clothes if she changed back to a male. He was about her weight. She smiled at the thought of being male; she could show Freddie a few tricks he didn't know yet.

At the door she remembered her sunglasses.

Her final look at the apartment didn't last long. The place was already fading into the distance. Too much had changed in the last few days to linger at this oasis of false security.

Freddie drew his weapon as he unlocked the door.

"Wait!" he said, pausing. "The receipt."

"Shit. That's right." She scrabbled among the matchbooks and condoms in the ashtray by the door. The receipt was there. As she picked it up, her heart fell.

On the side with the phone number and PIN code, more had been written. It read, in a tiny and precise hand:

I'm closer to you than you are to me.

Freddie was out in the hall, looking both ways. He turned to her. "Found it?"

Speechless, she pushed the receipt toward him. His eyes focused on it, and his expression sharpened. He snatched it from her and thrust it into his pocket. Switching the stun gun to his left hand, he grabbed her wrist and pulled her out. The door swung closed and locked itself behind them. They took the stairs fast. Halfway down, a pair of murmuring voices below them brought Freddie to a halt. He rounded the next corner slowly, stun gun extended. She saw that it was the Chinese couple whose daughter's face she had borrowed. At the sight of the gun, the two stopped talking and backed fearfully into an access door. Until they disappeared, Freddie's aim never wavered. They ran the rest of the way down.

At the curb outside the projects, a short Hispanic man was paying off a taxi. She pushed past the man and into the cab. Freddie joined her and shouted at the driver to roll. The driver shrugged her shoulders and the car jolted into the light traffic.

She turned to look out the back window as Freddie gave directions.

Bonito was there.

He was a man. Dark and smiling, dressed all in black, he jogged after them. The cab was slowing for the turn onto Delancey, and he was gaining.

"It's him," she said quietly. Freddie turned to her and then whirled around to face the back. His stun gun came up.

The cab turned right onto Delancey and sped up. Bonito fell back.

Freddie sighed with relief. "Thank God."

But Bonito was changing. His legs grew longer, ankles now visible below the cuffs of his loose black pants. His hips seemed wider, and he leaned down into a crouched run, bent almost ninety degrees at the waist. He began to gain in speed, to catch up again.

His run was horrifying and graceful, like some monstrous gazelle, long legs propelling him forward in a low-to-the-ground lope. His femurs seemed to stick up above his hips, as if they were jointed straight through his pelvis like the legs of a insect. His torso was parallel to the ground now, aimed right at their cab. His head arched back to face them, wearing a calm smile.

"Jesus Christ!" said Freddie. A spark flew between the two prods of the stun gun as his hand clenched nervously against the trigger.

Bonito was gaining.

The driver hadn't noticed him, but there was no point in warning her that she was being chased by the devil. New York cabbies drove as if they were anyway. But the driver began to slow, ready to turn, as they came to Sixth Avenue.

"Take the West Side Highway!" Freddie yelled like a maniac.

"Just to get up to Twenty-fourth?" the driver asked.

"*Yes!*"

"It's your money." They sped up. Lee looked ahead. All the lights were green.

Behind them, Bonito had left the sidewalk for the street. Lee realized that to the few cars on the street he would look like a roller blader, bent halfway to the ground and moving smoothly and inhumanly fast. Probably he didn't give a damn what they saw. He was only yards away.

She considered throwing a choke hold on the driver. The woman would probably slam her foot on the brakes, and Bonito might collide with the halting cab and injure himself. It was a shallow hope. More likely, the cab would wreck, leaving them at Bonito's mercy.

As Bonito closed the remaining distance, she noticed that Freddie was rolling down his window. Bonito reached out arms that were too long and threw himself forward. He straight-armed the taxi's trunk, somersaulting onto the roof.

Lee heard the driver's voice: "What the fuck?" Freddie fired.

With his arm craned out the window, he had connected the stun gun's prods to the metal of the roof. Bonito screamed above them. Then he fell, tumbling onto the trunk of the cab, one hand grasping the seam between trunk and chassis. Freddie fired again, prods against the trunk. Blue sparks skittered out from the gun's tip, and Bonito lurched and slipped off backward, disappearing for a moment. Freddie pulled the gun in, swearing. The heel of his hand was red, and the reek of seared flesh filled the cab.

Bonito appeared on the ground in the growing distance behind them. He rolled to a stop before another car hit him. A large Polish methane-burner, it crushed his legs before it skidded to a halt. Traffic piled up, but their cabbie drove on, speechless.

They pulled up in front of Freddie's building. Lee handed the driver, who looked to be still in shock, her last twenty. Freddie got out. He stood by the cab, inspecting something on the roof.

He leaned his head in. "Looks like we fried your sign."

The driver looked at him without comprehension. "Keep the change, he means," Lee said and got out.

Freddie shook his head as the cab pulled away. "I guess New York cabs aren't spec'd to take fifty-thousand volts. Apparently, neither was Bonito."

She looked down at the change the driver had given her, not remembering taking it.

"Speaking of which," he continued, "what the hell *was* Bonito? One of you?"

"Yes. He *is*. Don't count on him being dead yet."

He took her by the shoulder sternly and caught her eye. "You didn't mention that he was another changer. You've got to *tell* me these things."

"Sorry. I'll tell you the truth from now on."

"Good. So he's a changer like you?"

"The word for it is . . . *my* word for it is 'polymorph.' And he's much better at it than me." They started for the door.

"I'd gathered that," he said.

She supposed it was obvious, but her pride was wounded.

"So, how well do you know this guy?" he asked.

"We've had sex." She wanted it to shock him. It did.

"Great. This is your ex-boyfriend. I *hate* this town. I'm sleeping with the devil's ex-girlfriend. Perfect."

"He's not my boyfriend. Jesus Christ! What the hell do you think I am?" She went on, afraid he might answer. "It's just that I met him at the Glory Hole."

"The dyke club?"

"Yes, the *dyke* club. He's a woman sometimes."

"You mean, he. . . . That's right, you can change back and forth."

She was momentarily amazed. As smart as Freddie was, the basic facts hadn't penetrated his mind. "Yes, I can. And I do."

They climbed the stairs in silence.

When they reached the door, he looked at her, paused, and said, "Great."

"Sorry if it's a problem."

"I'm just a little confused," he said, opening the door.

"So what's so confusing?"

"Why that makes you . . . more interesting." He turned on the kitchen light and turned around to face her. He was blushing.

Amazement rose and fell again. She let the door close, crossed to him, stood close.

"But one thing you should know about Bonito . . ." she said in a teasing, quiet voice.

"What?"

"He's definitely a man at heart."

"How can you tell?"

"Because men are such *pricks*!" She spat out the last word, but Freddie didn't lose his composure.

"And you?" he asked.

"I spent the first fourteen years of my life as a female. But I refuse to define myself as such." She looked into his eyes. "But you wouldn't understand that, would you?"

"Sure I would. I spent the first seventeen years of my life as a virgin, and I refuse to define *myself* as such."

She laughed out loud. "That's a long time to go without getting laid, Freddie."

"It won't happen again."

"I suppose not," she said, leaning against him. Under his shorts, he was hard again. She encircled him with her good hand.

"Wait! Stop that. We've got to go." He pushed her lightly away.

"Go?" she asked.

He opened the refrigerator and leaned into it. "Go see Sam. The night hours are the best time to trace bank accounts."

"Freddie, aren't banks closed at night?"

"Banks don't close. They just don't let you do anything with your money after three o'clock. Because that's when *they* start playing with it." He pulled out a fresh two-liter plastic bottle of the coffee drink. "Look, if this Bonito guy isn't dead—"

"He's not," she interrupted. She knew it absolutely.

"Then let's get him while he's down."

CHAPTER 6

Sam

In the cab, Freddie swilled the coffee drink and explained that he had met Sam on AcNet.

"He was a customer?"

"Trespasser."

"Must have been love at first sight."

He ignored her irony. "Actually, he looked like a normal customer at first, several normal customers. He was using multiple identities, all lifted from legitimate users' accounts. The System had no idea. We wouldn't have caught him at all, but then I realized that some of my conversations were bleeding into each other."

"Your conversations were bleeding?"

"Well, you know in a crowded restaurant, when a topic comes up at one table, and it's compelling enough that it gets into the back of everyone's mind at the other tables. So you hear this conversation pop up first on one side of the place, then at another table right behind you, then—"

"Right, right. I get it. I've heard it happen. But the night you animated for me, you were doing that yourself."

"Exactly," he said. "But this time I was *not* doing it. Someone else was. And whoever it was couldn't have been just one person."

"You just lost me."

"You see, as an animator I can get a top-down

view of the conversation web: I know who's talking to who. And these topics would come up with one user, then another, then another, but there was no connection between them that I could see. At first, I figured it was some sort of chat line gestalt, like the System was having this sort of weird dream. I mentioned it to my boss, who thought I was maybe nuts. So I showed it to her. Finally, we figured that there was some hacker in the system. Someone who was more than one person."

"What do you do in that situation?"

"I sent out for a double espresso and decided to catch the fucker. I logged on with another identity, not ME, and set a trap for him."

"Like what?"

"An irresistible topic of conversation," he said. "I know 'em all. Reincarnation, subliminal advertising, Kemp assassination theories, the demons in virtual reality. Inevitably, if you bring shit like that up to a conversant, he'll bring it up to someone else. So I got all the spare monitors out and set up my desktop to show me every conversation on the network. Then I dropped a few irresistible topics into a group of conversants who were linked in a ring."

"A ring?"

"You know, person A was talking to person B, B to C, and C to A. Except this one went up to, like J." Both of Freddie's hands were moving, describing a jagged circular shape on the back of the driver's car seat.

"Naturally, the topic spread like wildfire within that ring. No surprises there. The tip-off came when one of the topics showed up in another group, even though there was no connection between the two. Then I backtracked to see who had introduced the topic to the second group."

"And that person . . . ?" she asked.

"Was also using an identity in the first group."

"What the fuck *for*?"

"Sam is a hacker. A compulsive hacker. It wasn't enough for him to hack into the network with someone else's ID. He was posing as four legitimate users."

"Don't you do that too?"

"Right, but that's my job. Anyway, I figured I'd scare him and he'd log off. So I told him I was the sysop coming down on his head with an FCC warrant."

"What'd he do?" she asked.

"He smirked. At least, he smirked as well as you can in text-only mode. He knew his line was secure. Then he asked me how I'd busted him. The System was attempting to trace him by now, so I figured I'd keep him on the line. I told him how I'd caught him. Then he told me how he'd gotten in. That started the most amazing conversation I've ever had." His eyes rolled up in a reverie. "Sam has got the Knowledge. But bad. He's been on the networks since they were new, half-made. Like when kids play in a building under construction and leave graffiti on the beams behind the unfinished walls. The graffiti gets covered over, and no one ever sees it again, but it's still there. Sam left a lot of graffiti when he was young. And now that the walls and all the locks on the doors of the networks are finished, Sam's graffiti still wait for him . . . and tell him things he needs to know."

His voice was very soft. He stared at an invisible presence past the grimy barrier between them and the cabby. The flicker in his eyes had become a hot burn. She realized that Freddie had a mystical side.

"It's like he can walk through walls," he said softly.

"Wait. What did you say about graffiti?"

"Well, when they first started networking computers in the 1970s, they didn't know shit about security. Basically, everything was open to anyone with minimal equipment and a phone. The companies setting up networks spent weeks just to train legitimate users to do a simple task. They never figured that thirteen-year-olds could come along and figure it out for themselves. So it was the heyday of the hackers."

"Yeah, I've read all about that. I thought it eventually all got shut down."

"Right. Famous and tragic arrests, especially after the Secret Service took over cybercrime investigation. But the folks who got busted were the aggressive ones, out to make a name for themselves in the hacker community. They published their ripped-off information, had their viruses leave messages on infected users' screens, went for maximum publicity. But there was another kind of hacker."

Freddie and his dramatic pauses. "Pray tell," she implored after a moment's silence.

"The other kind of hackers had a motto: Change Nothing. At least, nothing that anyone can see. They navigated just as extensively as the big names, but rather than screwing things up or leaving noisy viruses behind, they specialized in trojan files."

"Like the horse, I assume."

"The what?"

"Never mind."

"Anyway, these files hid themselves, or disguised themselves as harmless utilities. Some were so successful that they were ported over to new hardware as the networks advanced, recessive genes passed on to each new generation of machines."

"Besides hiding, what did they do?"

"Nothing. That was the point. They waited. For years, adapting and hiding, they copied themselves into new machines as the networks expanded. Unlike the viruses, the trojans were modest."

"And they wait for the people who made them?"

"Exactly. And they help them."

The cab pulled up in front of a large brownstone. They were on Central Park West.

As Freddie paid, she looked up and down the street. Sam's next-door neighbors included a racquet club and a large, brooding edifice surrounded by police barricades. The door of his building was heavy black iron and his windows had the HARD plastic look of a very unpopular United Nations mission. This was an expensive neighborhood.

"Sam's got some money."

"No kidding."

Freddie rang the buzzer. There was only one. These weren't apartments, this was Sam's house. Sam had a lot of money.

The intercom crackled. A strangely forced and nasal voice said, "Hello, Freddie." Freddie waved at the camera behind them. The odd voice said, "Wait, please."

When the door opened, she saw that Sam was small and thin. He was Japanese and looked younger than she had expected. He was wearing a black silk robe over a pair of bright-yellow pants. Freddie said, "Hello," with exaggerated clarity. He indicated her, keeping his face turned toward Sam. "This is Lee." As he said the name, the fingers on both his hands moved subtly. Sam watched the movements intently.

"Hello, Lee," he said in the same raw and nasal voice.

She started to say *Hello* but mouthed the word silently instead. Sam nodded his head and smiled as if she had spoken.

He was deaf.

They followed him down the wide hall. The floor was black-and-white marble, tiled in a checkerboard pattern biased forty-five degrees to the wall. Framed prints covered the walls. She recognized the twisted world map from Freddie's apartment. There were many other maps, world and local, showing terrain, demographic data, enterprise zones, political boundaries, network nodes.

They mounted a wide, carpeted staircase, and the exhibit continued. On the staircase walls were mounted a host of information displays: aerial photographs, cartograms, orbital tables, line graphs, flowcharts, architectural plans, pictographs, schematics. Along an upstairs hallway, a long series of tiny scatterplots led them to a large room lit only by the flicker of plasma screens.

It was a far cry from the place where Freddie worked. The AcNet office was smoothed over in clean corporate pastels, all the technology packaged in beige boxes. Here, the guts of the new century were on display. Freddie, pointing, named a few objects in a soft voice as Sam made tea. A fiber-optic hub studded with green LEDs; a miniframe stack, its optical core exposed and flickering; the microwave lattice that covered the ceiling; four workstations facing each other in the center of the room around a circular table. The computers visible in the room were half-stripped to reveal their motherboards—like models, city blocks from some exaggerated Tokyo— studded with coprocessors, custom cards, zip chips. She recognized the virtual reality visor at each workstation, smaller and sleeker than the ones at Hunter Library.

They sat on low-static plastic floormats. Sam poured a hot, yellow liquid from a twisted teapot into three exquisite *raku* cups. She blew on it and tested a few scalding drops. It was strong, made from barley. She detected a high caffeine content. That, at least, was unsurprising.

Freddie explained the situation to Sam, clearly enunciating every word. But Sam's eyes shifted between Freddie's lips and his hands. As Freddie spoke, his hands shimmered with a subtle play of fingers. She realized he was qwerting. As if he were inputting to a computer, without bracelets. Apparently, Sam had learned to read letters and words from the hand-dance of a fast qwertist. She remembered that Freddie had said he could qwert faster than he could talk. Sam's own hands occasionally queried Freddie with a flicker of motion. She wondered if their qwerted conversation matched the words Freddie was speaking for her benefit.

Freddie told Sam that she was being harassed by an ex-boyfriend, who had soaked her card. He asked Sam to track the soak back to its source, find Bonito, and hopefully spread a little counter-mayhem in his personal finances. He showed the receipt with the account number and access code to Sam, whose eyes brightened as he inspected it.

Sam turned to her and said in his forced voice, "This will go quicker if you give me your Primary Access String. But I will understand if you do not wish to."

The request made sense, but she was taken aback. There were several levels of access that could be given to someone else: Limited Withdrawal, ShortLook, Durable Audit, Power of Attorney. The access number she had stolen from Bonito was basically a single-account ShortLook, allowing only inspection of his balance. But from her first Home Ec class on, she'd been taught *never* to give anyone her Primary Access String. Someone who knew your PAS could do whatever they wanted with your money: buy with it, spirit it away to their account, hire a hit man with it. They could also change your other codes, even instate a new PAS and lock you out of your own affairs until you got a gene scan and a very serious court order. A PAS wasn't even stored on the chip in a smartcard, it was filed deep within the mainframes of the SEC.

Freddie saw her hesitation and spoke softly out of the corner of his mouth. "If you want Sam to go very deep, you should just give it to him. Remember, it's like giving your phone number to NYNEX."

But she had already decided. Milica Raznakovic was compromised in any case. Still, it was hard to vocalize the word. She hadn't uttered it out loud since entering it on an old, vaguely sticky keyboard at One Federal Plaza. They put you in a tiny, secluded cubicle when you were initialized, the walls papered with yellowing signs warning you not to forget the PAS, not to divulge it, not even to write it down. It was personal. She looked away from Freddie as she spoke.

"ABERRATION."

Sam looked puzzled—evidently it was a hard word to lip-read—but he nodded after Freddie's fingers clarified. He looked at her, and with all the sensitivity his tortured voice could carry, said, "Thank you." He held out his hand for her duplicate smartcard. She gave it to him with her mutated hand. He gave no flicker of notice to the hand's twisted shape.

They went to the machines.

Freddie handed her a visor, treating it as gingerly as his vinyl LPs. The gear was a tighter fit than she was used to, the visor almost as close as the lenses on a pair of glasses. She was relieved to discover that it was transparent. She could see the rest of the room as if through dark sunglasses.

At a croaked word from Sam, the workstations booted. The slender cyan grid lines of virtual reality appeared, superimposed on the room. When she turned her head, the lines in the visor shifted so that they stayed stationary relative to the room. While Sam and Freddie slipped on qwerty bracelets, a dialog appeared in the air in front of her. It prompted

her to calibrate the visor, asking her to respond when
two red dots, which soared together from the extremes of her peripheral vision, were exactly aligned.
When the points collided, a simple spoken *yes* suf-
ficed. Then the dialog prompted her to say a few
words for voice analysis: "bomb," "balm," "caught,"
"house," "about," "idea," and "water." She'd seen
this set of words before. It was supposed to prepare
the transliterator for ambiguities in regional dialect.

A new window appeared, hovering over Sam's
head. Characters scrolled onto it to form the words:

welcome to my home

She had seen Sam's hands move, qwerting the
words into the window. She realized what her own
SRT was for. She experimented with: "It seems a very
fine house indeed." He saw from his eyes that her
words had been transcribed over her head. His fingers flickered.

thank you

So this was how the talkative Freddie had stayed
friends with a deaf man.

Freddie's voice spoke from the small speaker in
her ear: "Nice system, huh?" She saw the transcription appear over his head. For a moment she wondered why the words faced her instead of Sam. Then
she realized the obvious; it was viewpoint-depen-
dent. In Sam's visor the transcription faced Sam.

It was strange as the three of them talked. Sam's
qwerted words scrolled by almost too fast to read.
Freddie's conversation manifested redundantly; she
could listen to it or read the text over his head. Perhaps most disconcertingly, Sam, and even Freddie
(out of habit, she supposed) listened to her with their
eyes trained just over her head.

After a few minutes of chatter, Sam said:

    lets go

His hands moved, and the gridded space before
them began to shift, to reorganize itself. The conver-
sational text windows shrank in size and moved
toward her, hovering in the lower quarter of her vision. The space over the table cleared of the cyan
grid lines. Sam swept her card through a reader on
the table.

Several wireframe cubes appeared above them,
joined by pulsating flowchart symbols. It was her financial schematic, familiar from the two-dimensional
version her own computer rendered. She felt vague
embarrassment at the hovering seals of the State of
New York that confirmed each rent subsidy and welfare waiver. But there was something reassuring
about Sam's intense eyes, the disinterested gaze of a
doctor upon a naked body.

Responding to the gestures of his braceleted hands,
a cursor probed each cube in turn, tracking the history of several transactions. It all looked straight:
drink bills, the cab ride to Pitt Street, prosaic bank
charges and the hourly compounding of interest, her
latest welfare payment—three hours early. That was
a first. A large window had opened directly in front
of Sam. It detailed the areas his cursor passed across;
each transaction, ratification, and parity check enu-
merated and diagrammed.

Sam's progress was slow, but she was strangely
fascinated with the probing of these effluvial data.
She had thought herself virtually data-invisible: no
job, no phone, no court record, no bulletin board
memberships, unregistered to vote or drive. But there
was a host of information here, just from the last few
days. She wondered what the financial schematic for

a wealthy and connected person like Sam would look like.

> you are very clean, Milica
> you make things easy for me

Freddie frowned at her, having just realized that her name wasn't Lee.

"Milica?" he said.

She pronounced it for him correctly.

"But I thought it was Lee."

"Names are bullshit, Freddie."

"Not to *me*," he said.

"Arbitrary signifiers."

They argued. Freddie called her a liar. It was odd to see the insult transcribed in his text window. Sam ignored them, remaining fascinated with the paucity of her data. He seemed to admire her purity. She wondered if Bonito had realized who she was when he had soaked her card. Probably no real person would have so simple a financial schematic. Monomorphs probably needed all the clutter to establish their identity. Another way to spot a polymorph.

> look at this

Sam's detailed view expanded before them. Among a cluster of government safeguards on her last welfare payment, a small parity byte icon was highlighted. "That shouldn't be there," said Freddie.

> I agree

"Track it!" said Freddie.

Sam's hands flickered.

The byte blossomed across the rest of the schematic, unfolding its own windows, dialogs, hyper-nodes. They were rendered in another color scheme, their fonts and layout different.

"What the fuck is this?" asked Freddie. Sam worked furiously for a few moments. Then he sat back, frowning.

    a subset of the INS mainframe

"Immigration? Bonito works for Immigration?"

    no
    this is his exit trail
    Milica is an immigrant

"Shit," Lee said. "What did he find out?"

    from here, your medical records are apparent

She swore again. Sam gestured, and in the air before her appeared X-rays, photographs, sonograms. She realized why Bonito had been waiting for them at her apartment. The details of Milica's damaged body would have left no doubt in his mind. Only a polymorph could fake the injuries she had.

"Jesus," said Freddie. "You sure pulled a job on these guys." He tried to sound convincing, for Sam's benefit, she supposed.

They searched the INS mainframe for an exit trail, but it was fruitless. The room was full of sprawling schematic before they gave up. The INS was a vast system, as chaotic as the New York Public Library. Bonito hadn't left a trail. They returned to her personal finances.

Sam worked for a while longer, then leaned back into his chair.

    that was it
    one byte was the intrusion

"Can you delete it, so I can use my card again?" she asked. "That is, without him finding me?"

> he is gone now
> but he still has card and numbers
> he can come back whenever he wants
> and do whatever he wants
> I suggest you deep format

She despaired. A deep format required X-rays, fingerprints, a retina scan, endless document work. A whole day at Federal Plaza in her crippled Milica Raznakovic body.

Freddie said, "What about Bonito's account number? At least we can strike back. Let's go fuck this guy." He tried to sound enthusiastic.

Sam considered this, a little hesitant at first. Then he flexed his fingers.

The rubric of her finances melted. It had been a village, a few huts and dirt paths.

It was replaced by a city.

It hovered around them, a megalopolis of blue whorls and red shafts, mottled clouds and bright suspended pixels. Thin translucent red lines connected everything, arcing over their heads, splitting off to other distant clusters that hovered beyond the walls of the room. Red lines shot straight through the three of them, seeming to reduce their bodies to phantasms. The dense crimson web pulsated in intensity.

"New York at night," said Freddie in quiet awe.

As Sam worked, the whorls deepened in complexity, shifted in size and orientation.

She asked for Eyemouse Help and probed the iconography. She learned that the red shafts represented transactions, aggregates of market activity between the various banks, S&Ls, government agencies, insurance companies, brokerages, currency houses, on-line individuals. The blue galaxies in their various forms—spirals, fractaloids, latticeworks, hexagonal mosaics—were large, highly regulated institutions. The dusty point clouds were more complex consortia, like mutual funds and university endowments. Here and there a lone bright pixel denoted a super-rich individual whose personal computers traded in the big leagues. The faraway clusters, seemingly several meters past the walls in the forced perspective of the VR visor, were other markets. Freddie pointed out Tokyo, Hong Kong, London, Hanoi, Moscow.

"This is what your money does at night," said Freddie. "Well, I guess not *your* money," he added a little condescendingly. Her tiny account was safely locked in an inflation-rate bond, one of the few remaining government-insured instruments.

Sam had Bonito's receipt in hand. He qwerted a few numbers and pointed. Near the center of an elongated point cloud that hovered near Freddie's foot, a single pixel flashed. A thin green line connected it to a detail window before Sam.

"Shit," said Freddie. "It's a Swiss Node. That's—"

"I know," she interrupted. "A numbered account."

Sam had blown up the detail window. As his fingers moved, highlights probed the window. Slivers of the red shafts emanating from the cloud turned white: Bonito's money at work. More detail windows appeared before Sam, and he probed each for a few moments. More connections were made. The fragile network of white lines expanded, extending new feelers to other clouds and other galaxies.

After ten minutes, the expansion stopped, and Sam leaned back to regard the detail windows that overlapped in an untidy batch before him. The white web now touched a few dozen financial entities. He frowned and gestured toward the swarm of windows, qwerting as he did so.

look at the names

For a moment she was confused. Then she realized that every detail window had a supertitle; a company name in bright SEC blue. They meant nothing to her: Transfund Ltd., World Enterprises, Global Custody, Universal Mercantile, Trade Internationale . . . none were familiar.

"I haven't heard of any of these," Freddie echoed her thoughts.

> exactly
> they are generic names
> front companies
> each transaction goes through dozens of them
> hidden dozens of times

"Shit, you're right," said Freddie. He had opened a copied set of the detail windows in the air before him and was qwerting madly. She tried to follow his progress. He talked while he qwerted.

"These entities are all custody houses, not brokerages. That is, they don't actually buy or sell, they just handle the money. And they bundle groups of orders from different clients, which makes it hard to trace an individual sale from public information. That's how they make a profit: holding on to a whole wad of capital until the last minute of an interest period, and then shooting it off all at once. Bonito's money gets mixed up with everybody else's making the same transaction, so you can't see where it's going." He looked at her. "With a system like Sam's, you can usually track a transaction. Sort of like finding someone hidden behind a tree by seeing their shadow. But Bonito seems to be unusually cautious. He launders everything about twenty times before it gets where it's going. Wherever the hell that is."

> yes
> he is as paranoid as Milica is fastidious

In their discouraged silence, a thought occurred to her. "Where did it come from?" she asked.

"What? His paranoia?"

"No, Freddie. His money."

"How the fuck should I know?"

"Can you trace it back to whoever gave it to him?" she asked.

"If you don't mind replaying every transaction on this account for the last year or so. We ought to get done in under a decade."

He turned back to the display hovering in the air above them. He and Sam began qwerting again, their desktops growing over with unruly hordes of green and blue transaction windows. They seemed to have turned their attention to a single transaction, tracing it through the maze of custodians between Bonito and its final goal. Freddie was muttering as he worked, oblivious to her presence. Her understanding became unfocused as she watched, her mind losing track of the individual commands they performed. She disabled her Eyemouse Help. There was a slow, cycling pattern to the play of fingers and virtual light, a repetition of the same series of steps as they followed the money from one transaction to the next. Apparently they had embarked upon some sort of brute force search, like taking every possible route in a maze to find the end. She was reminded of Freddie's search for Candy, culling the huge database for matches with the few clues they'd had. But this database was astronomically larger; opaque with all the muddy footprints of capital.

She remembered when the Public Access to Securities Act had been passed five years before. Bankers, brokers, and civil libertarians had all wrung their hands over the threat to privacy. But the other side had won; taxpayers were sick of bailing out looted thrifts and banks, investors sick of finding out their stocks were worthless. So the new rules made it possible for individuals to audit almost any legal transaction.

She looked at the multihued galaxy around them. It hadn't done much good. The profusion of data made finding anything impossible. A *Times* editorial had compared PASA research with taking a micrograph of every cell in someone's head and then using the data to sketch the person's face.

There had to be a better way. When she and Freddie had tried to find Candy, the most obvious clue had been staring them in the face, and they'd gotten lost in minutiae.

She decided to let Sam and Freddie continue until the search had almost exhausted them. When they were malleable enough to take a new tack, she would suggest another course. She drank tea, waiting.

Sam's eyes grew heavy-lidded, either from fatigue or in a meditative trance. Freddie's muttering got harsher as his throat dried.

Her barley tea grew cold and bitter, the leaves on the bottom of the cup a sickly mass of green. Freddie refilled his own tea with inhuman frequency. He must have a bladder the size of a basketball, she thought. As an hour crept by, punctuated only by the tiny *snicks* of qwerting, he developed a tick in one eye. She stood and moved behind his chair, putting a hand on one shoulder. He did not respond.

Sam was a slower qwerter than Freddie. The windows and dialogue boxes that littered the air before him moved more deliberately, without the pyrotechnic flutter that Freddie's had. But his concentration was more intense. He sometimes toggled among a small stack of windows like a nervous card player shuffling his hand. The time he paused before each little cluster of information was minuscule.

Absentmindedly, she grasped Sam's shoulders, felt the muscles and bone. They were as tense as Freddie's, but the muscles were taut all the way across

the shoulders, whereas Freddie's were bunched in
knots. She rubbed them lightly. He seemed more
fragile than Freddie, and she felt intrusive touching
him. The muscles relaxed a little, though his qwerting didn't slow. After a few moments he turned his
head a little and looked at her malformed hand.

She said, "Does it disturb you?"

He must have detected her voice through the tight
contact between hands and collarbone. He wiggled a
finger, bringing forward her dialog window, her
words time-stamped to show that she had just uttered them.

    no

came his answer.

    Im used to defects
    if I may call it that
    my deafness is also congenital

She didn't explain that the mutation was merely a
whim. She stopped rubbing but left her hands on
Sam's shoulders.

"Sam, what is it exactly that you and Freddie are
trying to do?"

    trying to isolate a single transaction
    not just the PASA filing
    but the locus of the actual debit/credit

"And that gets you into his system?"

    no
    but it shows us where the decisions are made
    so we can monitor all his transactions easily

"Why?"

```
to determine the algorithm of his investment
strategy
which we can manipulate with disinformation
and erode his account
in short: make him buy high and sell low
```

"But Sam, what if there is no algorithm? What if his investments are all just a whim?"

```
your friend Bonito is probably asleep
of course
his operating system is handling his affairs
for most people, you must remember
capital is the province of machines
of algorithms
```

"Oh, yeah. I guess not many people handle their finances themselves."

```
you are vanishingly rare in that regard
```

"I take that as a compliment."

```
it is
```

She resumed her massage, occasionally interrupting his work to ask a question. The shift from desktop manipulation to conversation didn't seem to break his concentration. His short, haiku-like answers were clear and direct. Apparently, his disability had trained him to make the most of few words.

Sam's labors gradually began to make sense to her. One window, always forward, showed the logical shape of the single transaction they had been tracing. As another hour dragged on, it grew into a twisted mass in the air before her, an impossible, Escher-like structure.

Bonito had wound his finances into a dense and

recursive forest of loops. Wherever they followed the maze of transaction, their path wrapped back onto itself, juggling their calculations, the different windows failing to add up. Sam explained that Bonito's operating system was buying and selling short the same shares of mutual funds almost simultaneously, hiding still other transactions in the welter of balance adjustments that the self-negating credits and debits incurred.

After another half hour, Sam stopped qwerting. He hung his head. Freddie went on another few minutes, then stopped. There was a moment of silence. Then came the *snick* of Sam's qwerting.

    this has been quite instructive

"Yeah, if you want to be the chief accountant for the CIA," Freddie sighed.

    at this point
    I wouldn't be surprised
    if that were Bonito's employer

"Great. The devil works for the CIA."

It was time to take charge. "Maybe we're going in the wrong direction," she said.

"What do you mean?" Freddie asked.

"Well, we're starting from this one account, which is just a little part of Bonito's life, and we're tracing all the minute effects this account has in the . . ." She waved at the virtual universe around them. "But we're not looking for the rest of his life; the stuff behind the account."

Freddie sighed. "But we can't even get his *name* from a numbered account. That's what Swiss Nodes are for. Even the bank doesn't know his name. It's all accessed by codes."

"Not his name, Freddie, or his address or his Social

Security number. But what he *is*. He's got all this money. So what's the story behind it? What's he doing with it? What does it mean?"

"It's money," said Freddie. "It doesn't *mean* anything. It just sits around making more money."

Sam looked thoughtful.

"But the way it's invested must tell us something!" She pointed at the twisted form before them.

"It tells us that he's a paranoid motherfucker!"

Freddie started to say something else, but an almost invisible gesture from Sam silenced him.

what are you suggesting, Milica?

"I think maybe you should forget the status bytes and the parity checks and all that little shit. Look at the big picture."

like?

"Like . . . how much money has he made tonight?"

Freddie shuffled windows with an exaggerated flourish. In a few moments he said, "He's lost money, actually. A few thousand."

"So," she groped frantically, "do we know why?"

"Why?" cried Freddie. "We can't even tell what he's buying or selling. We don't know *what* he's doing, much less why."

"But, Freddie," she said, trying to soothe him, "he's got to have a strategy. A goal."

Sam made an expansive gesture, and the air above their workstations cleared. In place of the chaos of dialogs and schematics that comprised the night's work, a long, thin window appeared. On its right edge a single red dot moved shakily up and down, a tracer of its recent path scrolling out to the left like a seismometer line.

Bonito's bottom line

"You mean, his account balance?"

correct

"It looks kind of like a heartbeat."
"The only one he's got," mumbled Freddie, stretching his arms.
She ignored him. "Does it follow a pattern?"
Sam flexed his fingers.

what sort of pattern?

"Does it correlate to some other account?"
Sam looked at her with tired eyes.
Freddie groaned. "There are millions of accounts open to PASA interrogation. Even Sam's system would take years to check them all."

months, actually

"Sorry, Sam. Anyway, I don't think we want to cast that wide a net. Even checking the Fortune 5000 would take an hour."

under 10 minutes

"For a fuzzy search? Bullshit. You'd have to leave a lot of leeway for a loose correlation. It would take at least forty-five minutes."

under 10 minutes, Freddie

"Bullshit."

bet me

"Forty bucks."

done

Another window opened, and Sam and Freddie started to define their correlation. They argued over the details. She lifted the visor and rubbed her eyes. Obviously Bonito still had the upper hand. Perhaps pursuing him was foolish. He was too powerful, too vicious. Possibly their probing had already alerted him.

She felt the weight of the last week intensely. Finding Bonito had changed her landscape. Now, only a few days into this new existence, she was very tired. Her cloak of anonymity had been a precious thing, but perhaps it wasn't lost forever. She could leave here tomorrow, find a new and remote existence. Or maybe the best thing to do would be to fade back into the Lower East Side and create a new persona, never sporting mutated hands again.

Sam and Freddie, laughing as they set some final variable, concluded negotiations on their bet. Freddie stood, done for the night. The wild goose chase was over. He flipped up his visor. "Well, I'm going to sleep. This is going to take at least half an hour." He turned toward Sam as he said the last words, mouthing them with exaggerated clarity.

But Sam wasn't looking at Freddie's lips or dialog window. There was suddenly an awestruck expression on Sam's face. His eyes were focused into the virtual middle distance. Freddie flipped his visor down. She did the same.

There was a correlation. Under the window that showed Bonito's balance, another had appeared. It bore the same red dot, rising and falling identically. In the supertitle of the new window was one word: "Americorp."

Freddie and Sam were silent.

"What's that?" she asked.

"A correlation."

"I know. But with what? Another generic company?"

"No," said Freddie. "It's the biggest corporation in the world."

CHAPTER 7

The King of America

"So why haven't I heard of it?"

"Because it's . . . everywhere. It's *the* multinational. They don't advertise; they just own everything."

"And there's a correlation? To Bonito?"

Sam qwerted.

it is a perfect match
his investment is ingeniously concealed

"Great. The devil works for Americorp," said Freddie.

"What?"

"You know how executives get incentive pay—linked to the performance of their company? This is some elaborately jiggered example of that."

"He works for Americorp? Why would he conceal it?"

"Maybe he's their hit man," said Freddie.

The thought chilled her.

at least his wealth is explained

Freddie rolled his eyes. "That's for sure."

"You mean he's well paid for whatever he does," she said glumly.

"To say the least. Americorp is the essence of profit. They own the license to the Universal Operating System. That's why they're so fucking rich. Ed King, their head guy, wrote the UOS when he was in college."

She took her visor off and leaned back into the firm grip of the ergonomic chair. She closed her eyes. A caffeine rush rose in a wave over her. The bright lines of the VR domain seemed stenciled into her brain. Ed King of Americorp.

She opened her eyes after what seemed a long time. Freddie and Sam had not moved. "Show me a picture of Ed King."

Freddie frowned, but Sam turned to his desktop and qwerted for a few moments. Then he looked back to her and inclined his head toward some invisible referent.

She put the visor on. Her eyes refocused. In the space to which Sam had gestured, a holograph floated. It was a head shot, oddly disembodied. King was wearing a blue business shirt and tie, just visible above the crop line. His hair was cut shorter than she remembered it. The holo was a public relations shot, with the heroic glow of a magazine profile. Ed King looked up, at something mystical and yet obtainable, just over her right shoulder. The Future. He was the young man from Candy.

"I know this guy," she said.

"You do?"

"His girlfriend is sleeping with Bonito."

Freddie groaned.

Suddenly, she realized it would be easy to leave this mess behind her.

She closed her eyes, rods and cones dancing with traces of virtual light, and relaxed herself. She began to neutralize the few hundred milligrams of caffeine in her system and emptied her mind. She allowed herself to forget Sean, Bonito, and Ed King. It had all been a fantasy: Milica Raznakovic was dead, her memories fading like phantasms.

But beneath the calm sense of completion was the tremor of a question. As her thoughts stilled, it grew in intensity and roiled to the surface of her mind. It pushed her eyes open.

When Bonito doppelgänged a person, what did he do with the original?

She stood up, a little unsteady now that the grid of cyan VR lines was gone from the floor.

"I need a drink," she said.

"Christ," said Freddie. "I need three days' sleep."

Sam pointed to the miniframe stack. She crossed to it and looked closer. The disks at its core were broken, dusty, ancient. She tugged at the casing and it popped open on smooth hinges. There was gin, vodka, sake, ice, glasses inside.

"Anyone else?"

Sam had pulled off his visor, a red line deep on his forehead where it had rested. She realized that he was deaf again. He croaked, "Good night." She mouthed the words back to him as he walked out of the room.

Freddie took off his visor and sat on the floor, head in his hands. He looked like he needed to recover from the shift to the merely real.

A drink in hand, she pulled her visor back on. She telescoped the SRT microphone in front of her mouth.

"Hang on a minute, Freddie. Don't pass out on me yet." He made a muffled noise. "How do I switch this thing from PASA filings to a library search?"

"Just ask it," he said.

"Library," she said. The desktop gave her a dialog box.

"First key word: 'Americorp.' Second keyword: 'King.' OK."

The citation count climbed into the thousands.

She sat back, Freddie curled at her feet, and started to read.

*   *   *

In a long night of cross-references, subject searches, and pure guesswork, she compiled the story of Ed King.

During the long stretches of inactivity—scrolling past irrelevant data or waiting for some distant library or newspaper to organize its files for her—she told Freddie everything that had happened in the last few days. At first, she had occasionally kicked him to make sure he was awake. He had an uncanny ability to stay awake with his eyes closed. Curled tightly at her feet, and then stretched out under the table, he listened without reaction. She described her first encounter with Bonito, his sudden shift at Candy, his relationship with Sean. Freddie moved only to drink, eyes still closed, from a cup of cold tea.

Hours later, Freddie took her to a room with a western bed. He had apparently spent the night there before. He knew his way to the room and found the light switch easily.

It was a little past dawn, the gray light of a cloud-choked sky brightening over Central Park. Freddie opaqued the windows. He pointed down the hall and said, "Bathroom." She stumbled as she walked, her depth perception addled by the long night in VR. She felt like shit.

They slept, her eyes still tracking phantom scrolling text like some digital bedspin.

The room brightened at two in the afternoon. Freddie had apparently set the windows to de-opaque. They were on the fourth floor. Central Park was aglow with bright treetops. To the north, the half-completed dome of Trump's Folly was just visible, rising out of the park like some ruin from the future. Freddie awoke with a kind of lazy ease. Eyes aflutter in the harsh green light, he tried to pull her back down to him. She was too nervous, though. She had learned that King was making an appearance in public that night.

There was work to be done.

They found Sam beginning breakfast. The kitchen was large, low-ceilinged, and bright, overlooking a partitioned courtyard. She looked out the window. Sam's building had the smallest section of the courtyard. The garden behind the building next door was large and gaudy, with statues and a bubbling fountain, but it looked ill-tended. Sam's garden was modest, a well-kept rock bed with low shrubs.

He was cooking rice in an elegant stainless pot that hummed a bright, tremulous pitch as the water boiled in it. In another pot, eggs were poaching in a mixture of water and red wine vinegar. While she and Freddie waited, they split a pear, juicy enough that they had to hold tea bowls beneath their chins as they bit. Between mouthfuls, Freddie qwerted to Sam, keeping a spoken commentary running for her benefit. They had agreed the night before to fill Sam in on Ed King's affair with Sean, as well as Bonito's apparent interest in them. Freddie left out any mention of shape-changing. Sam had little reaction to the story.

The rice and eggs were served together in white porcelain bowls. Sam and Freddie stirred with their chopsticks, blending the eggs into the rice, along with soy and Louisiana Red Devil sauce. They held their chopsticks the same way, thumb and forefinger at the middle of the sticks. She had been told it was a working-class habit.

She told Sam about King's appearance in public that night. She had subject-searched his name across a range of periodicals and found it in a Park Slope society on-line. He was attending the premiere of a Hillary Wilson opera. The article had listed a host of royalty, semi-royalty, and celebrities who would be in attendance at the Brooklyn Academy of Music. She spoke slowly for the benefit of his lipreading, but he nodded her on impatiently.

"But why approach King?" he asked.

"To warn him about Bonito."

"But Bonito may be working for him," he said, his voice cracking a little from the strain of speech.

She was silent. There was no way to tell Sam what she had seen in the Pitt Street nightclub. Bonito's stalking of Sean defied description. Freddie's hands seemed to grope for words.

She decided to let Sam in on a little more of the truth. "It's really King's girlfriend, Sean Bayes, that I'm worried about. But I don't know how to contact her."

Sam smiled. He knew they were still keeping something from him, but he was satisfied for the moment.

"Actually, I have four seats for Wilson's opera, but they aren't for opening night," he said. Her surprise must have shown on her face, because he added, "I'm a fan of Wilson's work. It's so . . . *visual*." The smile again.

"It should be fairly easy to swap your tickets, yeah?" said Freddie, qwerting in the air as he spoke.

Sam nodded, waved dismissively, and qwerted. "He's sure I can handle it," translated Freddie. "He'd prefer our company to his usual, anyway."

She waited until she caught Sam's eye, then mouthed, *Thank you*.

Sam left the room with a nod, and she and Freddie cleared the dishes in silence. She realized that despite his wealth, Sam had no servants. Perhaps his birth defect had made him value independence.

Down two flights of stairs, they returned to the still-booted computer room. While Freddie prepared to hack the BAM ticketing and reservation computer, she looked out the window. Sam was in the garden, raking the white rocks into wide, sumptuous curves.

He had dressed for the work in a loose white shirt and oversized shorts. He looked very small, and the attention that he brought to the task made him seem strangely distant. The night before, amid the web of data that he so effortlessly plied, she had thought him well connected, intimately attached to the worlds of finance and power. In the tiny garden below, he looked terribly alone. Staring out the window at him, the thought of a deaf man with opera tickets saddened her.

She looked at Freddie. His visor on, he was staring into the middle distance of VR. He looked a little like a village idiot as his fingers twitched codes of access. She paused to consider what they would have looked like to a real-world observer the night before; three demented inmates in their shared imaginary world.

She put her visor on and called up the notepad she had pasted together: news clips, videos, text: The Story of Edward King.

He had started his career as a Paper Boy.

As a lifelong welfare recipient, she remembered the crash. The Paper Boys (only one had been a woman) had made their fortunes in the margins of the faltering late-nineties economy. The country was swimming in dumb credit at the time. The Paper Boys swapped photocopied credit application forms among themselves and amassed photo albums filled with plastic. They canceled the cards as yearly fees came due and continually applied for more. She'd clipped an article from a Wall Street on-line that called the resulting composites "high-interest, unverified, instantaneous cash-advance portfolios." What they were was play money. If you made it big, you were rich; if you lost money, someone else was screwed.

The Paper Boys used the toy capital to make a killing in the gray market of school vouchers, Medicaid warrants, food stamps, and New York State tax refund script; all the varied specie of the privatized welfare state. The Kemp Plan had created a bold new market for the young entrepreneurs to play in.

All the social paper flying around at the time changed in value drastically with every election, each public opinion poll, and with Congress's midnight raids on the Social Security Trust Fund. Linked to illicit accounts on the Social Services Exchange, with one eye on the twenty-four-hour financial networks and the other on C-SPAN, the Boys easily outmaneuvered the hospitals, semi-private schools, and other large institutions on the SSE. It was an oft-quoted estimate that private involvement in the welfare markets had cost taxpayers a billion dollars even before the crash.

As she'd read the story to Freddie the night before, he'd interjected that he remembered all the Paper Boys being wiped out. But Ed King and some of the other more pragmatic Boys had foreseen the inevitable. They had shredded their cards and moved into real estate a few months before Congress had invalidated all privately held welfare paper. When the '02 recovery finally took hold, most of these Boys had acquired large holdings in Manhattan and Boston office buildings, some of which had been empty for a decade. The small fortunes they had made in social paper were soon dwarfed.

But King had taken a different course. He'd had a dream since a freshman job at the Dartmouth computer lab. In the mid-nineties, surrounded by the chaos of incompatible platforms—a menagerie of strange beasts with names like UNIX, Chicago, Macintosh, and Windows—he had written a few thousand lines of code that would change the world.

The Universal Operating System was the first true cross-platform protocol. Effortlessly, it could leap the dark chasms of incompatibility that severed the realms of cyberspace. With a few brilliant algorithms, the UOS not only made every software system fully compatible with every other, but anticipated in principle every possible system. Later, King's discovery would be compared with Chomsky's or Saussure's. In short, he had discovered the universal grammar of silicon. As a college student, he had grasped the importance of his work, but he kept his discovery to himself. He didn't want to become another Lanier.

After the crash, he returned to his dream child. With his sudden millions, he took what had been an academic curiosity and forged of it an empire. For a few hundred thousand dollars, a small army of lawyers wrapped the basic concept in four gigabytes of patents. Then he hired an engineering team to port the UOS to every platform in existence, refining and expanding the original premise into a usable product. Then, his creation perfected and secure, he gave it away.

It became available at 5:37 P.M. 11/1/02. For the taking on a hundred bulletin boards, scattered by King's Paper Boy friends onto the ubiquitous tributaries of shareware, and shipped with every cheap clone whose manufacturer King could bribe, the UOS standard module was thrown away like rice at a wedding. The module moved quickly, its universality allowing it to duplicate like an implacably persistent virus. It was so successful that, within a few hours, the National Sysop had made a panicked phone call to the Secret Service, reporting that the backbone was under a terrorist hacker's attack. The UOS spread faster and faster as previously incompatible computers were joined through it. In a few days, it had realized the dream of a single, integrated network. It eased the boundaries between old machines and new, reconciled exotic systems with the mundane, and made old rivalries between megacorporations moot.

It also erased a measurable percentage of the
world's wealth. Proprietary operating systems had
formed the basis of some of the world's most profit-
able companies. In the course of a week, what had
been the most valuable intellectual properties in the
world had become worthless. The world stock markets (their own trading computers suddenly linked
by UOS) roiled for months as the damage was
assessed.

King's only intrusion to the whole messy process
was to charge an almost invisible tax: one dollar on
every licensed shipment of the UOS after 1/1/03.
Every computer, car, oven, telephone—every commodity whose basic processor used those few thousand lines of code—was licensed. The world hardly
noticed, but Ed King got very rich.

In the days before Americorp went public, the
stock exchanges in Tokyo, Moscow, and New York
slumped. Investors pulled their money out of stocks
across the board, freeing up capital to buy Americorp
shares. Even with Ed King maintaining 40 percent of
the corporation, Americorp was overcapitalized from
its first hours. With its ready money and free use
of the UOS, its influence was irresistible. King's pet
projects, the smartcard, Vivid TV, the networking of
India, were merely spikes against the background
noise of Americorp's dominance. Even in markets
where its competitors won, they did so using the
UOS, and Americorp still profited.

As the story approached the present, the name
Sean Bayes began to appear. An installation artist
from the DUMBO scene, she met King at a Japanese
embassy party. She had recently created an installation for the Mitsubishi/Benz headquarters in Kyoto.
The Japanese government was honoring a sampling
of Americans who were addressing the trade imbal-
ance. King with his licensing billions and Bayes with
her single commission were at the extremes of the

guest list. According to hacker gossip culled from old Internet backups, they had gone home together that first night.

The relationship was infrequently in the press. King's extraordinary wealth enforced a certain amount of secrecy around his movements. Sean had been a fairly obscure artist before they met, and she used King's wealth to remain aloof from the art world. She also used it to create ever-larger installations, strange re-creations of urban shopping areas— bodegas, delicatessens, discount drugstores—all filled with fictitious merchandise that Bayes created herself. The fabricated products were burlesque parodies on the theme of commodity capitalism. The irony that they were financed by the richest man in the world was not lost on Bayes's critics. In *Art Forum Online*, Lee found that Bayes had more detractors than supporters. She also discovered that King had recently bought an entire warehouse loft for Bayes's next installation. For her security, or as a marketing ploy, its location was a closely guarded secret.

Making herself a drink from the miniframe bar, Lee leaned over Freddie's shoulder to see if he'd made progress with the BAM tickets. He was outdoing himself. A model of the opera house filled the center of the room. Bold red marker points hovered over several of the box seats at the extreme ends of the first mezzanine. He was peering at the virtual contraption from different angles, tracing lines of sight among the various boxes.

"Jesus, Freddie," she said. "We just want tickets. We're not going to assassinate the guy, just talk to him."

"Fine. But think about it. How are you going to get close to him? His security is tight as shit since his mother got kidnapped."

Freddie had done a little homework on his own.

"I just figured I'd think of something. I usually

do," she said. Freddie looked hurt. He had been pouting since her rejection that morning. "Well, what would you suggest?"

He gave a look that read, *I've got it all worked out.* "Look, Sam's season seats are usually here."

A tiny sliver in the orchestra highlighted.

"And the Americorp box is here." It was on the same side as Sam's seats, almost directly above. "Actually, they're great seats for an assassination. You could lob a grenade just like this." A cursor swept in a tidy arc from Sam's seats to the box.

"Very funny."

"But not good for looking."

"So where do you suggest we sit?"

He waved a finger. A box across the theater, on the same level as King's, flashed.

"How are you going to get us box seats?"

"They are gotten." The hacker's smugness in his voice.

"Freddie," she said, "don't you think the legitimate occupants will raise a stink if they show up and find out their box seats have been given away? It is opening night."

"Relax," he said. "They're comps. Press passes for some critics. I transferred them to Sam's usual seats and e-mailed apologies that they had to miss opening night. I told them they were getting bounced by some of the Kennedy-Schwarzeneggers."

"Great," she laughed. "And I thought my last boyfriend was the devil."

Freddie rolled his eyes. "Boy, you can't please some people."

"So," she asked, "why the direct line of sight?"

"Well, if Bonito can doppelgäng, why can't you?" The suggestion chilled her. "What do you mean?"

"You want to get King's ear, right?"

"*Just* his ear."

He frowned. "I don't mean doppelgäng *King*. I mean someone close to him."

"It's not that simple, Freddie. People aren't just appearances. They've got mannerisms, ticks, memories, not to mention voices."

"So I've gathered over the last twenty-two years. What I mean is, someone he doesn't know. But someone who could get close to him. Look." Text fields sprouted from the other boxes above stage right, listing ticketholders by name and smartcard number. There was a bevy of aristocracy, heads of state, and celebrities around the Americorp box. "Pick anyone you want. The more famous, the better. Ask for a meeting during the break. Isn't that how it's done?"

"I suppose so. But this isn't as easy as you think."

"Sam owns some *very* good binoculars." She wished he would quit italicizing words at her. It reminded her of Bonito.

"That's not what I mean," she said. "Where would I change?"

"In the box."

"With Sam there?"

"I hate to be the bearer of bad news, but he's got it halfway figured out already."

"You told him?" The gut feeling of violation rose quickly. Her hands flexed, and she felt close to violence.

"No," he said. "But listen. He knows about Milica Raznakovic, right? So he knows that Milica Raznakovic just came out of nowhere. Any fourteen-year-old hacker could've figured that out. But Milica has medical records that patently do not match your body. So where did her body come from? I told him I met a woman with hands that were different. Now you show up, but only one of your hands is different. You've managed to make enemies with this Bonito, an Americorp hit man or whatever. Is this normal? He keeps asking me who the hell you are, *what* the hell you are, and all I can say is I can't tell him." He leaned back, sighed, and ran his fingers through his hair. "But I know Sam; he'll figure you out a hell of a lot quicker than I did."

A wash of red came down over her vision, so thick that she thought it was in the VR. She pulled the visor off, but the red mist didn't clear. After what seemed a long time, she felt Freddie's hands on her. When she could see, she looked up at him. Thankfully, his visor was off.

"Don't you understand?" she said. "For so long, nobody knew." Her voice sounded strange and tinny in her ears. She breathed deeply and regained control. "Now Bonito. And you . . . " She choked.

"Make friends with Sam." He said it softly, simply.

She went to the window and watched the little man below arrange the rocks and tiny statuary. His motions were elegant and precise. He seemed to be waiting.

She turned to Freddie and said, "Let's go."

In a room on the third floor, its russet carpet washed blood-red by sunlight filtered through pink drapes, she pulled her hand back into a normal shape, the expressions on her face sharp and unguardedly inhuman as she did so. Sam watched with exquisitely focused attention, asked no questions, and held the new hand for a long time afterward.

When she could stand, she left the two of them together and returned to the bedroom to sleep a few more hours before the show.

CHAPTER 8

BAM

A black stretch limousine, garishly red inside, appeared within ten minutes of Sam's call. The table between the seats had the dull look of an LCD flatscreen. There were two handsets and three phone lines. A microwave matrix checkered the back window. Its ride was quiet, with the even acceleration of a fully electric.

They stopped first at Freddie's apartment. Sam was already dressed in black tie, formal wear exaggerating the fragility of his frame. He had changed his glasses. The lenses were thinner and they were silver-rimmed. He wore black qwerty bracelets pushed back into his coat sleeves. She realized that he would always carry them: to make a phone call; to use a bank machine. More and more machines had begun to talk as she had grown up, but she'd never considered who had been disenfranchised by the disappearance of buttons and readouts. She saw him take a small speech transcriber from the drawer of a doorside table as they left. Sam's left qwerty bracelet trailed a silver modal antenna, dangling two inches out of his sleeve. He kept pushing it back in, but its winding mechanism was apparently loose. The bracelets were sleek, expensive-looking. She wondered if they were a formal set (for the opera?) or just a better brand than Freddie's.

They stopped by Freddie's apartment to change.

Freddie wore a double-breasted black suit. He didn't have a tie or a real dress shirt, so he wore a black boxneck. She had salvaged only one dress: knee-length and low-cut, silver Mylar and silk. It wasn't exactly formal, but then again, this was Brooklyn. It would have to do. At least it was cool. She'd need that when she changed.

They went back out to the limo. Sam was standing on the sidewalk calibrating his binoculars. They were military field glasses—large, camouflage-mottled, their lenses trimmed with brightly reflective lines of optical circuitry.

"A little extreme for opera glasses, don't you think?"

Sam sensed that she had spoken and looked at her questioningly. Freddie started to qwert, but she stayed his hands and mouthed the question again.

"When you can't hear," Sam said, "vision can become a fetish."

She acknowledged with a nod.

The sun climbed back above the horizon as the limo passed over the Brooklyn Bridge, the sky bright red behind them and pale yellow overhead, and she tried to remember the last time she had left Manhattan. In the limo, it didn't seem so far to go. From the bridge, they could see the Pei skyscraper rising over the old LIRR station. Across from Freddie and her, Sam was looking back at the soaring towers of the financial district. She turned back and squinted into the sunset, but could distinguish only the prominences of the World Trade Towers, the Mitsubishi/Benz Building, and the Morgan Heliodrome.

They descended into Brooklyn.

Traffic began to choke as they neared BAM. News trucks, satellite dishes raised high on telescoping ceramic poles, loitered in the blocks around the academy. The limo driver took them the long way around, through wealthy brownstones ringing Fort

Greene Park and past the uniformed guards of the Brooklyn Arms Luxury Complex. The entrance way to BAM was aswarm with paparazzi, clustered around the line of arriving limousines. A few smokers in their opera clothes looked on. A man with a palm-size video camera ran over when their limousine rolled to a stop. When they emerged he looked at them, frowned, and lost interest.

Freddie picked up the tickets at a window labeled "Media" while she and Sam stood in a long line for champagne. The buzz that filled the huge, crowded lobby had a sharp edge. It was opening night.

There were gallery types, their formal dress leavened with eccentric touches: a bright-red silk cravat, a black bowler and walking stick, the subtly shifting colors of VSGA jewelry. There were Downtowners, threadbare in black and gray, hair shorn or polychrome. There were tight, fawning knots around hidden celebrities, and a few lone patrons looking down at their watches as they waited for friends to arrive.

Freddie joined them in line for a moment, but then headed back to the media window to make sure the tickets they had displaced were torn up. "The last thing you need is to be surprised in the middle of a change by an enraged opera critic," he muttered as he walked away. She laughed and mouthed the words for Sam's benefit.

The champagne came ice-cold, served in longstemmed plasticware stamped with a biodegradable symbol. They climbed the stairs to the mezzanine level.

The air of anticipation in the crowd mixed with her nervousness. She had never tried to substitute herself for another human being, even briefly. The goal of her changes had always been anonymity, motion across the barriers of identity. She had never been interested in personalities. Her eye was best at focusing on the landscape—the scene—and her goal had always been to blend in, to lose herself. Mimicking seemed like a cheapening of her ability; merely to re-create the limited whole of a single identity.

The butterflies in her stomachs felt like the onset of a change, and she calmed them with champagne.

Their box was above the extreme right of the stage. There were five seats in the box, three in front and a pair behind. They were directly over the orchestra pit, but their view of the stage was partly cut off by the proscenium arch. She realized that the point of the box seats was not their view of the stage, but to see and be seen. The view of the audience was commanding. Freddie crouched behind the back pair of seats, setting up a small tripod for the field glasses. He swore once or twice as he fumbled in the dim light. Sam was looking at the curtained stage with a tiny opera glass. With it still to his eye, he leaned toward her.

His whisper was harsh, but not as tortured as his full voice. "The box where Ed King will sit is directly across the opera hall. At the moment, there are two men sitting there." She started to look, but he held out the little opera glass to her. "Please, use this. Subtlety is best. Its focal direction is fugitive."

"Its what?" she asked.

"Just point it toward the stage and look through."

The glass looked like a little telescope. It was surprisingly heavy, made of natural wood with brass fittings around both lenses. A thin leather strap was looped through a brass ring on one side. She looked through it. At first the view was dark and fuzzy. Then her eye focused, closer, and she realized she was looking at the palm of her own hand. She turned the glass end over end and looked again.

Instead of the orchestra pit, the center of the front mezzanine came into view. She twisted the glass slightly in her hand, and the view shifted up to the second and third balconies. She took her eye from the lens and looked at the instrument. There was a minute hole in either side, in which she could see the bright sheen of reflective glass. Apparently there was a two-sided mirror at a forty-five-degree angle between the lenses. It redirected the line of sight out the holes in the side. She oriented it toward the stage curtain as Sam had done, her palm out of the way. The box seats directly across from them came into view. The small glass magnified the view slightly. A box one level above their own was occupied by two men in black suits. They were wary-eyed, with earpieces and a bulk that implied kevlar vests.

"Nice little contraption," she said, looking down at the glass. "Something you invented?"

"Hardly. It dates from the eighteenth century, when people appreciated what opera was all about."

"Watching other people?"

"Watching them subtly. It's called a palemoscope." He articulated the syllables of the word a little unsurely, as if he'd never said it out loud before.

"I could have used this once or twice in my life. Watching people is part of my . . . avocation." She spoke in normal tones, realizing that she was more comfortable speaking to him. She no longer mouthed the words with exaggerated clarity.

He closed his tiny hand over hers. "It's yours."

She suppressed a start. His hand was very cold. She looped the instrument's little leather strap around her neck.

The hall darkened slowly, the audience hushing as the lights dimmed. Freddie joined them in the seat next to her.

The overture began, a long, slow wash of chords from the five keyboardists in the pit. The volume was at the threshold of audibility. An occasional stifled cough came from the audience. Then the percussionists lifted their sticks. She braced for a torrent of sound.

But the percussion began softly: a scraped cymbal; snares set lightly ashudder with jazz brushes; a tentative roll on the concert bass drum, as subtle as a subway train's rumble heard from aboveground.

A few minutes passed in the miasmic wash of sound. She looked out over the darkened audience. The vast array of faces, still and intent, disquieted her. She put the palemoscope to her eye and brought the box seats Sam had indicated into view. The only light in the house was from the orchestra pit. It was still too dark to see King clearly, but the silhouettes of his two guards had been joined by a third shape.

The curtain began to rise.

Red suns flared among the bank of spotlights arrayed beneath the mezzanine. A quintet of saxophones growled in densely voiced, lushly consonant chords. The curtain opened on a giant upright checkerboard, from which two dozen or so performers hung. Their costumes were brightly reflective; gilded with metals, mirrors, rhinestones, Mylar, whole sheets of VSGA. They were attached to the chessboard by elaborate harnesses like parachutists'. Most of them were moving; stepping between rungs placed on the chessboard, bringing mountain-climbing clips down onto black plastic handholds with loud snaps.

Six of them—four men and two women—were stationary. They were turned toward the audience, their costumes exceptionally bright even on that effulgent grid. They began to sing.

The percussion section settled into a simple rhythmic figure. The saxophones followed in the repetitive arpeggios that had typified opera for the last twenty years. The singers' voices were softly treated with some sort of flanging effect, their ornate throat mikes plainly visible. The keyboards remained mired in their long chords.

She strained to catch the words, but she couldn't

quite place the language of the text. Leaning to Freddie's ear, she asked, "Is that Italian?"

"It's Esperanto. But I don't think anyone's supposed to understand it. That's the point. The text is drawn from some UN treaty on oil spills, or something like that."

One of the singers was replaced on his square by one of the moving performers, who turned around and began to sing herself. A few minutes later, a knight's move away, another singer lost her place to a moving performer. The displaced singers turned their faces to the board and began to move.

Lee tried to find a pattern to the performers' movements. Halting and meandering, they shifted in fits and starts, one move often canceling out another. If she concentrated on one climber, she could almost begin to predict the next change of direction, but each seemed to move under a different set of rules.

Whenever a moving performer arrived at a square with a singing one, the stationary one was replaced, so the number of singers remained at six, though the makeup of the chorus changed. Over the next twenty minutes or so, she broadened her attention to the whole board, hoping the pattern would become clearer. She noticed that the women singers were slowly gaining in number. For a long time, the chorus had remained even at three men and three women. Then a man was replaced by a woman, and still another. The last man left singing was in the upper rightmost square.

A young Asian soprano (one of the original six singers, since displaced) was making her way toward him. The music gained in intensity as she approached. Just before she reached him, however, another woman singing in the center was replaced by a barrel-chested tenor with a full beard.

Over the next ten minutes, the women slowly lost their lead.

She lifted the palemoscope and focused on the box across from them. Shielded from the glare on the stage, her eyes adjusted to the darkness. King's box was close to the glitter of the stage, and he was clearer now. She recognized him from Candy.

She leaned back to Freddie. "Did you point the field glasses at King?"

"No," he whispered. "Someone else you might want to see. Hillary Wilson."

"The composer?"

"The woman of the hour."

She took his point. If anyone could get into King's box tonight, Wilson could.

"And," Freddie added, "she's got the same haircut as you."

Lee made her way to the back of their box, careful not to kick the legs of the little tripod. She knelt there in the darkness and carefully brought her eyes to the lenses.

Through the glasses, vision was the grainy green monochrome she associated with war footage, some sort of low-light enhancement. The image was framed by administrative debris in dim yellow: scattered numbers, a battery level, a hatched line along the bottom labeled with degrees.

Hillary Wilson was seated alone in the highest box. She was thin and Anglo, with slicked-back short hair, dressed in a dark suit and a tight-necked white blouse. Her eyes were closed. She seemed to be in her late fifties.

Lee felt Freddie next to her, and looked up at him. "This isn't what I would call a good picture, you know. I don't think I can see well enough to impersonate someone from this distance." She spoke directly into his ear to be heard over the music.

"Wait, here's the controls." He handed her a small remote. It had six hard icons and a trackball, contoured for a smaller hand than hers. "Here's the zoom. This other icon brings up a resolution palette menu. Just make selections with the ball, and . . ."

"Thanks, Freddie. The zoom will do fine."

She leaned to the lenses again and pressed the hard icon Freddie had indicated. The image grew a little larger. She held the icon down. In a series of little jerking steps, the image filled the screen.

The woman's face was suddenly clear and unexpectedly beautiful. It was sharp and aquiline; her nose and cheekbones high and aristocratic. She wore dark eyeliner. Above the exaggerated eyes, her eyebrows were plucked bare, or possibly washed out by the image enhancement. It made her forehead seem strangely high, like some noble alien. She was touched by wrinkles only at her neck.

Her eyes were still closed, but she didn't seem to be in a meditative repose. Her back was straight, her lips tight. At this extreme magnification, Lee could see a flicker at the corner of her mouth at each downstroke of the concert bass. Her head was shaking a little. The music was reaching a climax of some kind, growing more rhythmic and driven. Even the keyboards had become insistent and staccato. Lee could hear that the men had become a majority of the singers.

Lee sat back. Her neck was sore, and she relaxed it. She covered her eyes to keep them adjusted to low light.

The field glasses didn't show enough. The picture of Wilson's basic facial structure was clear, but what surface details were missing from the electronically rendered image? There could be an uneven tan, freckles, liver spots, characteristic wrinkles when Wilson smiled. Freddie simply didn't grasp how rich the human face could be.

Perhaps that was the trick: to rely on the poor eyes of monomorphs. She hoped King didn't know Wilson personally. If he did, this plan would be a disaster.

Her voice, clothing, eye color, hair—almost anything could give her away. Even Bonito required weeks (was it months, *years*?) of stalking to replace someone fully. She would have to keep her approach to King limited to a few people, celebrity gatekeepers who would recognize the great composer, but would not know Wilson well.

She looked back into the glasses. Now Wilson's eyes were open. They were unwrinkled, the flesh below them a little taut from a surgical tuck. At least that was easy to emulate; it looked the same on everybody. She pushed the other icon Freddie had indicated, and Wilson's face was replaced by a palette of colors, four-by-four. The trackball moved a small arrow among them. She found she could select colors with a little press on the ball. Wilson's image returned after each press, rendered in the various hues. At first, the pictures seemed the same. As her eyes adjusted, however, the images took on subtle differences. She went through the hues on the palette one by one. In the reddish colors, she could make out perspective in the lines of Wilson's slicked-back hair. The nose looked even sharper than she'd thought, upturned a little puckishly. The bluer colors flattened Wilson's features but brought out the aged skin's texture in greater detail. The yellows were almost the same as the grainy green default hue, but sharper, making Wilson's small nervous movements easier to see. The last option, a bright purple, exaggerated the imperfections of Wilson's face. She suddenly seemed a wrinkled crone: cheeks sunken below their sharp armature, neck hideously mottled, eyes radiant with crow's-feet.

Lee wondered if this horrible rendering was what Wilson actually looked like. She swept the glasses across the rest of the audience, hatches counting off degrees at the bottom of the view, the autofocus optics whining as she panned. On the purple setting, the field glasses transformed the crowd into an audience of leering monsters, grim corpses, lesioned PWAs. Lee wondered what the hell the setting was for. She switched back to the default.

After a few moments she found Wilson again. The woman had again become beautiful, elegant, aristocratic. A picture was solidifying in Lee's mind.

The music was still building, its climax developing—as everything seemed to do in this opera—with maddening slowness. A quick census of the checkerboard revealed that there was only one woman left singing, the Asian soprano, still in the upper right-hand corner. (In a sudden stroke of intuition, it occurred to her that the rules of movement made it harder to displace a singer in a corner.) But two men were approaching, and the music grew thinner and harsher as they worked toward her, weaving and stuttering like half-autistic mountaineers.

As far as she understood the logic of the piece, she had to work fast. She didn't want the house lights to come up while she writhed half-formed on the floor.

The chemicals of change were impelled by her nervousness. It was the first time she had done it in public. The proximity of Freddie and Sam, the rapt audience a few meters below, the public scent of industrial carpet all drove the change. Pain wrenched her face into a featureless mask with a harsh jerk, her own ragged cry at the distant edge of her awareness. She pulled it into the aquiline Anglo visage that had formed in her mind. The grainy, unsubtle colors had given Wilson's image a strange poignancy, an immediate and pointed verity: like a surveillance video, a home movie, night battle footage. She had always invented the faces she wore. Now, the raw material of voyeurism gave her mental image a strange new confidence.

Excitement took her body quickly into a supple state.

The face was easy. It swept over her, possessed her. Her skull shifted into sharp, flat planes, the skin clutching hard to them. Her eyebrows thinned, hair subsumed by greedy pores, and she stretched the skin beneath her eyes with rivets of cartilage like a surgeon's staples. With a tightly controlled burst of melanin she lined her eyes. The body she extrapolated from Wilson's thin neck and arms: a brittle skeleton, its frame a little taller than her current one, covered less generously with skin. She kept the muscles fit and lean, letting the breasts sag just a little.

When the hard work was done, she textured her hands and neck with age. Then she lay still.

Sweat covered her, cool and unabsorbed by the mylar dress. The music had passed its climax, and the six voices of the chorus were now replaced by a vocal solo. Still gasping for air, she pulled herself up to see.

The Asian soprano, at last cornered by the two men, had escaped. She was flying, hoisted up with terrible slowness on invisible monofilament. A host of white follow spots lit her with blinding ferocity, the performers on the chessboard gone silent, their faces turned up in awe.

The aria rang with passing dissonances, her voice bell-like over the wash of five keyboards. The score thickened with complex harmonies, but resolved again and again to a strangely harsh unison between her and the keyboards. She had risen so high that she was almost hidden by the top of the proscenium arch.

Lee leaned to the binoculars again. Her eyes took long seconds to adjust after the blinding spectacle. Hillary Wilson's eyes were closed again, but now her head was thrown back. Pain seemed to rack her features; her hands were at her cheeks, fingers splayed.

She was biting her lower lip, head shaking a little feebly. The fingers flexed in time with the pulsing decrescendo of her music, pulling the lower eyelids down to reveal irisless whites. She looked a thousand years old.

Lee turned away, from Wilson, from the spectacle on stage. The audience below was awash with light reflected from the ascending diva. From down in the orchestra seats, they could still see her rising into the flyspace of the old opera house. The hundreds of upturned faces were raw in their attentiveness, sharp with the emotion of that abstract, enormous, dramatic moment. Lee had to turn away again, dropping her eyes to her own hands. Their form was unmutated, but they seemed very old.

She heard a brief gasp, a sharp whisper over the music, almost in her ear, and looked up to meet Freddie's eyes.

And saw her change reflected in them.

The shock on his face was unhidden, undiluted. He had never seen her with another body. At last, he was faced with the profundity of her talent. She looked for horror or sudden distrust in his eyes, but they gleamed only with unguarded excitement. She saw Freddie take conscious control of himself, slowing his breath.

Sam was also looking. His gaze was more critical, taking the measure of her. When their eyes met he nodded in appreciation. "Very precise," he mouthed soundlessly. An opera fan, he had probably seen Wilson's picture before.

The music was dying in a hush of synthesized white noise, like some distant beach beaten by waves. The loud rush of the audience's applause came before the sound had completely subsided. It was dark for half a minute before the house lights rose for intermission.

Freddie offered her his hand.

Her legs were unsteady, but the muscles had formed well balanced, and she felt a sinewy strength in her arms. She was probably sturdier than her twin across the house. She smoothed her dress and took Freddie's coat when he offered it. It fit better than she expected, and the padded shoulders lent her authority. She realized that silver Mylar was probably out of character for Wilson.

She paused at the door.

"Freddie, what happens if we run into the real Wilson?"

"She's a recluse. Doesn't give interviews. She won't be wandering around. But stay away from reporters. They'll give their left nut for video of you tonight." Freddie was nervous.

She hesitated. "Maybe we should have picked someone less famous."

He started to say something but lost his voice. "It's really weird to talk to you. You're so . . ."

"Different," she completed, and opened the box door.

Freddie followed her out of the box. As they walked, he hung a step back, as a personal assistant would. She took the lead, assuming an air of confidence. They followed the curve of the hallway toward the other side of the opera house.

Halfway there, they reached a crush of audience members exiting the mezzanine. There were soft mutters of recognition around them. A few people caught her eye and smiled. She smiled back. She calmed a rush of adrenaline, an unfamiliar exhilaration as the crowd parted before them. Fame.

Suddenly a man was in their way, his face alight. He grasped Lee's hands in his.

"Hillary." A German accent. A seductive smile.

Lee turned her fear into a smile and leaned forward into his offered hug. His hair was slicked back with something that smelled like lemon.

"It's wonderful, Hillary," he said, his eyes sweeping down her.

She looked down at the Mylar dress, afraid to speak. She had made no changes to her voice.

"Not the dress, Hillary, the opera!" He laughed, joined by a few other people arrayed a step behind him. Like him, they were dressed in well-pressed black: suits, boxnecks, evening dresses. One of the women looked like a man in drag. Lee forced herself to laugh along with them. Freddie put his hand on her arm and started to say something.

"There's just a few people I would like you to meet," the German interrupted. He stepped a little to the side, his arm extending like a game-show host's.

"I'm sorry," she said, her voice coming out crisp and tight, "but I don't know who the fuck you are."

His smile stayed on his face, but something behind his eyes crumpled like a house of cards. He made a little rubbing gesture with the fingers of his extended hand, as if he was trying to remember a name, a phone number, a simple word that was somehow eluding his grasp. He started to speak again.

Freddie's grasp tightened as he said, "Ms. Wilson has an appointment." He pulled her free of the little knot of embarrassed faces. She smiled as they moved out of her way. One of the women smiled back, a twinkle in her eye as if she'd won a bet.

Lee felt a rush of strange pleasure. It was the delight of illicit power. She'd had a girlfriend once who could get bogus smartcards, and the feeling reminded her of the thrill of charging a purchase on one. But this was much more visceral. She guessed it was something Bonito would understand.

They moved quickly through the rest of the crowd. She glanced back at Freddie. He was ashen. His hand still grasped her arm, as if for support.

They reached a series of doors set flush into the

curved hallway, deep mahogany like the one that led to their box. A pair of suits flanked one.

Freddie cleared his throat. Their expressions didn't change. He started to speak, but instead his grasp tightened.

"I am Hillary Wilson," Lee said. "And I would like to meet Mr. King."

One suit looked at the other, his eyebrow raised. The shorter one's face bore a look of recognition. He made a little half bow. "Wait just a moment, please," he said. He had a corporate accent as smooth as a CitiBank machine's.

He put a finger in one ear and muttered something almost silently. He had a bead in the other ear. He listened intently, nodding, smiling politely when he caught her eye. Confirmation flickered in his face.

As they were ushered inside, the other suit waved his hand just behind her, at the periphery of vision. Something in the hand chirped a little, probably at the brass fittings on the palemoscope around her neck.

Two more suits inside stood shoulder to shoulder, shielding King from her view. They smiled politely and waited for a signal from the guard with the metal detector. Then they parted. Behind them was King.

He looked older than he had at Candy. In the yellow incandescent houselights, his boyish features were showing their age. But his enthusiasm was undimmed.

"Thank God you've come," were the first words out of his mouth.

It wasn't the greeting she'd expected.

"There's a discrepancy, you know." He pointed meaningfully at the paper notebook on his lap. It was covered in a welter of scrawls, looping curves in several colors. "But I mean, that could be the point, right?"

He seemed desperately to need an answer. The silence grew, second by second.

She held her hand out for the notebook. Maybe somewhere on it was a legible word, a drawing, any clue at all. He handed it over eagerly, saying, "I mean, I thought I'd cracked it in the first movement, but then you threw in those diagonal exceptions. Quite logical, really. I should have seen them coming . . ." He was waiting for a look of understanding from her.

Beneath several layers of swirls and loops of ink, she saw a grid, eight-by-eight, a diagram of the opera set. Over the grid, the movements of the singers had been traced, elaborated, extrapolated. She gathered that each color was one singer, though there seemed to be too many colors. She pretended to study it carefully, nodding her head and biting her lower lip as she'd seen Wilson do.

King waited expectantly. He was chewing a thin plastic pen whose end was ringed with a color dial. It was a cheap item, popular with kids a couple of years before.

The diagram staggered her. This was how King had seen the opera: chaos to be mapped and domesticated. She had looked for the pattern herself, but it seemed intentionally overcomplicated—as if to resist determined analysis, forcing attention onto other issues. She had let her intuition predict the movement of the singers, concentrating on the waning fortunes of the women rather than the rules of motion. But the pattern had been no match for King and his multicolored pen.

Beside the scrawls that recorded the performers' raw movements, a set of formulae had been inscribed. The handwriting was minuscule; letters, numbers, flowcharting rubric, all neatly boxed and marked with symbols vaguely familiar from Senior Logic. On the facing page, numerous precursors to these final formulae had been scrawled and scratched out. *Christ*, she thought, *how did he have time to watch?* She cleared her throat.

"There's no discrepancy," she calmly disagreed. Out of the corner of her eye, Freddie looked horrified.

"But," King blustered, "the girl at the end . . . when the two lateral-movers hit adjacent corners, their movements would have been totally recursive after that. I mean, they were stuck. She was safe, wasn't she? *Indefinitely* safe?" He pulled the notebook back out of her hand and looked at it again, his head nodding a little as if checking old and certain facts.

Maybe all his doodles had discovered something interesting. "So how's that a discrepancy?" she asked. "All the rules were followed."

"Well, I mean, sure. It was all by the rules until she . . . flew away. That wasn't in the rules. And she was safe. So, why did she have to escape?" He asked the question almost desperately.

She knew the answer right away, as surely as if she really were Wilson. But she let the moment linger.

Then she smiled and said, "Because, Mr. King, she was just sick of the whole thing."

His face stayed blank for a moment, and he looked almost dumb as the thought sank in. Then the liveliness in his features, the sure intelligence, returned, and he broke into a grin. "Ms. Wilson," he said, "would you like to have a drink?"

"Please." She took the seat next to him, leaving Freddie standing. He retreated a step, giving them a small area of privacy.

She took the notebook back and spread it open across her knees, caressing the sprawling loops. She could feel the incisions of the penned lines in the heavy bond paper. "How odd that *you* should use a paper notebook," she said.

"It's an old habit." He fondled the plastic color

dial of the pen. "Really a marvelous piece of technology: open architecture, pen-based, low power."

She laughed. Drinks appeared; two champagnes in real glass, thin and fluted. "I hope you don't think it's perverse," she said.

"What?" he asked.

"That my soprano flies away from a danger that's not real. Well, it's very real, but not as imminent as it looks. I really didn't think anyone would figure out the pattern. Not on opening night, anyway."

He looked a little embarrassed. "It's a curse, really. I can't just sit and watch something so exquisitely . . . *rule-governed* and not try to figure it out."

She looked out over the house as if in thought and caught the glint of the field glasses back in their box. She thought she saw Sam's small form behind them. Of course, he would be watching: zoomed in all the way, lipreading.

She remembered how Wilson's face had looked at the end of the act.

"It's governed by a lot of other things, too," she said. The champagne was ice-cold, as dry as dust.

For the first time King seemed hesitant. "She escaped partly because . . . I mean, it had to do with the fact that she was . . . a woman. Right?" He bit his lip, unconsciously imitating her gesture.

He suddenly seemed terribly innocent. It was amazing that he had missed the point of the piece. The rise and fall of the women's fortunes had only been obscured by his page of colorful squiggles. She laughed again, and he started. She wondered if her apparent age intimidated him.

"Yes. It always matters."

"Damn. I wish Sean were here. She's much better at catching that kind of stuff than me."

Lee realized that he had a point. Sean was probably the wiser of the two. In Candy, he had dominated the conversation, charming and animated, but Sean was the better listener. At the Loisaida Social Club, Sean had parried her queries, controlled the conversation.

King had found his subtle discrepancy in the rules of Wilson's opera, but he had missed the glaring inconsistencies when Bonito had replaced Sean at Candy. How could she explain Bonito to this man? Bonito was something monstrously irreducible, undiagrammable; utterly not rule-governed.

King's world was too coherent to admit Bonito. She had to talk to Sean. King could only provide an introduction.

"Sean Bayes?" she asked.

"Yes." He brightened instantly. "You know her?"

"I admire her work, but we've never met."

"That's wonderful! She really would have been here tonight, except . . . she's working on a new show, you see."

"I've heard. Supposedly, it's quite secret."

"Not really. Sean just doesn't like to work in all the publicity that I've created for her."

"I'd love to see the work in progress."

"Really? Let me introduce you, then." The promise fell into the air. She wondered if it would fly.

They drank their champagne in silence for a few more moments. She tried to think of a way to return the conversation to Sean. She was about to speak again when the houselights flashed twice. King looked up.

"Ms. Wilson, would you do me the honor of watching the second act from my box?"

"Well . . ."

She felt Freddie's hand on her shoulder. "Ms. Wilson has to go on stage after the last curtain. It is opening night, after all."

Freddie's ears were sharper than she'd thought. It was a good thing he'd thought of that. If the real Wilson had taken a curtain call while she was still here with King, it would have been difficult to explain.

"Freddie is right, of course."

"I understand." King rose.

She decided to forgo politeness. "But I would like to meet Sean Bayes."

"Certainly," he seemed charmed at her insistence. "Give me your number?" He raised his pen.

"I don't take outside calls, actually. Please give me Ms. Bayes's number."

Her voice was flat, direct. Freddie's hand clenched a little as she spoke.

King smiled. It was a knowing smile. Of course, he approved of Sean's proclivities, was turned on by them.

He wrote the number on a corner of the tangled diagram. With a little flourish, he tore it off and handed it over. It was fifteen digits, complete with a call-screening number and a Brooklyn area code.

"Thank you, Mr. King. Enjoy the second act."

His handshake was firm and lingered a little, releasing her reluctantly. He seemed to be looking for something in her eyes. She turned away from his gaze.

The guards parted, and the door was opened by one of the men outside.

As they strode down the hall, Freddie fell in behind her again. He seemed a little awestruck. She realized that, among hackers, King was at least a minor god.

As they rounded the slow curve of the hallway, the knot of people around the mezzanine doors became visible. She steeled herself to pass the German man she had offended. As they reached the crowd, it parted for her again.

Suddenly a woman blocked their way. She held a palm-size corder and wore an omnidirectional throat mike.

"Excuse me, Ms. Wilson, but I'd like to ask you . . ."

Lee was momentarily paralyzed. She didn't want her own voice recorded coming out of Wilson's mouth. Without hesitation, Freddie swept around her and placed his hand over the corder's lensing surface.

"We're sorry, but I'm sure you know that Ms. Wilson does not give interviews."

The woman started to protest, trying to pull the corder away from Freddie. He kept it in a firm grip. Deeper in the crowd, she saw another corder lofted high and pointed at them. It was bulky and bore the logo of a local cable channel. The crowd's murmur became excited.

Freddie, still politely remonstrating with the woman, gestured with his eyes toward the exit stairs. Lee started down them, then turned and grabbed his wrist, pulling him after her. She was afraid to be caught alone in Wilson's body. They rushed down the stairs together.

"Boy, this was a good idea, Freddie! Doppelgäng Hillary Wilson, at the opening of her own opera. Great disguise!"

"Thanks. At least we got in to see King."

The plushly carpeted stairs ended between the orchestra seats and the main lobby. The crowd was thin here, but the lobby ahead was filled almost shoulder to shoulder. Freddie took her hand and pulled her forward. Another staircase faced the one they had just descended.

"This goes back up to the mezzanine," he said.

After only a few steps, Freddie halted. At the top of the stairs, a man stood with a large video corder. He was flanked by more paparazzi.

"We're surrounded," said Freddie. "We can get lost in the orchestra seats."

"No way, Freddie. What if Wilson's still in her box and sees us?"

"Well, shit, let's go straight through these guys."

He attempted to charge ahead, but she restrained him.

"Freddie, the lobby!"

"But there's no way back up to the box from there!"

"So what? We need to get out of here. I don't know if I can change again tonight. Let's get a damn cab."

"And leave Sam?" he asked.

"Sam is *fine*." She pulled him back down. The woman with the throat mike was at the bottom of the stairs, wiping the lensing surface of her corder with an oilcloth. Lee ignored her and pulled Freddie into the lobby.

It was crowded. Every elbow she jostled seemed connected to a plastic cup of white wine. They made their way aggressively through the crowd, trailed by whispers of recognition. The doors were open to the warm, humid night. They rushed down the stone steps to a line of idling limos. Some were leaving. She looked up and down the street. Incredibly, there were no taxis.

But, she realized, there were more paparazzi than she could count. Lounging on the stairs, standing in small knots, drinking beer outside the bodega across the street, they held low-light corders, satellite packs, long-lensed still cameras.

So far, she had not been recognized.

"Put your arm around me, Freddie. This way." She steered him toward the edge of the crowd.

"We can't go too far. This is a pretty scary part of Brooklyn," he said.

She smiled despite her adrenaline. Freddie was a wimp. "I can be pretty scary myself, you know."

He considered this silently.

They reached the corner of the building and turned

into sudden darkness. The sidewalk led along the featureless brick of the academy's side wall. After the crowds, it seemed strangely deserted. Then her eyes adjusted, and she saw a small group directly in front of them. She slowed Freddie with a tug on his arm.

It was four males, gathered in a tight circle. The two facing them looked up, a little startled. She felt her body readying for a quick and silent fight—hand muscles bunching, pupils dilating to adjust to the semi-darkness. If they attacked, perhaps she could scatter them with a few deep scratches. Then she saw the red ember that one cupped in his hand. A whiff of sweet, heavy smoke confirmed her relief. The men had just stepped around the corner to smoke a joint.

But they were paparazzi. As they turned, she saw corders and various lenses dangling from straps around their necks. Bright-red LED fireflies glowed evilly from the equipment.

"Hey, you're Hillary Wilson," one said. His accent was broad, midwestern.

"No, I'm not," was all she could manage.

The others looked at their colleague and then squinted at her. One flicked a belt control, and suddenly the scene was seared into her brain in bright cobalt colors. The unexpected light was devastating to her dilated pupils.

Freddie must have recovered his sight first. She felt herself pulled into a run, his hand on her shoulder. As they passed the group, she heard the whir of corders and a few clipped commands that one of them muttered into his throat mike. She willed her pupils out of their sudden contraction and opened her eyes to the desolate street before them. The colors were wrong, her cones still jangled by the burst of light.

Freddie pulled her through an open gate. They were inside BAM now, in the space between the opera house and the music school. The alleyway angled down.

"We can outrun them. They're carrying a lot of shit."

"Freddie, I think they called in reinforcements."

Freddie slowed. "Shit. Well, maybe we should just give an interview. Or tell them to fuck off."

"I don't want to be on camera at *all*, Freddie. What if Wilson sees it?"

"So, she figures she's got a twin. Or a bent admirer with money for plastic surgery."

"Right, and she complains to the press that they interviewed an impostor. So it's a big story. Or Bonito sees it on TV. And you, who he's seen before, are standing next to me."

It sank in.

They ran. At the end of the alley was another gate, locked. Flatbush Avenue was in front of them. A trio of cabs sped across their view, ten meters away. "Shit," Freddie panted, "I hate this town."

A news van pulled up onto the curb before them. They turned back. A pair of the pot smokers were at the other end of the alley, one casting shaky illumination from his shoulder floodlights as he walked.

Freddie pointed toward a stage door they had just passed. He ran to it and fumbled in his pocket. He swept his smartcard through the reader. The access light stayed red.

"Nice try," she said.

"Hang on, it's *thinking*." He waited, counting under his breath, and then ran the card through again. With a heavy click, the light turned green.

He yanked the door open with a grunt. As they entered, he held up the card for her appreciation. "Pretty smart, huh?"

"Pretty smart. You figure any of those reporters got a card that smart?"

He frowned. "Maybe. But I think we're on home turf now. Let's just wait until they leave."

"Let's just find another exit and get the fuck out of here."

They were standing at the end of a dimly lit hallway. The walls were white and shabby, the floor tiled with scratched institutional gray. They were in the BAM music school, an old Salvation Army building that the academy had annexed a few years before. She started down the hall.

As they walked, Freddie checked the locked doors to either side. Through the small safety-glass panes set into them, they could see offices, classrooms, a small phone bank. This was the deserted administrative wing of the building. They moved quietly. An encounter here might be as bad as one with the paparazzi outside. They might run into someone who knew Wilson personally. She hoped any confrontation would go down as theatrical lore—the Phantom of the Opera. At least it wouldn't get uplinked for broadcast on the news.

Their wandering path led them from the grim hallways into darker, more mechanical areas, from institutional to industrial in feel. A long, sloping hall led them down, back toward the opera house. Large black machines from another century hulked in cramped spaces lit by red incandescents. Once, a harried prop hand ran past, taking no notice of them. They could hear the orchestra warming up. It sounded as if it was directly overhead.

"We're not heading toward an exit!" Freddie whispered harshly. "We're just gonna get lost down here."

She moved ahead more slowly. Around a corner, they surprised a pair of stagehands wearing headsets. The two were speechless for a moment, and then one said, "Curtain in one minute, Hillary." The other looked embarrassed.

She smiled at them, and she and Freddie picked up their pace.

Around more corners, down another hall, they found themselves in a large room. Its circular walls were filled with hand levers, dials, and banks of power outlets, crowded with unruly bunches of thick cable. The worklights here were blue.

In the center of the room, a black machine squatted. It didn't seem to be in working condition. Rooted on great iron legs, it looked like a giant dead insect. Cutting laterally through its center was a huge gear, parallel with the floor, mounted on a broad shaft that ran from floor to ceiling. She realized that they were below the opera house. The mechanism had once been used to rotate a circular section of the stage.

Upstairs, the orchestra began to play. There were no slow washes of sound to begin this act; a driving, arpeggiated rhythm had leapt into being, fully formed.

Out of the corner of her eye, she glimpsed motion.

She grabbed Freddie and indicated the figure with a jerk of her head. Visible through the machinery, it swayed in time with the music. Freddie started to back away unsurely, but she held on to his arm. They needed a guide out of the building.

Assuming the air of confidence she had managed upstairs, she rounded the girth of the machine. She struck a casual pose before the figure and cleared her throat. The woman lifted her head a little unsteadily.

Lee realized two things simultaneously.

The woman was booting up. A dermal injector was strapped to her bare left arm, counting off its delivery in sharp ticks, her sweat aglow in the light from its LCD readout. Her eyes were glazed and wide.

The woman was also Hillary Wilson.

Lee said nothing. She heard Freddie gasp behind her. She heard the orchestra above suddenly halve its tempo, slowing into a determined grind.

Wilson looked up, and her eyes filled with terror. She raised one hand to her mouth, as if to scream.

"Wait," said Lee.

Wilson didn't scream. She seemed paralyzed by the directive.

Lee scrambled for something to say.

"There's a discrepancy, you know," was all that would come.

Wilson blinked her eyes, once. The injector slipped from her fingers, clattering on the cement floor.

Lee took a step forward, put a hand on Wilson's shoulder. "She didn't have to escape. She was safe, Hillary."

Wilson nodded. "I know." Her voice cracked a little. It was high, like a child's, slurred by the drug. She seemed hypnotized. Lee decided to keep talking. The music above had settled into a short, repeated figure, quiet and almost soothing.

"So why did she fly away? Tell me, Hillary."

Wilson stood. Her hands were shaking now. Her face was shiny in the blue light, filmed with sweat. She opened her mouth as if to speak, but no sound emerged.

"Why did she fly away?" Lee spoke calmly.

"She was tired . . . of singing. She had to leave."

Lee nodded. "Good. That's what I thought. She was sick of it, right?"

"Yeah. She was sick, all right." Wilson winced. "She was just about ready to explode. There was some kind of pain inside her."

"What kind of pain?"

"Lee, stop," said Freddie.

Wilson ignored him. She put one hand to her head and said, "It was a bad pain. It hurt like shit. It was from tearing herself apart." Her voice grew still higher.

"And she was sick of the whole thing, right?"

Wilson nodded. "She was sick, because she knew

that if she didn't escape she would turn into something else."

"Jesus Christ, Lee," came Freddie's voice.

"Shut up, Freddie. Turn into what?"

"Turn into what she most hated."

"What was that?"

Wilson put a hand on her stomach. She grimaced. "I have to leave now. It's started." She looked up.

Lee smiled. "We can leave anytime you want," she said. "Why don't we get a taxi?"

Wilson looked straight into Lee's eyes and seemed to see something. For a moment, some apparition was reflected in Wilson's face. A chill rose in Lee.

Then, with a cry, Wilson turned and ran.

She was fast. Whatever designer chemical she'd injected had hopped her up. She was out of the room before they could move. Lee was first after her, cracking a shoulder against the frame of the low doorway Wilson had taken. She heard Freddie following.

The pursuit led through the winding bowels of BAM, past a startled stagehand, through a room full of half-finished sets, up a flight of stairs. Lee suddenly imagined that Wilson was headed for the stage. The three of them would burst out into the blinding light, and the audience would turn and stare.

Then she felt Freddie's hands on her arms, trying to bring her to a halt. She spun, and her fist connected with his mouth. He was thrown back, his face blossoming with blood. Her fist hurt. The blow had landed unexpectedly hard.

She stopped, took his shoulders.

"Why the fuck are we chasing her?" he said, his breath ragged. His words were thick with blood.

"She's headed out, don't you see?" she shouted at him.

Freddie looked after Wilson. She was almost

through a set of double doors at the far end of the hall. They followed her again at a dead run.

When Wilson burst through the doors with a crash, Lee caught the glimmer of a streetlight outside.

"Come on," she said, shoving Freddie before her.

They ran down the hallway. As Freddie pushed through, he coughed, and blood spattered the handrails of the doors. They were on Flatbush Avenue. Cars sped by a few yards ahead, their tires shushing on the wet roadway. It had rained.

Wilson was nowhere in sight.

They stood there a moment, looking up and down Flatbush, gasping the cool, dry air. Then Freddie's arm was up, and a taxi hydroplaned to a stop before them. Inside, Freddie started coughing again as he tried to give his address. She put her arm around him and said, "Manhattan."

CHAPTER 9

Surrender

It rained again during the ride home, and Freddie's mouth would not stop bleeding.

The cab was a new Ford that smelled of tobacco smoke and cleaning solvents. The wipers arced grime and wet streaks that blinked mercury-vapor orange under the struts of Manhattan Bridge.

The driver, a small Hispanic woman dwarfed behind the Ford's steering wheel, passed back a handful of tissues wordlessly. Freddie blotted his nose clean with a wad of them, holding his head back. Lee cradled him against her shoulder. She and the driver talked about the rain, drifting back and forth between English and Spanish.

As they approached home, she dug money out of Freddie's pocket. The meter had hit twenty even, and she tipped the driver with the few dollars she had left of her own money. Freddie fumbled with the keys at the outside door and seemed unsteady on the stairs.

Upon entering the apartment, he opened the refrigerator but closed it empty-handed.

They showered together. More blood ran from Freddie's nose when the water hit his face. He didn't notice. He met her eyes with a look that was intense, cautious, reticent. He seemed continually about to say something, but it never came.

His gaze fell to her body. She had varied her skin

with the diverse textures of age; it was here and there wrinkled or discolored. To conceal her strength, she had woven her musculature into multiple conduits: tight, dispersed cords discretely threaded among her sharp bones. Still, her body was spare and healthy looking, its surface seasoned with age.

He held her, pressing tight. The water ran between them, around them, tracing the connection of their bodies.

"Lee?"

"Yes."

"What the fuck were we doing to her?"

"To Wilson? I don't know. But I knew she would take us out. We had to escape."

"But what about her?"

"I have no idea," she said. "What would you do if you looked out a window one day and saw yourself? Your own face looking back?"

He frowned. "I guess I'd scream at first. But then I'd just figure it was you."

She laughed, and he kissed her. They held each other until the water started to grow cool.

In bed, they kissed for a long time. He explored her mouth carefully, with teeth, lips, and tongue. She realized the source of his fascination: Her lips were thinner than they had been. He was trying to measure her change, if only in this one trivial particular. The kisses lasted as her passion rose, and she pushed him down to her breasts, still sensitive in their newness. He licked them, tenderly bit. As he moved across her body, she felt a reluctance in his attentions. She moved down to kiss his shoulders, adjusting their position until she could reach his groin, ran her fingers through the soft hair above his cock. He was flaccid.

"What's the matter? Don't you like older women?"

He raised his head but looked toward some point beyond her.

"I'm fascinated."

"So what's the problem?"

"I just keep seeing the terror in her eyes."

There was a stab of pain, almost like a physical intrusion, in her side. Freddie was only half with her. He also lay with Hillary Wilson, in effigy.

For the first time, she had stolen a body. Now came the price. Anger toward Freddie rose in her, a sense of betrayal. But there was something subtler than that, an almost imperceptible dislocation of self. The feeling was like the odd sense when a new body mimicked her in a mirror, but broader. Usually, a new body was like a new apartment, an empty shell that had to be filled before it was comfortable. But this body was already claimed, furnished with all the baggage of being Hillary Wilson. She had seen that reflected in Freddie's eyes.

Something seemed to slip away from her. Her mind tried to grasp exactly what it was, but it was too soon out of reach.

She held Freddie until he fell asleep, his breathing heavy and slow against her chest, and waited for the feeling to go.

When she woke, Freddie was up, dressed and sitting cross-legged on the floor, drinking something from a coffee mug. He was staring at her, his eyes glazed. She reached out one leg and poked him with a toe. He smiled, blinking.

Looking down at herself, she flexed her hands, the muscles in her arms and legs. The usual awkwardness of a new body was absent. In the last week, she had become physiologically accustomed to frequent changes. But she felt a physical toll. She relaxed her muscles and did an internal census of her major organs. There was a disquieting ache near her stomachs, from the place where the fire of a change usually started. A seasick feeling, so subtle that it went away when she concentrated on it. It was evident only in the peripheral vision of her mind's eye.

She reached out and took Freddie's mug, lifted it to her lips. It was strong coffee, hot and sweet, flavored with something like hazelnut. It cleared her head. She wrapped one hand around its warmth and propped her head on the other.

"What's with you?" she asked him.

"It's odd to sleep with the same person in two different bodies."

"Two so *far*, Freddie." She had picked up his habit of italicizing words.

He smiled again, leaning back against the closet door. She drank, the events of the previous night going through her head. Visions from the vivid and effulgent opera colored her memories with a fantastic light. The whole evening now seemed overacted.

Freddie watched her think for a while and then said, "What do we do now?"

She had already decided. "I've got to talk to Sean."

"But what the fuck are you going to say?"

"I don't have the first idea, Freddie." She drummed her fingers on the side of the mug. "The way I see it, Bonito may want Ed King's money, or power, or whatever, but he wants Sean's . . . identity. Because Sean's the only person close to King who still lives in the real world. The rest of his friends are corporate clones wrapped in the Americorp security blanket. Bonito's only route to King is through Sean."

"So?"

"So, our only way to get to Bonito is through Sean. He's only exposed while he's stalking her. If we can warn Sean about Bonito and get her on our side, we can find him. Then we can hurt him."

"*Hurt* him? Are you serious? Last time he fucked with us he ate fifty thousand volts and then got run over by a car."

"Merely a body thing. He changes bodies like you

change clothes. I'm talking about fucking up his *life*. Hitting him where he lives?"

"If he doesn't live in his body, where the hell does he live?"

She thought about it. Freddie waited silently.

"Something's got to be important to him. Whatever is a constant for him: his plans, his home, his heart's desire."

Freddie rolled his eyes. "What was it that he did to you again, Lee? Stole your smartcard? Wore a dick in the wrong bar? I mean, I agree that he's the devil. I can *see* that. But we could just warn Ed King and let him handle it."

She considered this. King, if they could convince him of the danger, would be formidable. But this wasn't just between Bonito and King. It was her business now. She heard the steel in her voice. "Freddie, I thought I was the only one, the only polymorph. Then Bonito appeared and showed me that there were more of us. He destroyed my innocence. And then he abandoned me."

"And you want revenge."

"That's part of it. I want his ass, and I also want to know everything he knows. About us—him and me—about polymorphs. He knows about the others, Freddie. I have to know, too."

"But Lee, what if they're all *just like him*?"

Oddly, Freddie's sudden vehemence didn't surprise her. She couldn't remember voicing the question to herself but felt as if she had already considered it.

"Then *I'm* just like him. And if that's the case, it's something I want to know."

Freddie was stunned. "But you're not . . ."

"We'll see," she said and went into the bathroom.

She stayed under the shower until the water turned cold. As she dried herself, she felt a rush of release. In the mirror, she saw she had been crying.

* * *

Freddie was in the kitchen, the smell of burned toast joining that of coffee. He was spreading jam thickly with a plastic knife.

He looked at her and spoke as if there had been no interruption. "If you wanted to warn someone, why didn't you just tell Ed King about Bonito last night?"

"He's too literal-minded. You computer geeks never see the forest for the trees. I have to talk to Sean."

"But what the fuck are you going to *say*?"

"See what I mean? Shut up, Freddie. I don't *know* what I'm going to say yet. But I'll think of something."

He grimaced and swilled coffee. "It's too bad we don't have proof."

"Proof of what?"

"Of Bonito's power. Like a video of him changing into Sean."

"Don't be stupid, Freddie. Any fourteen-year-old with PixelBoy 1.0 could make a video of that. Besides, we do have proof: me." She began to pace. "But I take your point. Maybe a demonstration is in order."

"I thought you didn't want anyone to know about you."

"I don't want anyone to know about *us*," she said. "Me or Bonito, and the rest of us. But Sean's in deep trouble. Sleeping with Bonito isn't what I'd call safe sex."

Freddie rolled his eyes. "Who would fuck this guy?"

She ignored him. "If I showed her a change, she'd be ready to listen."

"You could change so you looked like Sean. That'd get her attention. Worked pretty good with Wilson." He didn't laugh.

"Great idea. She'd probably run like hell, too. Probably the best thing to do is stay as Wilson. Since King gave me Sean's number, he might've mentioned to her that he's met Wilson."

"So call." Freddie went to the door, where his jacket hung. He fished his phone out of a pocket and handed it to her.

She found herself reluctant to make the call. The impersonation the night before had gone so utterly awry.

"What if this doesn't work?"

Freddie smiled. "You could always doppelgäng Bonito. Then she'd let you in. They are fucking, after all."

She shuddered. "No, thanks." She hit the phone's power switch.

"Just a second," interrupted Freddie. He went into the other room. There was the whine of a RAM count as he booted his Sony. She sipped her tea and waited, still nervous about the call. He returned.

"Just thought I'd trace the call."

"We've got the number, Freddie."

"Yeah, but *just* the number. If she's cellular, we can get a location. Plus, I thought I should scramble the caller ID."

"Freddie, that is *so* illegal."

He flinched mockingly. "Ouch! Remonstrance from the welfare queen."

"It's a question of privacy, shithead."

"Outdated, bourgeois concept."

"Your French accent sucks." She punched in the number. Freddie went back into the Sony's room.

Sean answered on the third ring.

Lee tried to affect the same aristocratic accent she had used with King the night before. "Good morning, I hope it's not too early to call."

"No. Been up for hours. Who is this?"

"This is Hillary Wilson."

Sean was silent.

"You see, I met Mr. Edward King last night and remarked to him that I admired your work. He gave me your number and suggested I call you. I hope you don't mind."

There was still no response.

Something was wrong. "I trust you and Mr. King are still friends?" There was a pause. She heard a distant car alarm from Sean's end.

Sean's voice sounded very small. "Who is this again?"

"This is Hillary Wilson."

"That's bullshit."

Lee was stunned by her vehemence.

"This is a really sick joke," said Sean.

Lee cleared her throat. "It most certainly is not, young lady." She wished that Freddie's little phone had video.

"The fuck it isn't. Who is this?"

"Hillary Wilson," Lee said, stamping her foot on the tile floor.

"Yeah, right. Listen, asshole, I just got the paper. Hillary Wilson blew her brains out last night."

Lee dropped the phone, a cry caught soundlessly in her throat.

PART III

The Principle of Force

CHAPTER 10

DUMBO

She changed in the bathroom, kneeling naked in the tub. The porcelain was still wet, the air hot and humid from her shower. The change came quickly, almost effortlessly, but as she rested from it the strange sickness in her abdomen rose, along with the taste of bile. She vomited, at first to ease the pain but then uncontrollably. When the heaving stopped, she opened her eyes. A thin, bloody mucus filmed the pores of the bathtub drain. Despite the agony in her gut, she probed the bile with a shaking finger. It smelled of stomach acid and coffee and had the texture of thick olive oil. She'd never seen anything like it before, neither in an anatomy textbook nor in vivo.

Freddie was there, his hands on her shoulders. He handed her a warm, wet towel. She rested her face in it and tried to take control over her raging body. After a while, her head stopped spinning, but the nausea was unabated.

She made herself stand.

The mirror on the medicine cabinet showed a pallid, sweaty face. Her eyes were filmy, the muscles slack. But it was the face she wanted. It was beautiful, strong-jawed, Italian. And her eyes were vivid green.

She was Bonita.

Freddie looked at her, as awed as he'd been at BAM. But this time the awe was tinged with horror.

She whisked the shower curtain across his view. Cold water slowed her metabolism, washed away the sweat and bile. Soon, the agonizing pain in her gut subsided to a dull throb. She paused under the water to release a measure of morphine analog into her blood. The morphine didn't really still the pain, but soon it was less noticeable, the raging of a faraway madman.

She dressed in her own clothes, in a loose black coverall like the one Bonito had worn at the Loisaida Social Club. Freddie had boiled a package of ramen noodles and asked her if she wanted any. She shook her head and sat heavily in the chair across from him.

He looked up from eating, paused, and said, "Lee, I've got to go to work. I've skipped my last two shifts."

She smiled. "That's okay. I need to see Sean alone."

"But you should wait until I get off tonight. Something might go wrong."

"Like what?"

"Like Bonito might be there."

She felt her smile turn evil. "Then I'll kill him." The morphine was buzzing in her head. "What's the address?"

"Do you really think you should—"

She reached across and grasped his shoulder, hard. "What's the address?"

Freddie sighed. "All right, it's still on the VTV. But you should take my phone. Say 'work' into it and it'll speed-dial my AcNet number."

"Thanks, Freddie. By the way, why don't you work at home? You might as well."

"It's a deal AcNet made with the city. They get a tax abatement if they keep workers in commercial property."

"Typical," she said, and smiled. "God, I *hate* this town."

He smiled back, started to say something, and thought better of it.

"Good-bye, Lee."

On Freddie's VTV was an address and a street map, showing that Sean had taken her call at a warehouse in Brooklyn.

She was hungry, but she didn't think she could keep any food down. There was milk in the refrigerator, and she whitened a cup of hazelnut coffee with it until she could sip the mixture without gagging. She stared out the front window for an hour or so, watching Chelsea pedestrians pass.

She found Freddie's cash easily, a thin, tight roll of twenties in the battery case of the alarm clock by his bed. It wasn't a very original place to hide money.

She put on her sunglasses and slipped the trench knife into a pocket as she left.

The taxi driver was a large man with a skin condition and a five-syllable last name. His cab was small and had the bright smell of an electric with a leaking battery. He frowned when she got in. She frowned back and said, "DUMBO."

He drove for a few blocks and then slowed. "What is DUMBO?"

"Down Under Manhattan Bridge Overpass. Brooklyn."

He frowned again and drove.

It was a bright, clear day. Canal was lined with stalls of cheap Asian toys, synthetic leather, and fresh fish. A crush of pedestrians slowed the cab until they reached Manhattan Bridge. As the cab rose above the city, she could see the Domino Sugar factory, the Pfizer drug plant, and the FEMA barracks across the river. As they descended into Brooklyn, the noon sun glimmered in bright moiré patterns through its struts and catwalks.

She hadn't gotten Freddie's printer to work but

had sketched the map from the screen. After ten minutes of slowly trolling the DUMBO neighborhood, they found the warehouse. She handed the driver a twenty and said, "Keep it."

He frowned and drove away.

She walked around the warehouse once. It was from the middle of the last century. Paneled industrial windows looked out from the third and fourth floors. A coal chute climbed one of the walls. The neighborhood had a few fancy delis, holdovers from the turn of the century, when DUMBO had been fashionable among loft-dwelling artists displaced by Manhattan rents. The riots had hit harder in the outer boroughs, though, and most of the warehouses were empty again.

The buzzer was next to an old loading bay door. It was labeled "S. Bayes." She pressed it. No answer. She pressed it again, holding it for a solid five seconds, and waited. Then a whir from the shadows caught her ear. She adjusted her eyes and spotted a camera in a dim corner of the bay. It moved again, focusing on her face. She waved at it.

She was about to buzz again when the door opened.

The man was wearing a pink knit shirt, short-sleeved and well pressed. His khaki pants were neatly creased. He had the same relaxed look as King's guards at BAM. Even in his casual clothes, he had the unmistakable air of a suit.

"I thought she was going to meet you in town," he said, still standing in the doorway.

She had tuned her voice to Bonita's low, throaty rasp. "She said she'd be here."

He smiled a receptionist's smile and pulled a phone from his pocket. "Let me see if I can reach her for you."

She smiled and took a small step forward. He took no notice. Her kick caught him squarely in the groin, lifting him off the metal floor a little. His eyes met hers with an expression of surprise as he fell. She kicked him twice on the side of the head and caught the door before it closed.

He was heavier than he looked, a kevlar vest tailored skintight under the pink shirt.

Just inside the door were a wide staircase and a freight elevator. The ground floor was a vast unlit space, littered with old boxes, trash, large rolls of bubblewrap. Her arms goose-pimpled in the chill of the air conditioning. She shoved the guard into a corner, looking around for a way to tie him up or to secure the elevator door. There was nothing in sight. Then she checked his pulse. He was dead.

She leaned against the warm metal of the outside door and breathed deeply. Her head began to spin again, but her adrenaline remained under control. The pain in her abdomen took on a new edge. She released another dose of morphine analog. Reaching up to wipe the sweat from her face, she found, horribly, a smile on her lips.

She carried him easily, rolled him into a sheet of bubblewrap that popped desultorily a few times as he turned.

Climbing the stairs at a dead run, she felt like she was flying.

The second floor was living space. A large kitchen surrounded a central island, a forest of bright stainless hanging from the ceiling. Past a wall of shojin screens, a low bed faced a two-meter video monitor. The monitor was flanked by bright-red omnidirectional speaker columns. On the bed were four identical remote controls. Two cats lounged among them, one ash-gray, the other a bright apricot. They looked at her disinterestedly.

The next floor up was almost empty. It had the clean, renovated look of a SoHo loft, the gray industrial floors relaid with pinewood. The windows on the west side reached from floor to ceiling. Facing the view was a single loveseat, lonely on the vacant expanse. She crossed to it. There was an ice bucket filled with water, a champagne bottle floating empty in it. The gold foil from the bottle lay on the floor, glinting in the light of the lowering sun. A phone rested on the loveseat. The only other object in the room was a black onyx ashtray, filled with butts. All were marked with the same deep-red lipstick.

The fourth floor was the installation.

Lee had been to New Jersey once. A lover had taken her by rented motorcycle out to a new megastore. Beside an eight-lane interstate, a huge, low building had risen out of the lush wetlands. It was bright, clean, and white—like its clientele. The merchandise was arrayed with uncanny precision and almost heroic redundancy, row after row of the same products, as if they could sell themselves by sheer weight of numbers.

The same disquiet that she had felt in that Jersey megastore visited her now. The floor and walls of the installation were painted an unambiguous, reflective white, shadowlessly lit with broad panels of fluorescent ceiling tile. The shelves were constructed of white HARD plastic sheets suspended from the ceiling by monofilament, all exactly aligned. As she walked, a little awestruck, among the aisles, she saw that Sean had realized another fearful symmetry: every product bore her own image. The smiling girl on a can of Italian tomatoes, a fuzzily lit woman on a box of pantyhose, the energetic supermom on the display over a rack of antidepressant dermal injectors—all had the face of Sean Bayes. In the neat rows of boxes, cans, packets, shrinkwrappers, bottles, jars, even on an aisle of romance novels, their covers gaudy with holographic illustrations, Sean's face looked at Lee from a thousand vantages.

Lee backed out of the installation warily, the commodities suddenly alive with Sean's penetrating stare. In one corner of the floor, she found the workshop. Half a dozen monitors were still booted, their screen savers churning out slowly morphing globs of colored light. There were printers, scanning beds, a 3-D fabricator, a digital camera, various tools of desktop design. Littered among the scraps on the worktables were pictures of Sean, retouched, bitmapped, and morphed into a dozen different scenarios. On one table she found a draft of the installation's catalog, entitled *COMMODITY DREAMGIRLS: Emblems of Desire/Whispers of Inaccessibility.*

She brought it to a window and read:

Commodity-land dreamgirls, angels of billboards and emblems of desire, recess into their own empty stares. Their inaccessibility, of course, simply enflames the desire for access, compelling the purchase of the commodity pitched. Though the product is infinitely acquirable, one can never deplete the product's elusive double, the dreamgirl on its surface. Thus one's desire is never entirely exhausted—there is always more, just out of reach, for tomorrow. The value of such a bottomless cup is immeasurable. Dreamgirls sing the inexhaustible value of what you can't possess though it's in your own hands.

The annoying question must be raised: What about the "real" women whom these dreamgirls purport to imitate? Is there such a thing as a "real" woman? Can her body be trusted to mean anything when it has been, for centuries now, the emblem of a desire which deceives? The iconography of insatiability results, predictably, in a body meaning only desire.

By now it's a well-known conundrum in the wranglings of feminist theory: the female body has historically signified masculinity (as the repository of masculine desire) while women are excluded from the privileges accorded that term. Thus, a "woman" striving to be other than representative of the phallic order can find herself striving to be disembodied. The drive toward phantomic, or disembodied, presence resonates with the phantasmic scene of the commodity, with which, in image, she so often finds herself doubled. All of this is reminiscent of late 20th-century feminism's unpacking of the secret that the female body, or she who lives within it, is not, *cannot* be, that which she is given to appear to be. (Schneider, *Explicit Body*,1997)

It was like going back to old anatomy texts she had once read fluently and discovering that now they only hinted at prior meanings. She stared out the window, watching the sunlight flicker on the East River, unable to decide what to do next.

Some time later, the phone in her pocket rang. It took a moment to clear her head. It was Freddie.

"What's happening?"

"She's not here. I'm waiting for her."

"Well, I called because there's something you should know."

"What?"

"Sam called me. He said the correlation shifted."

"The what?"

"The correlation between Bonito's account and Americorp's stock value."

"You mean he sold off? He's given up?"

"No. The correlation is still there, but it's no longer positive. It's negative. He's short-selling. And Sam's done some more work. He says the margin is very high. If Americorp stock goes up even one point, Bonito's wiped out."

"And if it crashes . . ." Her brain was responding slowly.

"Then he makes billions."

She felt her head-spins returning, put out a hand,

and leaned heavily against the window ledge. "We don't have much time, do we?"

"Sam doesn't know. Bonito's taking a big risk, unless he can do something that will crash Americorp's stock in the next few days."

"The guard here said that Sean went to meet Bonito." There were a few moments of silence. Then she said, quite calmly, "Sean isn't coming back, is she?"

"I don't know." Freddie sounded defeated. "Not if Bonito's making his move."

The sunlight was warm on her hand. "Freddie, how do we find them?"

He thought for a moment. "What did the guard say, exactly?"

An image of the guard, rolled in bubblewrap three floors below, stole her breath for a moment. She allowed herself a little more of the morphine analog. "He said that Sean had gone to meet me. He thought I was Bonita, of course."

"So they must have spoken on the phone. Sean called Bonito or Bonito called Sean."

"So?"

"So did Sean take her phone with her?"

"No. It's here."

"Bring it to my apartment. I'll be there. We'll soak her phone, drag up her stored outgoing calls. And if *he* called *her*, we'll trace the account and soak the NYNEX mainframe. Listen, this is the easiest hack there is. If they talked on the phone, we've got him."

She turned back and headed through the installation. "All right, Freddie. I'm coming home."

The rows of products watched her passage with mocking stares.

CHAPTER 11

NYNEX

In the deserted caverns of DUMBO, it took almost half an hour to find a cab. Finally, one rounded the corner twenty meters ahead of her and stopped when she gave an inhumanly loud shout. She threw two twenties at the driver and said, "Chelsea. Drive like a maniac." Then she lay across the backseat and concentrated on not throwing up.

Freddie was already home, qwerty bracelets on his wrists. He popped a small square box of coffee drink with its straw and led her into the Sony's room. He took Sean's phone from her and slammed it against the side of his workstation chair. The molded plastic case split down the middle. He picked through the electronics with a kind of bored grace, pushing aside the grosser elements of speaker, microphone, power supply. The motherboard resisted his prying for about a second, then popped clear of the case with a loud snap. One edge of the board was copper-colored. He fitted the edge into the pickup teeth of a short, fat scuzzy cable that he pulled out of a cluttered drawer. He jacked the cable into the back of the Sony.

The Sony's screen saver cleared, and a few lines of alphanumerics appeared.

"Matsushita 990. Crappy phone," said Freddie. "Got a scrambler. Easy hack, though."

His hands flickered. More lines of text filled the Sony's monitor.

"That's the last number she called," he said. The last line of text was a eight-digit number.

"Couldn't we have just pressed Redial?"

He gave her a look of infinite patience. "And when someone answered, what would we do? Ask for Bonito?"

He qwerted a little more. "Besides, it's a Chinese restaurant."

"How the hell do you know?"

"I've got a copy of the Five-Borough Directory in numerical order. Standard equipment. I figure Bonito's not in the phone book, but looking up numbers makes it easier to pare down the list."

She tried to follow the text on the screen but was lost. This wasn't a user interface, like Sam's elegant financial schematic or even the New York Public Library's cluttered network. This was the operating system of a small, sophisticated machine, rows of numbers scrolling down the screen without any clue to their meaning. Freddie seemed at home here, though.

A few minutes later, he spoke again.

"Here's the last 256 numbers she called." They scrolled by. "Just let me chop the listed ones."

"They probably talked today," she prompted.

"Good point. Only four are time-stamped today. Let's see, Mexican for lunch, Chinese for dinner— eats a lot of takeout—a call to a listed number in Brooklyn after that."

"She's from Brooklyn," Lee said.

"Yep. Anita Bayes. Mom, maybe. The last one's a call to a voice-mail service. No Bonito here."

"What if he'd left her a message? Can you hack her voice mail?"

He raised his hands. "If need be. But let's not get

too complicated. Bonito may have called *her*, you know."

"Does her phone save its caller IDs?"

"Only the most recent one." He leaned forward and squinted at the screen. Then he hissed. "And it's the fucking Chinese restaurant calling her back. Couldn't they find the place?" He sighed and leaned back.

"Actually, her warehouse *is* pretty hard to find," she said.

"Let me check the other 252 outgoing calls." His fingers moved into a blur. The screen rolled with text, too fast for her to follow. She looked away, her head beginning to spin again. She sat down on the bed and considered another jolt of morphine. Instead, she shut her eyes and relaxed the knotted muscles in her gut.

Freddie didn't take long. "Only one of these is unlisted. It's a very secure mobile line based somewhere in Manhattan."

"So that's him."

"Right. It's a thirteen-digit number with a microwave prefix and a security code. Like a movie star would have."

"Like someone who wanted to keep a low profile would have, you mean."

"Yeah, and she calls it about three times a week."

"Can you get the address?"

"Like I said, it's unlisted, so we gotta hit the NYNEX mainframe."

"That's hard?"

"A fucking piece of cake. Four-year-old could hack it."

As he qwerted, she curled herself into a tight ball. The pain was duller now, but it was larger, more expansive. It had been a long time since she had thrown up involuntarily. She remembered a bad time at age twelve—five beers with an older girl who lived in the Gompers projects. They'd found two six-packs hidden in a storage cage behind the laundry room and had drunk them too quickly, wary of being caught. Afterward, they'd gone outside, where sundown pinkened the brick of the towers, the cool air beautiful to breathe in her adolescent intoxication. Then they'd run to the swing sets. High into the air, standing, thrusting harder and harder until her hands were burning with the pattern of the chains, it had been glorious.

Until they'd stopped.

The feeling had come as if from far away, a revolution fomenting in some distant province of her body. She fought it, marshaling her unformed talent against the rush of nausea, holding on far longer than her older companion. But the whole time there was a certainty in her gut that she had lost control, that her body was building toward some vast explosion.

The feeling now had that same inevitable, sovereign edge. But she kept it down.

Freddie talked while he worked, and she listened with half her attention as a distraction from the pain. As far as she could follow it, he opened Sean's account easily, pretending to be an audit warrant from the Phone Harassment Complaints Bureau. He verified the audit request with the chip from Sean's phone itself, and the last 1024 numbers that had called her rolled by, time-stamped and fully open to interrogation.

"Here we go," he said a few minutes later. "The fucker likes his own name."

"What?" She struggled to clear her head.

"Bonito Visconti, 564 East Sixth Street. Got three lines, call-waiting, an incoming screen code—"

"He lives on Sixth Street?"

"Has for seven years."

So close. He had been so close all along.

"Got a nice alarm system, too," Freddie continued.

"Got a dedicated phone line for it. It's set to call his personal mobile line if anyone breaks into his house. It doesn't call the cops. That's unusual."

"Guess he values his privacy. Can you disconnect it?"

"Can't disconnect the alarm system's line. Need a court order for that. But his mobile phone's an easy hack." His fingers fluttered, and he smirked with satisfaction. "No more incoming calls for him tonight."

"What about Sean? Did he call her today?"

"Right before the Chinese restaurant did. 4:38 P.M."

She tried to think clearly. "I got there about six o'clock, so let's say she left to meet him around five. They've only been together for two hours or so. They could be at his apartment."

"It's a house. But they're probably not there."

"Why not?"

"According to NYNEX, he made a call from the West Side Highway mobile cell fifteen minutes ago."

"Shit. They're headed somewhere."

"Bonito is, anyway."

"Can we track him? Like you did Sean?"

"No. His phone's got a real scrambler. PGP. Not like this piece of shit." He dropped the remains of Sean's phone onto the floor.

"So how do we find him?" she asked.

Freddie leaned back, his voice taking on a professorial air. "Well, we could through-put the NYNEX audit and get all the numbers that Bonito's called in the last month. Then, if there's any toll-free calls, we could check them against the 800 directory for credit card customer service. From there we hack the credit card company's records and see what he pays for with plastic: where he eats, any hotel bills, deliveries to another address, whatever we find."

"You do this kind of shit a lot?"

"Not since I was a little kid."

She thought it over. "How long would it take?"

"Days."

"Freddie! This is happening *now.* I know it is. I say we go to his house."

"He won't be there." There was fear in Freddie's eyes.

"He's got to come home sometime," she said.

Freddie wiped a braceleted hand across his mouth and cleared his throat. "That's what I'm afraid of."

She smiled. She wasn't afraid. Somewhere in a place distanced by the morphine, she mourned: Hillary Wilson, the security guard, and whatever part of herself was dying painfully in her gut. But the immediate part of her, the self she was wearing now, was impelled by the chemicals of change, gone ferocious with overuse. The new self cried out for action. "Freddie, we need a gun."

He considered this for a moment. "There's a high school up the street. Ronald Wilson Reagan Vocational."

"Good. Get something with a lot of stopping power." She threw the roll of twenties to him. He looked at it for a second, the slightest frown crossing his face as he realized that it was his.

"While I'm doing that, you're gonna change, right?"

The pain in her gut sparked at the thought. She fought to keep it down. "I don't think I can, Freddie. Too damn many changes lately. It's kind of starting to . . . hurt."

"Hell of a disguise, don't you think? Sneaking up on Bonito as Bonito?"

She sighed. "I guess we have to count on shock value."

Freddie picked up the roll of money wordlessly. He went to the door. His hand on the knob, he turned back. "Whatever you say."

While he was gone, she searched the apartment for other weapons. She figured that a gun could knock

Bonito down, but killing him would be a different story. She had no idea what it took to halt a polymorph's metabolism. She could empty the gun into his head, but he might have rearranged his vital organs. She had considered developing a backup for her own autonomic functions but hadn't known where to begin. With Bonito's powers, he might have a spare medulla oblongata, distributed brain tissue, a whole extra braincase; anything was possible. The point was to kill him good. On the kitchen table she arrayed Freddie's stun gun, a spray bottle of 7 molar D-Con rat poison, a ten-pound maglight, the trench knife.

Bonito was expendable now.

She'd realized it since Freddie had soaked the NYNEX mainframe. The CANDY account had given them only a thin sliver of connection to Bonito. Now they had him cold. Freddie could compile a history of his movements, his phone calls, his finances; somewhere in the ocean of data had to be a trail that led to another polymorph. Even if every lead turned up dry, she could still wait in his house, with his face. Sooner or later, some polymorph friend of his would come by.

She didn't need him to find the rest of her kind. He was in the way.

The thought calmed her pain.

She was contemplating the array of weapons when Freddie came back.

"Jesus," he said, surveying the table. "Got a stake?"

"No. Get the gun?"

He pulled it out of the crumpled paper bag in his hand. It was about thirty centimeters long, with a snub nose and a magazine grip that was longer than the gun itself. There was a spare magazine taped upside down on the grip.

"Two hundred and forty bucks," said Freddie.

"Totally ridiculous. Little shits tried to tell me it was Israeli. Israeli, my ass! Fucking Zairois copy of a Chinese police pistol. I *hate* this town."

She picked it up.

"How does it work?"

"Point it and pull the trigger. Pull it light and it shoots one bullet. Pull it harder and it goes fully automatic. For about two seconds, that is. Then it runs out of bullets."

It was improbably light. The barrel was just wide enough to stick a pencil into. She held it by the grip, her finger on the trigger. An illicit thrill leapt through her.

"There a safety catch?"

"No."

She took her finger off the trigger. "I like it," she said.

"It's yours. I hate guns."

"How come you know so much about this one, then?"

" 'Cause I'm a boy."

She stood and found that the gun fit into the pocket of her coverall. "Let's go."

CHAPTER 12

Victim

They cabbed to Tompkins Square Park. The tops of its few remaining trees were bright with the setting sun. There was a trace of coolness in the air. A breeze stirred foul smells from the park as they walked past. There were sounds of activity inside, shouts and the pop of a police radio.

They passed a bar she knew at Seventh and B. She wondered if Bonito had ever unknowingly exchanged a glance with her there. Her hands in her pockets, she clutched the pistol's grip. The pain in her stomachs had turned into a sickly fear. Freddie looked pretty nervous himself. He had taken the trench knife from the backpack of weapons and pocketed it.

Bonito's house was on the south side of Sixth, between Avenues B and C. It was a three-story redbrick building, an old church. On an ancient sign above a basement door were the words "Loisaida Living Center." The building seemed abandoned. The windows were dark. The closest streetlight had been shot out.

A door at street level was the only part of the building that seemed kept up. It was a meter and a half wide, jacketed with smooth, black HARD plastic. Beside it was a large and graffitied card reader. There was no buzzer.

Freddie whipped his card through the reader,

waited a moment, then swept it through again. The access light clicked green. Freddie smirked and started to say something. Then, with a whir, the card reader split down a central seam to reveal a retina scanner.

"Shit," said Freddie. "Serious about security, isn't he?"

"Can you hack it?" she asked.

"Maybe with my Sony and some extra hardware, say about a thousand dollars' worth."

"Fuck."

"Probably should download the manual for the scanner off the net and spend a couple of days reading it, though."

"I will take that as a *no*," she said, stepping back to view the building again. An accordion roll of razor wire snaked its way around the building between the first and second floors. Loiter spikes glittered on every window ledge. She wished that her control over her body extended to retinal patterns.

"You sure you disabled the alarm system?" she asked.

"For all intents, yes."

"I'm gonna climb in, then."

"Are you nuts?"

She ignored him and jumped the fence beside the building. There was a narrow dirt path between Bonito's house and the community garden next door. The lowest tier of the fire escape was about five meters overhead. She looked around to see if anyone was watching, and then she jumped.

Her fingers grasped air the first time, a few centimeters short. Freddie whistled at the height of her jump. She smirked at him. She had done much better. Concentrating, she made it easily the second time.

As her fingers closed on the edge of the escape, she gasped with pain. She fought the impulse to let go and hauled herself up. As her head cleared the edge of the escape she saw that it glittered with broken glass set into mortar. She rolled onto the escape and looked at her hands. They were lacerated and bloody, but fundamentally sound. Stopping the bleeding was easy. She paused to reconstruct a muscle in her right index finger and released another measure of morphine to fight the pain.

Sitting up, she waved to Freddie. It had grown too dark for him to see the blood.

At the next landing up the escape, the windows were boarded over. Behind the weathered wood and dirty glass, she saw a hinged metal gate. It was certainly weaker than the HARD plastic front door, but she didn't think she could kick it in. She climbed another level, to the top of the escape.

There was no wood here, just window glass and another metal gate. She took off her sneaker and beat the glass in. It was new and double-paned, webbing for a moment like safety glass before it shattered and fell through the gate. She wrenched the window frame out. In her haze of pain and morphine analog, she ignored the border of broken glass that ringed it. The slats of the gate were spaced too tightly to let her hand through. On the side opposite its hinges, a panel of solid metal was welded to it. On the panel's other side would be the fire safety release. She closed her eyes.

The change inflamed the pain in her gut, turning it from a dull, even throb to fiery agony. She pushed one of the tightly threaded cords of muscles in her right hand through a rent in the skin, forming a short, grotesque tentacle, strong but only dully sensory. It had a patch of skin at its end, but the length of muscle itself was nerveless. When it was formed, she lay on the escape and gasped. Unlike the pain from injuring her hands, the agony of changing wasn't affected by the morphine analog. The high was a distraction, but it didn't push the torment out of her mind.

After a minute, she had recovered enough to push her tentacle between two of the slats. She probed the other side of the metal panel. The lock was a deadbolt. She wrapped her tentacle around it tightly and twisted. It turned, and the lock opened. The gate pushed open.

With her left hand, she drew the pistol. She changed again, pulling the muscle harshly back into her right index finger. It only took a few moments, and she ignored the agony of it.

The room smelled of dust. There was an overstuffed chair and a short couch, its cushions threadbare and shapeless. It looked like furniture found on the street. She paused at a crowded bookshelf. The anatomy texts were familiar. The collection included a leather-bound Gray's. There were also technical anatomical journals, hole-punched and organized by year into blue binders. One shelf was devoted to works on vivisection.

The door of the room opened onto a dark hallway. Pausing to adjust her eyes, she leveled the pistol before her. The other rooms on the top floor were similarly appointed: old furniture, books, one bed with a phone beside it. The windows of the rooms were all gated, letting in only thin ribbons of the streetlights' sharp orange glow.

The stairs creaked as she descended, but she took them quickly. If Bonito were here, he would have heard her by now. Intuitively, she knew he was gone. The house was too still to harbor a presence like his.

On the second floor, she found Sean.

Unlike the shabby upstairs, this floor had been renovated. It was all one room, the floors finished in industrial gray plastic. The walls were crowded with file cabinets, a workstation, rotating files, a glass-fronted stainless-steel cabinet filled with surgical instruments.

At the center of the room was a steel table, high and wide, covered with butcher's paper. Sean was there, her wrists and ankles bound by calf-leather restraints. She was naked, dead.

He had opened her up.

A tray beside the table still held his instruments. They were the tools of a pathologist: a surgical hand-saw, a laser pencil, a rotary scalpel; all meant for a corpse. But Sean was very tightly bound.

Lee realized that Bonito had also grown tired of monomorph anatomy lessons. At some point in the past, he had learned all he could from cadavers.

There was a long table beside his workstation. On it were arrayed Sean's vital organs in Ziplocs. They gave off the bright smell of embalming fluid. A digital camera on a tripod surveyed them.

She felt Sean's face. There was some warmth left in the dry skin. The incisions in her torso and limbs had a bright sheen; fixative had been sprayed to keep them sterile and bloodless. The surgical work was neat and precise. Her fingertips had been burned off, probably to keep the body anonymous when it was dumped. A patch of blackened skin in the corner of one closed eye implied that Bonito had taken the same precaution with her retinas. Lee turned away, a shudder rising at last.

One of the filing cabinets was wooden, older than the others. She opened it with her eyes closed, a little afraid of what might be inside. The smell of old paper reassured her. It was crammed with spiral-bound scrapbooks. She opened one. Bonito's hand-writing was almost illegibly small, but as precise as his surgical technique. The entries were dated as far back as the 1960s. She realized that Bonito was older than he looked. He might be very old indeed.

As she flipped through the scrapbook, it tended to

open onto pages where mementos were glued. There were newspaper articles, photographs, a missing-person flyer. Most of the photographs were posed studies of faces. Had Bonito recorded his various guises, or had victims unwittingly sat for him? The articles mostly seemed to be profiles of the wealthy and powerful. A few, however, concerned unsolved mutilations, unidentified bodies. One page was filled with a study in aging Polaroids, set in a surgery far cruder than the one around her, a suburban garage. The victim was a young boy, maybe eleven or twelve. Nobody particularly wealthy or powerful.

None of the notebooks was more recent than the late 1980s. She closed the cabinet and went to the workstation. Its power light was on. It had an old qwerty keyboard, and the monitor brightened at the touch of a key. The screen filled with a digitized photograph. It was Sean's tattoo.

There was an eyemouse monocle next to the keyboard. She clipped it to the bridge of her nose and quit-blinked. The screen cleared and then filled with thumbnails, other photographs of Sean. She chose one at random. It was a video of an exposed leg muscle flexing, visible through a long incision. Another: Sean's hand, spasmodically twisting to some unseen stimulus. Another: a still photograph of the same hand, flayed with the inhuman precision of a laser pencil set wide and low. They were cold, technical pieces of work. There was nothing desirous in the camera's gaze. They looked more like medical documentation than snuff quicktimes.

She was glad there was no audio.

She quit-blinked a few times, finding her way out to Bonito's desktop. It was a fast machine, better than Freddie's system. There was a lot of storage space. She searched the drive for askies. They were all together, eleven megs of text files in a volume called "BONITO." She smiled grimly at his egotism.

She directoried the askies by date. One or two files
had been created each day since 2/1/1989. It was the
continuation of his journal. She opened a file at
random.

Finally got up my nerve today. Waited for an hour
by the exit ramp off FDR. The car was small, only
doing about sixty. Had started to do it four or five
times, but lost my nerve as each car rushed toward
me. Cars are far more powerful than I had given
them credit for. Finally, I gave myself until noon to
do it. At 11:51 (exactly: my watch was crushed) I
jumped.
Made sure there were no head injuries, but my
guts were a mess. It came again. The shock of massive trauma brought it to me. I could mold myself
so easily. This was better than the bullet.

She shuddered in fascination. There would be
plenty of time to read these after Bonito was dead,
but she couldn't pull herself away from the screen.
The important question was, Did Bonito really
know other polymorphs? She was almost afraid, now
that his secrets were lined up before her, that he had
been lying, that they were alone in the world.
She called up a search dialog and stared at it for
a few minutes, thinking. Then she reached out to the
old qwerty board and typed the word *us*.
The machine's drive access was almost silent, just
a breath of sound. Then a window opened. A para-
graph was highlighted:

There are fewer of *us* than I would have thought.
Fully one percent of humans have the organelle. It
seems that most simply aren't smart enough to use it.
If not developed in childhood, the change apparently
cannot be learned, even under the greatest duress.

She smiled. There were other polymorphs. Bonito had found them. She blinked for another search.

Apparently, most of *us* don't begin to change until age six or seven. Again, I am exceptional. I was shifting my entire body at an age when most of *us* can only manipulate an isolated area.

Six or seven years old. She hadn't started making faces until she was eight. She wondered when Bonito had started. What would it do to someone, to be able to change so early, before identity had been defined at all?

She'd once read that most serial killers shared a childhood profile: as children, they had been moved among many different foster parents. Bonito had gone one better. He had moved among different bodies. Perhaps he was not so much warped as absent, never having taken time to form inside a formless vessel, his humanity so thoroughly lacking that he had nothing left to miss it with.

She continued to read.

A pounding below interrupted her. She realized that in her fascination she'd forgotten Freddie. He probably thought the worst by now. She took the stairs quickly.

Something was hitting the HARD plastic door hard. Freddie must have picked up an iron pipe. She yelled, "Wait a minute."

The controls on this side were simple. She pressed a large green button, and the door sighed and clicked as a series of bolts slid. It burst open.

There were three suits before her, riot tasers leveled at her head. Behind them, another pair of suits aimed real guns. A couple of long black limos were pulled onto the curb at hasty angles. Freddie was nowhere in sight.

She dropped the pistol.

One of the suits said, "Where is she?"

She realized that she was wearing Bonito's face. They were here to find Sean.

"She's upstairs."

CHAPTER 13

Jersey

Once they hit the Florio Memorial Traffic Grid, the limousine drove itself.

There were three suits in the car. One was in the back with her, holding a taser wand a centimeter from her throat. She had decided not to dare the taser. She'd seen what had happened to Bonito when he'd been hit by Freddie's stun gun. When the car took over, the suit who had been driving turned around and kept watch, relieving the other suit in front, who rubbed his shoulder and bitched about his neck. They lacked the easy confidence she had seen in King's personal guards. Maybe they were second-tier security, or perhaps they were just spooked. She figured they'd seen the video of her killing Sean's guard. And they had seen Sean's body.

It was in the other limo.

They hadn't gotten Freddie. He must have faded as the two big cars pulled up. Smart boy. In retrospect, it had only been a matter of time before King's men tracked down Bonito. The suit guarding Sean either hadn't reported in on schedule or had been carrying some sort of deadman switch. However it worked, Americorp security knew that she'd killed him. The camera by the door must have been recording. And they'd taken only a little longer than Freddie to find Bonito's address.

Actually, she'd done a pretty good job of framing
Bonito. Unfortunately, he wasn't around to take the
rap.

When they hit the artificial wetlands outside of
New Brunswick, she panicked for a moment. Maybe
they were just going to shoot her and dump her here.
She calmed herself. This wasn't the Mafia getting revenge. This was refined, big-corporation security,
who, more than anything else, wanted to know who
the hell she was. And Freddie had said that Americorp headquarters was in New Jersey.

It was dark. She closed her eyes, settling back into
cool leather, and focused on calming herself. The
pain in her abdomen had lessened briefly in Bonito's
surgery, her fascination having driven it away. Now
it was back, dulled but just as persistent. During the
long drive, she had formed a small organ to synthe-
size a steady dose of the morphine analog. It coun-
tered the pain and let her mind skim the mortality
of her position, but fear would occasionally shoot
through her, vibrant in the bright colors of her
intoxication.

She was worried about the pain. If she came face-
to-face with Ed King, changing would be the only
way to convince him that she wasn't Bonito. But she
had never pushed herself this far before. The pain
might mean she was near crippling herself. Another
shift in her body would tell. So she waited and tried
to relax.

She awoke when the car slowed, exiting the highway down a long tree-lined private road. After a few
kilometers, they reached a steel gate flanked by
guard boxes. The red eye of a scanner flickered across
a bar code on the windshield, and they were waved
past. Another kilometer farther on, a building rose
out of artfully engineered rolling hills.

She was reminded of the shopping mall many

years before. The building was long and low, white in bright halogen floodlights. There were few windows, the walls featurelessly blank. As they drove around to the building's rear, a moiré of cables shifted above it, a vast microwave antenna array. The parking lot was almost empty of cars, but a small group of men waited in a floodlit turnaround. The limousine was still driving itself as it pulled into its parking space.

Her door was opened for her. The night air was cooler here. An insect buzz came from the dark trees around them. There were perhaps ten people in the waiting group, a wheeled stretcher among them. No one spoke. She recognized King, flanked in a doorway by his two guards from the opera. He didn't look at her. He was watching the other limousine. When it rounded the corner, lights off, every head turned. It slid into place as neatly as if driven by a ghost. Two suits got out from the front seat and moved away from it.

King and his guards stepped out into the light, and the suits around her stiffened. One took her arm.

When they reached the other limo, one of the guards raised a remote and the back window slid down. A light went on inside.

King leaned into the window. He reached one hand in, briefly. Then he pulled himself out and turned away. There was a brief conference that she couldn't hear over the buzz of cicadas. Then King nodded and they went to the trunk of the limo. One of the suits opened it, shining a flashlight. King stared inside, his face transfixed. There was a long pause and the suits began to fidget. A distant helicopter flew over. Faces looked nervously upward.

Finally, King turned away from the trunk and walked back to the door. He went inside without even having glanced in her direction.

Once he and his guards were gone, the suits went

into motion as if released from a spell. Three of them walked her toward a large service door painted with red stripes. Over her shoulder, she saw the others pulling on tight plastic gloves. As she and her escorts entered the building, the squeak of the stretcher's wheels came from behind her.

The room they put her in was not a cell. A conference table dominated it, ringed with brown chairs that gave off a heady smell of leather. In front of each chair was a telepresence projector. She'd seen one before, used to pipe a distance-learning lecturer from San Francisco into a Hunter classroom. A wide projection well was at the center of the long oval table, and two of the walls were screens. There was also an easel holding a large pad of drawing paper. Ed King and his pen-based technology.

A window ran the length of the room, and she'd considered putting a chair through it. But it would be bulletproof at least, and the door was teak, magnificent and impenetrable. So she sat in a chair, one hand on the table, drifting in and out of a morphine dream.

It was still dark outside when the table booted. It was a subtle effect—a hum felt through her fingertips, a glow in the central projection well. It woke her instantly. Backlighting for the controls in her chair's armrest flickered on.

Across the table, one of the telepresence projectors activated. A wash of static filled the chair opposite her, resolving into Ed King. He was wearing a gray suit, his tie loosened slightly. He looked tired.

"Who are you?" he said.

"My legal name is Milica Raznakovic." He frowned, and she spelled it for him. He looked into the middle distance for a moment, and then back to her.

"That's a false identity. Handicapped Serb refugee, my ass."

"That is correct. I use it for welfare purposes."

"So who are you really?"

She paused, struck by the complexity of the issue. He frowned again. "Just tell me this: Who do you work for?"

"No one. I'm on welfare."

There was a long moment of silence. Then he spoke, cold as ice. "I am doing this myself because you are, or seemed to be, a friend of Sean's. I have professional interrogators at my disposal."

"No doubt." She sighed.

"Why did you kill Mark Andrews?"

"The guard at Sean's loft?"

He nodded.

"That was an accident. I had to talk to Sean. I was trying to save her." She paused. "I guess I didn't do too well at that."

He snorted. "Sean's fine. I just spoke with her."

"Sean's *fine*? Who do you think that was in the trunk?"

He seemed to suppress a shudder. "We aren't sure what that is yet. I was going to ask you. As you know, it's a close approximation of Sean, without retinas or fingerprints, but with Sean's DNA."

"A close approximation! It's got her *DNA*, dumbass!" She was shouting now. "Who do you think it is, her long-lost twin sister?"

He looked at her unflinchingly. "It's some kind of accelerated clone. Obviously, you were going to fake her death and provide a body. But you weren't finished. You hadn't gotten around to constructing fingerprints or retinas yet. Our question is, Why?"

She put her head in her hands. Missing the forest for the trees was too limp a metaphor. King was missing the devil for the flames. "Sean is *dead*."

"I just talked to her," he said.

She looked up into his eyes. Even in the limited resolution of telepresence, she could see the certainty there. He was afraid to know the truth.

She tried anyway. "What you talked to was a . . . doppelgänger."

"A doppelgänger? How quaint."

"It won't be very quaint when it gets through being Sean and decides to doppelgäng *you*."

He rolled his eyes. "This is ridiculous. I just talked to Sean, and she's on her way here."

She groaned.

"The person on *his* way here is Bonito. He can change himself into any form. I know, because I can change myself too."

A look passed across King's face, as if he was considering for the first time that she might be insane. His hand moved toward an invisible object, a cutoff switch on the other side of the line.

"Maybe we should talk later," he said.

"Wait!" she shouted, and he hesitated for a moment. Her mind raced for the statement that could hold him for a few more minutes.

"I was—" she started, paused, and then it came to her. "The last singer, in Wilson's opera, she didn't really have to escape. It was a discrepancy."

King looked at her silently. His hand remained motionless, halfway to the invisible switch.

Despite her panic, her thinking was hazy. Memories of the night before formed slowly. Then, a snatch of their conversation found her lips, verbatim.

"Mr. King, she was just sick of the whole thing." Her accent was the same, but the voice was still Bonito's. She gathered enough strength to shift her vocal cords.

His hand withdrew from the switch.

She continued, in the voice she had used as Wilson. "That's why she flew away. Like I said, there was really no discrepancy at all. She was just sick of it."

He looked down. "I guess I still don't understand. The opera, I mean." He looked at her again, his eyes intense even in the imperfect resolution. "What the fuck are you?"

"I don't know, Mr. King."

They stared at each other for another moment.

"We know you're different," he said. "Your heart rate is abnormally slow, your blood pressure way too low. We thought it was the drug."

She gave him a startled look.

"The room you are in is designed for meetings with representatives of other companies. It is elaborately equipped to record what goes on in those meetings. The chair you're sitting in can take your heart rate, body temperature, blood pressure, can measure and analyze your sweat. We know you're on some kind of opiate. It's rampant in your perspiration. If you put your hand on the table, I can even tell you if you're lying."

She rested one hand, palm down, before her.

"Sean is dead," she said.

He looked away for a moment, at something in the room with him. His eyes did not change.

"When the drug wears off, we can get a more accurate reading."

She put her head in her hands.

"One more thing," he said after a pause. "Did you kill Hillary Wilson?"

She could see the question in the air. She blinked her eyes and it disappeared. A sudden hallucination. "No . . . yes . . . by accident."

Strangely, he nodded as if accepting her answer. "I'm sorry I never actually met her."

"I'm sorry I did."

King looked away from her suddenly, into the middle distance at the other end of the connection.

"Sean's here." He stood, his head grotesquely attenuated by the upper limit of the projection area.

"It's not Sean," she said, but he was gone.

The table stepped down, went dark.

He hadn't seen the forest.

Chapter 14

Teeth

An hour later, she decided to sleep.

The phones in the chair armrests were all dead. She'd pushed the hard icons on all the control panels in the room. There was no response, no way to get a line out.

She curled up on the thick shag under the table, the fetal position containing and comforting the pain in her gut. It didn't even feel like pain anymore. It was an insistent presence, but it didn't hurt. It was an intrusion, like the dull bass throb from a stereo in another apartment. But it had no pulse, did not change. It seemed to be waiting.

Finally, she slept despite it.

She woke to fear.

Someone was in the room. Not telepresent but standing at the open door. It closed, quietly. The intruder's feet looked like a woman's. They walked to the table and halfway around it. Lee remained silent, letting adrenaline build slowly in her, trying to keep control.

Then the woman knelt. It was Sean's face, close in the darkness below the table.

"Well, hello there." Bonita's smile hadn't changed.

Suddenly, the space under the table seemed horrifyingly small. Lee rolled out, away from Bonita. They both stood, across the table from each other.

Lee screamed. It was piercing and inhumanly loud. She took a ragged breath and reformed her larynx slightly, then screamed again, louder still.

Bonita smiled.

"Darling, please. Aren't you glad to see me? It's been so long. And I hardly had time to get to know you."

Lee filled her lungs, expanding them flush against the limits of her rib cage, and screamed again. Her larynx was torn by the cry. Someone must have heard.

Bonita put a finger to her chin. "You know, I'm reminded of Oscar Wilde. 'We can bear the absence of old friends for years at a time, but to be separated even for a few moments from those we have just met is agony.'" She said the last word with bared teeth. "Or something like that." She shrugged.

Lee tried to scream again but lost control of her breathing. She began to cough—deep, brutal spasms from the bottom of her lungs. Someone must have heard.

"And we really *have* just met."

Lee slowly regained her breath. She spat into one of the leather chairs. Her lungs were under control now, but she couldn't scream again. She turned her concentration to her hands. A fire built in them, branching from the palms toward the fingertips.

"Good. That's enough noise. After all, this is the Americorp boardroom. It's built for privacy. You could drill the other side of that window with a jackhammer, and you wouldn't hear a thing in here. That's what Eddy said, anyway. He's been bragging that he thought of sticking you in here. I guess they don't have a proper Americorp dungeon. I'll have to fix that, won't I?" Bonita smirked. "In any case, this little talk will be very private." Her eyes were filled with delight.

Lee cleared her throat and spoke, her voice breaking raggedly. "Fuck you."

Bonita leaned forward, hands flat against the table. "Say *please*."

Lee felt the change realize, cartilage extending out from each finger, sharpening. She smiled back at Bonita and cleared her throat again. "Come and get it, bitch."

Bonita moved a second before the words were out. There was no flicker of warning, no slight drop to show that her knees had bent. Just a smooth, effortless bound over the table. Lee watched her reaction from a strange remove, morphine, adrenaline, and instinct making a distant spectacle of it. She threw one hand between them, a sideways blow that sliced across Bonita's neck. The newly formed claws opened up the flesh, and blood spouted from Bonita's jugular.

Bonita struck her with arms outstretched, the full force of her bound behind the blow. Lee was thrown back against the window, the breath knocked out of her. Then Bonita was upon her, a terrible force pinning her chest and limbs.

Bonita's face was only a few centimeters away. Blood spurted from the torn flesh for a few slow heartbeats. It soaked through Lee's coverall, warm against her skin. Bonita giggled, the sound bubbling in her throat.

In seconds, the wound had healed itself.

Bonita forced them toward the floor. Her body, sized to Sean's petite frame, seemed to weigh too much. They slid together down the window, smearing blood behind them, Lee's legs powerless to keep her standing.

Her arms were crushed against her sides. Her claws flexed uselessly. She closed her eyes and tried to focus for another change. The fire came quickly, caressing the muscles and bone of her jaw. She made her teeth longer and sharper than she ever had before, extending the canines until she tasted the salty warmth of her own blood, then hardened the tissue inside her mouth until the bleeding stopped.

They had reached the floor. Bonita's body was wrapped around her like an octopus. Their faces were close, Bonita's breath hot. Lee felt a warm, tender kiss on her cheek, then another on her closed mouth. The kisses were slow and long, Bonita's lips wet and throbbing. The lips were inhumanly prehensile, pulsating with a wormlike inner motion as they caressed her neck.

Eyes still closed, Lee turned her face toward the lips, responding as well as her stiffened facial skin would allow. The kisses became heavier. Lee parted her lips and felt a long, hot tongue venture into her mouth. She suppressed a gag as it slipped deep into her throat.

She bit.

Bonita's body stiffened. Lee turned her head to the side, tearing out the last few strands of muscle and spitting the tongue out, gagging. It had writhed, disconnected, for a moment in her mouth. Lee turned back to Bonita and realized with horror that her face was beatific: eyes closed, the picture of pleasure, blood dripping from one corner of her mouth. Lee felt panic take her. She thrashed her limbs in a useless frenzy and strained her head forward to bite Bonita's face. Her fangs found purchase in the cheek, tearing another mouthful of flesh.

Bonita's eyes opened as she screamed and rose from the floor. She stumbled back, one hand over the gaping hole in her face, and fell into a chair beside the conference table.

Lee sprang to her feet, claws and fangs ready.

Bonita's body was like a fluid, reforming in some liquid dance almost too fast to see. It shifted from a bulky, indefinite mass to a long-limbed creature. Lee took a step back as it moved forward. Bonito's fist swung out, in an inhumanly fast roundhouse, and struck the side of her face. There was a moment of blackout, and Lee felt herself falling.

She came to as Bonita lifted her from the floor. Her vision blurred at the sight of Bonita's ghastly ruin of a face.

The words were slurred. "You're so predictable, and I love you for it." Blood sprayed with every syllable. Bonita seemed to be weakening. Her eyes were glassy. Lee shook herself free and stepped back, her head still reeling.

Bonita was pulling her own shirt off.

Lee tried to thrust a claw toward Bonita's throat, but her arms didn't respond. Bonita easily parried the blow and shoved her backward. Lee was thrown onto the table, her head snapping back to hit the hard wood. The pain was a white light in her brain. Her morphine organ shifted into full gear, out of control. Her head began to swim with hallucinations, and she gave herself a rush of adrenaline and endorphins to keep her mind together.

She felt Bonita cover her again. She was powerless to resist. Bonita pulled her limbs akimbo, holding her wrists with steely hands, her ankles in prehensile, grasping talons. A coarse tentacle wound itself around her neck, tightening just enough to brighten the pain in her head. Lee could open only one eye. The other was shut by swelling from Bonita's blow. Lee felt other extremities at work, ripping her coverall apart unhurriedly. One of her cheeks seemed to have a hole in it, torn by her own fangs when Bonita had struck her.

Bonita's facial wound still gaped, but the bleeding had stopped. Her skin was ghastly white, as though she had withdrawn the blood flow from her face entirely. Lee could glimpse bone through the hole.

She thrust upward to bite again, but the tentacle

whipped her head back against the table. It stayed tight for a few moments, until red clouds formed at the edges of her vision. It relaxed before she passed out.

"No, darling, I want you awake," came the slurred words.

As Lee gasped for breath, she felt something. It was subtle, at the threshold of awareness. The table was purring beneath them. She turned her head toward the projection well, and the tentacle reflexively tightened. Before redness clouded her vision again, she saw a faint glow in the well. The table had booted.

Bonita was oblivious to it. She had pressed her body against Lee, her face as white as death. Lee could see that the tentacle around her neck emerged from Bonita's chest. Another had formed between his legs. He had stripped, and Lee's clothes lay in rags around her.

The penetration came, oddly tentative. The member was thin, sinuous, ribbed like a cheap bodega condom. She felt its corded length slip slowly into her, then branch into distinct threads. They probed her with a strange tenderness, growing finer as they split and split again, exploring ever wider as if to exhaust the spaces inside her. She wrenched her vaginal muscles trying to expel the tentacle, but it was too strong.

Lee's face and head throbbed from their injuries, and she closed her eyes and focused her pain into her groin. She began to strengthen her vagina, stealing muscle from her thighs, her back, impressing into sinew the flesh of her buttocks. She took shards of bone from her pelvis and began to set them into the hard new muscles.

Bonito's flowering cock slid forth nervous tissue. It began to fuse with Lee's nerves, first in her vagina, then penetrating deeper; her stomachs, solar plexus,

spinal column. As his nervous pattern imprinted itself on hers, she began to feel Bonito's pleasure. It
was wholly unlike the glow of her morphine buzz
or any sexual pleasure she had ever felt. It was as
flat and sharp as an Arctic wind; it blew across a
broad and empty place. In the mind's eye of her morphine fugue, she was vividly there, in his pleasure.
It was intense, brutal, barren.

He was working his own change inside her. The
disaggregated cock had merged into a few strands,
which forced their way farther inside her. They
reached for her solar plexus, the seat of her pain.
Somehow, he had taken control of her body. Her
abdominal organs shifted aside as his cock approached its goal.

For a moment, the change in her groin was stalled.
She fought his advance, straining to weave more
muscles around the base of his cock. But his intrusion
surged forward again, deep enough to interfere with
her breathing, and the change was halted.

He reached his goal inside her. His branching
cocks grasped the ball of her pain like fingers. The
nervous connection expanded, until she could feel
him from the inside, a ghost body on top of hers,
like the phantom of an amputated limb. She felt his
hot, corrupt breath on her face again. Against her
will, her eyes opened.

"Live inside me," the dead face said. His cock's
grasp tightened and began to draw her out. She
would die now, she knew.

Trying to speak seemed to mean nothing. Her
awareness of her own body was diminishing. The
ghost sensation of Bonito became stronger. She felt
his chill pleasure increase, rising toward orgasm.

Her hands clenched, fighting the pleasure. The
claws cut into her palms. She focused her will on
them, commanding them to close tighter, to wound

her deeper. She felt him feel the pain, and they gasped together.

For a moment, she found her own voice.

"Stop him. He's killing me," she whispered.

Bonito's eyes opened. There was a look of suspicion in their glassy depths.

The door slid open. She closed her own eyes, saw through Bonito's. Two men with guns, leveled at his head. One started to say something.

Bonito screamed.

She felt the scream bubble up from his throat, rising from an organ between larynx and glottis, a mutated voice box of supertaut folds. Bonito's ears closed as it began, and hers did so instinctively, but still the screech was deafening, punishing. Its effect on the guards was paralytic. One went to his knees, the other fell as he tried to back out of the room. She had once heard a FEMA cruiser let loose a paralyzing blast from its crowd-control siren during the riots. In the close and soundproofed room, Bonito's scream was exponentially more disabling.

But for a moment, she was free.

The new muscles in her vagina pulled tight with wrenching force, their leverage against her pelvis threatening to snap it. The shards of bone she had teethed them with cut hard into Bonito's cock, tearing at its knotted flesh. His pain doubled back through their nervous connection. It was blinding, shattering, and she reveled in it, pulling her muscles tighter.

His scream had cut short with her first contraction, dying on his lips with a startled gag. She opened her eyes. Above her, his mouth was still wide. In it, fangs were forming, long and sharp, his jaw slackening as its bone was hurriedly depleted for them. The tentacle around her throat uncoiled and wrapped around her head, slamming sideways to expose her neck to his bite.

She wrenched herself with one final contraction. The feedback of his pain stopped. The connection, his control, was cut. His cock was sundered.

At the same moment, a spray of bullets hit his head. The gun was less than a meter from him, firing again and again. His skull shattered, he was thrown off her onto the floor.

The man was one of King's guards from the opera. His face was ashen. He dropped the gun and put a hand on her shoulder.

"My God," he said.

She fought to speak, feeling air and blood escape from the hole in her cheek.

"Listen," she whispered.

She grasped his arm and pulled him closer, forced her tongue to move. "He's still alive."

His eyes widened, and he was pulled from her grasp, disappearing below the edge of the table. His screams seemed sadly faint after Bonito's paralyzing screech.

She sat up. Her abdomen felt bloated with Bonito's riven cock. She grasped the gun. It was like the one Freddie had given her, but the magazine was longer. The other guard had fled. Somewhere, an alarm was ringing.

The struggle under the table hadn't lasted long.

She found she could pull herself into a kneeling position. The alarm cut off, and it was eerily silent. She jerked her head one way and then another, trying to see in all directions. The room began to spin in a waltz of pain, morphine, and adrenaline.

Then, at the head of the table, Ed King resolved into focus.

"More help is on the way," he said calmly.

She clenched her wounded cheek shut with angry teeth and said, "Thanks for the timely rescue, shithead."

"I thought it might reveal itself to you. I just wanted to know why Sean died."

She spat blood and started to speak, but he interrupted. "It's moving toward your right."

Two tentacles came over the table edge, long and spined with cartilaginous teeth. She pulled the trigger again and again as they scuttled toward her, chips flying from the dark wood of the table. One tentacle split as a bullet hit it and drew back, broken. The other wrapped around her waist, its hooked thorns tearing her flesh. She didn't resist. She threw herself over the side toward it, clutching the pistol.

Bonito had repaired his face enough to show surprise when she landed beside him. He had normal arms as well as his tentacles, a taser wand in one. The right side of his mouth was still fanged, but the left had been shattered. His head was lopsided, half blown away.

She didn't waste time with his head. She put four bullets into his chest, just to push him away. He dropped the taser.

She pointed the gun at his solar plexus, at the place he had reached for inside her, and squeezed the trigger hard. It went fully automatic.

When help arrived, she was bent over his bloody form, recharging the taser wand and thrusting it into his wounds one by one.

CHAPTER 15

Ambulance

She didn't dare pass out.

The concussions were bad enough to kill her. She dealt with them slowly and surely, after she'd stopped all the external bleeding she could find. King had told the paramedics not to touch her.

She was in an Americorp limo, headed toward a Jersey City hospital. At first she had hallucinated that Freddie was beside her. But it was another man, old for a paramedic, who held her hand as she healed herself. His eyes were glassy with shock. He must have seen the boardroom.

She laughed softly to herself. She was reducing her morphine level slowly but was still hopped up. She now realized that at some point during her battle with Bonito, she'd had a mild overdose.

The new muscles in her vagina took only minutes to force the remains of Bonito's cock out. Repairing her groin, she discovered a hairline fracture in her pelvis from the stress of her final contraction. Two ribs had been broken at some point, and several teeth were missing from her mouth, snapped off in their thinned and sharpened state.

The internal organs of her abdomen were a mess. Bonito's efforts there had been even more brutal than she'd realized. One stomach was collapsed, her spinal column was low on fluid, and the walls of her vagina and uterus were badly torn.

But the changes came with an ease she'd never known before. The fierce pain of change had been replaced by a fluidness, her body shifting facilely beneath the bloody sheet across her. The damage she'd sustained didn't lessen the pleasure her new powers brought her. She was lightened by the realization that her body meant nothing. What was it Bonito had written? *The shock of massive trauma brought it to me.* She lay there, exploring the splendid mobility of organs and tissues, the exquisite arbitrariness of form. This is what Bonito had found, or had always possessed: a pristine detachment from the trauma of discarding oneself.

And finally, there was respite from the pain in her gut. It was as if the hot center of change at her solar plexus had exploded, spreading throughout her body. In its absence, a coolness covered her mind, like a blanket of snow.

By the time they reached the hospital, she was fit enough to make a run for it. They had to use a taser to bring her down. The shock shot through her deliciously, and she laughed as they wheeled her to her room.

CHAPTER 16

Down

She changed in the shower.

As he dried himself, he realized how good it was to be back at Freddie's. The dingy bathroom was a pleasure after the antiseptic hospital suite. It felt like home.

The coarse fabric of the towel across his back brought a twinge, a sense-memory of the spinal tap she'd been subjected to a few days before. Americorp's physicians had tested her mercilessly for two weeks: CAT scans, sonograms, fiber-optic insertions. She had carefully controlled what they withdrew from her, even during the spinal tap, and had destroyed the nanomachines they'd slipped into her body. Of course, they didn't really need her. They had what was left of Bonito.

He shuddered. On a walk in the hospital corridors, limited to Americorp's private wing, she had encountered a dolly stacked with cryostasis canisters, misting like dry ice. They could have been anything—plasma, transplant-ready organs, a superconducting coil. But for a moment she had imagined the line of Bonito's jaw, his green eyes. The newsnets were full of Americorp's big new push, a shift away from information services to biotechnology.

He stepped from the bathroom, a little nervous about Freddie's reaction to the change.

Freddie sat at his new workstation, visor over his eyes, his frame sparkling with the nodes of a full-body input suit. A million dollars bought a lot of toys. The cash had arrived by FedEx the day she got home from the hospital. The return address was in Belize; black money from one of Americorp's off-shore operations, Freddie had guessed. There was no thank-you note.

Lee suspected it wasn't thanks at all. More like a down payment on services yet to be rendered. He was out of the hospital, but Americorp's surveillance was always present. Like a watchful parent, it hovered at the edge of awareness, unintrusive, making itself known subtly yet surely. They knew that if he slipped through their fingers even once, he would disappear forever.

Soon he would be able to lose them, if he really needed to. But that would mean leaving Freddie behind. Also, Ed King had Bonito's papers and his data. They would have to be bargained for.

Freddie was too deep into the net to look up. That was probably best. Lee dressed in jeans and a white T-shirt, looked through Freddie's leather jackets. The jeans were too new looking. They were going to the Glory Hole that night.

"Interesting rumors on the net about our friends," Freddie said from the workstation, his right hand making the faintest gesture toward the sky. "They're starting a price war in the retina scanner market. They're working on one that can read your eye from a meter away. No more bending over. Some guy hacked their PR copy before it was released. 'A scanner for every door, every ATM, even smartcard points-of-purchase. Security for the twenty-first century.' "

A subtle message from Ed King. The retina scan was the one kind of ID he couldn't beat. Not yet, anyway.

"Anybody up in arms?" Lee asked. His voice was lower, but Freddie didn't seem to notice.

"The usual suspects: the EFF, New.ID.org, the ACLU."

"Send New.ID a hundred thousand dollars, in my name."

Freddie didn't turn around, but his fingers stopped moving.

"A *hundred* thousand? That's like their operating budget for a *year*."

"Yes." Lee's tone didn't invite argument.

"Don't you think we should make this particular contribution anonymously?" Freddie asked.

"Open wire." He could send King messages too.

Freddie flipped the visor up and turned around, about to say something. He paused at the sight of Lee's new form, looked him up and down.

Lee was suddenly embarrassed by his stare.

"Surprised?" he asked Freddie.

"Where'd you say we were going tonight?"

"Glory Hole."

"Thought that was a dyke club."

"Not on Wednesday."

"Ah. Wondered why you were taking me." Freddie smiled a little, as if laughing at himself. "I've heard about the swimming pool. Too good to be true."

Lee put his hands on Freddie's shoulders. "We can still go in the pool." He leaned forward and kissed him.

There was just the slightest shudder in Freddie's form, but he submitted to the kiss. When Lee drew back, Freddie's smile had faded.

Then Freddie laughed. "Man, I *hate* this town."

They laughed together. Freddie turned back to his workstation, and Lee massaged his shoulders for a while, letting him grow used to contact with the new body. Lee's changes usually turned Freddie on. He figured this one would eventually.

The monitor clock neared midnight. Lee kissed Freddie on the ear and said, "I'm going out for something." Freddie made an inarticulate noise of assent.

He climbed the stairs to the co-op's roof. The air in the stairwell was hot and smelled of Spanish cooking. Someone had padlocked the roof door since the day before. A blow to the door snapped the hasp.

Outside, the air was cool and still. The Empire State Building was lit red, white, and blue for the anniversary of the Intervention. In the clear night sky, he could see a widely spaced circle of planes in the La Guardia holding pattern. A few car alarms held forth in the distance. He paced the roof a little anxiously, preparing himself with a few shifts in his musculature, reinforcing his ribs to protect heart and lungs, hardening his cortex. Finally, he let his morphine organ expand a little, breathing deeply as the rush hit him.

He went toward the back of the building, which overlooked an unlit airshaft. It was seven floors down, but at night the shaft looked infinitely deep. He knew that the bottom was paved with crumbling concrete, but free of broken glass and garbage. He took the T-shirt off.

To the west, a VTOL freighter landed with a sovereign roar.

He jumped.

The moments of free fall were unexpectedly calm. There was no sense of hurtling downward as in a falling dream, only weightlessness. He had expected himself to tense as he fell, but instinct relaxed him utterly. For a second, the fall was timeless.

In his ears, the sound of the impact was gigantic.

After a brief incoherence, he awoke to a body awash in activated chemicals. Adrenaline, morphine, endorphins, and the rich rush of change buoyed him out of unconsciousness. His legs were badly broken, one femur splintered. A lung was collapsed, fragments of rib piercing it. He concentrated on its repair, trying to control the rattling cough that threatened to turn thick with blood. As he did so, poisons ran riot in his abdomen, where a ruptured kidney cried for attention. He turned from one crisis to the next frantically. His mind slipped closer to panic, until a mist of red gnats swarmed before his eyes.

And then he felt it come. Control swept through his body like the rush of an aircraft's acceleration, lifting him out of incoherence, thrusting a picture into his mind.

He saw shattered bones swim, sinuous, to reform themselves. He saw organs flow like sand into their apposite shapes. Twisted muscles loosened, rent skin zippered closed. Almost casually, he coughed fluid from his lungs into his mouth, and swallowed.

After he was healed, he lay for a while, a calm like the free fall having overcome him. Muscle and bone continued to shift as his thoughts wandered, a play of surfaces and forms under his taut skin. His morphine organ pulsed for a while and then slackened like an expended cock. His eyes opened and he smiled. He was ready to go out.

He climbed the building easily.

When he got back in, Freddie was dressed for the Glory Hole; he'd put on a black T-shirt and chinos. He looked at Lee's jeans. They were scuffed and dirty, and despite his best efforts, blood had stained one knee.

"Hurt yourself?" he asked.

"Took a fall."

"That's one way to break 'em in," Freddie said with a smirk.

Lee stuck his tongue out at him, eight inches studded with tiny pseudopods. Freddie's face went briefly ashen, and he turned away.

Lee smiled. Still buzzing from the fall, he was not in the mood for Freddie's squeamishness. He put a hand on the boy's shoulder. There was the slightest tug away.

For a moment, the rejection hurt her, deep inside. Then, almost as a reflex, the morphine organ responded with a tiny burst. A flush of satisfaction filled him, and the dark look on Freddie's face only prompted his desire. He took both shoulders, hard, and pushed Freddie against the wall. Through his fingers, he slipped filaments of nervous tissue into the bare shoulders, felt the flutter of Freddie's heart, his confusion, the buzz of the speed he'd taken before going on the net. Lee looked into Freddie's eyes, trying to connect. He saw his desire reciprocated, with a hint of terror.

He moved forward, his mouth at Freddie's throat.

When he allowed himself to be pushed back, his grip still firm, he saw he'd marked Freddie's neck. The terror in the boy's eyes remained.

Freddie wasn't used to the new habits yet—the casual shape-shifting, the mood swings, the sudden violence.

But he would learn.

Coming From Roc Books
in December 1998
The new book from Scott Westerfeld

Fine Prey

Chapter 1: School

The bed woke me with deliberate care. First a soft vibration that swept from foot to head repeatedly, then a gentle rocking, and finally a low chime that pulsed as the windows de-opaqued. The orange sun was still halved by the forested horizon; the bed's painstaking ministrations could not hide the fact that it wasn't yet six.

It took a full ten seconds of staring sleepily at the low orb, its shape burned into blue tracers on my retinas, to remember that it was the last day of school.

With that, I leaped from bed. My roommate, Alex, was already gone, following to the last his perverse schedule of jogging for an hour before sunup. Of course, the run was his only freedom; at Aya School, every moment of daylight was carefully prescribed. I had tried to join him at the beginning of semester, but it quickly became one discipline too many.

I began heating the ceremonial morning meal, mindlessly uttering an appropriate Ayan votive. Out of the corner of my eye, the sun was slipping above the trees, and I rushed the prayer to conclusion. The meal stood ready when Alex, naked and sweaty, bolted in from his run. He grimaced at the sun, fully clear from the trees, and muttered, "Thanks for waiting."

I whacked him halfheartedly with a rolled-up hunt magazine. He had been collecting too many infractions lately. We had drawn a room in the Salutatorian Seniors' residence next year, and I didn't want to lose it. The building enjoyed an extra half hour of morning shade from the tall poplars at the edge of campus, which, according to the Ayan method of laying out the day, meant thirty minutes more sleep. Talking out loud in English was punishable by 144 demerits. As Juniors, we were supposed to speak, think, and shit in Ayan, twenty-four hours a day.

He muttered a short, breathy trill which Hogson's text series always translated as: "I respect the violence with which you have illuminated my error." At school, it pretty much meant something between *ouch!* and *fuck you*, but he lofted it to the register of an affectionate mode.

I didn't attempt to answer. My mouth was too dry in the mornings to really give the language its due. Alex was by far the better speaker. He had a natural feel for the airy vowels and glottal frictives of Ayan. His father had been on the original contact team, and I figured some of the collateral radiation had gotten into Alex's genes, his language ability some perverse recompense for the bizarre cancers his dad had succumbed to. We were complimentary forces at school, his natural ability and slovenly working habits and my grim, scholarly discipline. That, and the fact that we had both lost our fathers, comprised the unspoken core of our friendship. Of course, we were also both riders of the fine hunt, but *that* we talked about all the time.

We crunched through the morning meal in silence

and then dressed. The school uniform was a skintight, smart-fiber coverall, light gray for Juniors. The
garment was lined with a colony of engineered bacte-
ria that cleaned the skin, regulated our metabolisms,
and protected us from any collaterals coming off our
native Ayan teachers. Its hidden abilities were leg-
endary in the rumor mill of the school. I'd personally
seen a student's life saved by her suit. She had over-
dosed on a cortisone-based designer drug engineered
to foil the suit's substance monitors. The drug had
slipped past the chemical censors well enough, but
had also had the unfortunate side effect of stopping
her heart. The suit registered the cardiac arrest and
called the medics. Before they arrived, it stiffened
and compressed bizarrely around her, forcing the
blood from her extremities into the oxygen-starved
brain. Her face turned a bright pink around bluing
lips, her eyes agog and red with broken blood ves-
sels. The med drones arrived a few minutes later and
pumped her with jolt juice, and she was almost normal the next year.

The real purposes of the suit were far more insidi-
ous, though. It protected us from being swayed by
the human rhythms of bathing and menstruation,
and from the adolescent scourges of zits and a sex
drive. Aya School was total immersion, our young
heads held under the water as if by some ass-kicking
Baptist converting the heathen. Of course, this was
the only way to learn a language born under an alien
sun. I'd been a star student in the curriculum since
I was five years old, and my speaking proficiency
compared to a native was roughly that of a polite
but moronic adolescent.

After eating we sat in the middle of the room, gnomon between us, and drilled a little. It was simple

stuff, prattling parallel niceties across the authoritative, and attendant modes. Alex badgered my demonstration mercilessly—my nominal hand movements were getting soft again—and I retaliated in the mercantile. He was better at the old modes, the ones that measured status and obligation by the drop. Today, though, he was just as facile with the egalitarian mercantile. That was good to see. I was half afraid that he would snap today and screw up an exemplary (for him) semester.

Three years as his roommate had endowed me with a healthy dread of last-minute fuck-ups. I was probably being paranoid. After all, the testing today was relatively trivial. The school didn't follow the human academic rhythms of crunch and finals time, because that would have been very un-Ayan indeed. But even for a human, Alex had been jumpy lately.

By now, the ceiling was transparent, and the shadow of the gnomon had reached the jewel at First Call. The little fleck of stone was imbedded in a resonant cavity in the hard floor. It sang softly, converting stored solar energy into sound. The jewels were beloved by the Aya because their singing sounded a little like Ayan: a whispery, airy shushing. They were the mythological source of the Ayan language, although with the Aya the line between myth and history was pretty fuzzy. The lack of a literal mode was one of the profoundly dirty tricks the language played on its human students.

As we waited a few moments before taking the Call (punctuality was not tolerated at school), Alex wished me good luck with rattling frictives of excessive gravity. I joked back at him in an imperious mode, cocking my head in the human equivalent of a coutier's tail twitch, but he took my wrist and spoke in English, dead serious.

"Can't you feel it?"

"What?" I said, then swore, realizing I'd answered in English. I looked nervously at the intercom.

"We are *this* close," he said, demonstrating a milimeter between forefinger and thumb, "to riding again."

Despite myself, I smiled at him. I'd almost not let myself think about it. With the end of school came the riding season. Actually, it had started a week before, but Alex and I always missed the Milan shows; Aya School ran a full month longer than the rest of the world's elite academies.

It was part of Alex's job as the bad boy in our relationship to throw this in my face. I, the good student, had suppressed how soon we would be in competition again. The constrained world of elegant cycles, hushed hallways, and byzantine grammar was about to shatter, the shushing of Ayan replaced by the squeal of prey on the killing ground. I felt the heat of it prickle my skin inside the modulated cool of the coverall. It was a very un-Ayan explosion of joy. I put my hand into Alex's, breaking the loop of his tensed fingers.

"Yes, my love. We'll be hunting soon."

RoC

THRILLING SCI-FI NOVELS

☐ **EXILE by Al Sarrantonio.** It is the end of the 25th century. Human civilization has expanded into the Four Worlds of Earth, Mars, Titan, and Pluto. Recent progress in terraforming promises to turn Venus into the Fifth. But for Prime Cornelian, usurper of Martian rule, there will be no rest until all planets bow before him. "A very talented writer."—*Washington Post Book World*   (455215—$5.99)

☐ **FLIES FROM THE AMBER by Wil McCarthy.** An Unuan mining expedition has discovered an alien mineral they name centrokrist—a stone of incomparable beauty. Yet when the Earth scientists at last arrive to investigate, they find a phenomenon eclipsing the centrokrist crystals. For this double-sunned solar system is nestled right next to a black hole.   (454065—$4.99)

☐ **BEYOND THIS HORIZON by Robert A. Heinlein.** This classic tale portrays a utopian Earth of the future, in a time when humanity is free of illness and imperfection. Yet even in paradise there are some like the privileged Hamilton Felix who harbor deep doubts about the very point of human existence.   (166760—$5.99)

Prices slightly higher in Canada.

Buy them at your local bookstore or use this convenient coupon for ordering.

PENGUIN USA
P.O. Box 999 — Dept. #17109
Bergenfield, New Jersey 07621

Please send me the books I have checked above.
I am enclosing $_____ (please add $2.00 to cover postage and handling). Send check or money order (no cash or C.O.D.'s) or charge by Mastercard or VISA (with a $15.00 minimum). Prices and numbers are subject to change without notice.

Card #_____ Exp. Date _____
Signature_____
Name_____
Address_____
City _____ State _____ Zip Code _____

For faster service when ordering by credit card call **1-800-253-6476**

Allow a minimum of 4-6 weeks for delivery. This offer is subject to change without notice.

CUTTING EDGE SCI-FI NOVELS

☐ **CINDERBLOCK by Janine Ellen Young.** Alexander's amazing ability to log onto the Web without the use of computers makes him unique—and very valuable indeed. Especially to a mysterious, shotgun wielding revolutionary named Cinderblock who is plotting against the Virtual tyranny. And Cinder's scheming might not only spell the end of reality—it might also get her and Alexander killed. (455959—$5.99)

☐ **NO LIMITS by Nigel D. Findley.** Samantha Dooley is a hotshot pilot with a thirst for adrenaline, and she's out to buck the ban on women fighter pilots. But when her beloved grandfather passes away, he leaves behind a secret that's going to require more than fancy stick work to figure out.
(455258—$5.50)

☐ **TWILIGHT OF THE EMPIRE by Simon R. Green.** Once the Empire spanned light years, uniting far-flung mankind in peace and harmony. Now it is rotten to the core, and a half-mad Empress rules with a fist of iron. Before the rise of Owen Deathstalker, other heroes defended this perilous galaxy. Their exciting stories are told in three action-packed novellas set in the amazing *Deathstalker* universe. (456491—$6.99)

Prices slightly higher in Canada from 🖼️

Buy them at your local bookstore or use this convenient coupon for ordering.

PENGUIN USA
P.O. Box 999 — Dept. #17109
Bergenfield, New Jersey 07621

Please send me the books I have checked above.
I am enclosing $_____ (please add $2.00 to cover postage and handling). Send check or money order (no cash or C.O.D.'s) or charge by Mastercard or VISA (with a $15.00 minimum). Prices and numbers are subject to change without notice.

Card #_____ Exp. Date _____
Signature_____
Name_____
Address_____
City _____ State _____ Zip Code _____

For faster service when ordering by credit card call **1-800-253-6476**

Allow a minimum of 4-6 weeks for delivery. This offer is subject to change without notice.

OUT OF THIS WORLD ANTHOLOGIES

☐ **BETWEEN TIME AND TERROR Edited by Bob Weinberg, Stefan Dziemianowicz, and Martin H. Greenberg.** Take a terror-laden trip to a dark, hidden place where fear feeds on the mind and science devours the soul. With contributions from acclaimed science fiction, fantasy and suspense writers, this riveting collection is a free fall of fright that speeds you through one magnificent story after another. (454529—$4.99)

☐ **ALIEN SEX** *19 Tales by the Masters of Science Fiction and Dark Fantasy.* **Edited by Ellen Datlow.** In these provocative pieces of short fiction, best-selling and award-winning writers explore the barriers between men and women that can make them seem so "alien" to one another.

(451422—$5.99)

☐ **ROBOT VISIONS by Isaac Asimov.** From the Grandmaster of science fiction, 36 magnificent stories and essays about his most beloved creations—the robots. And these "robot visions" are skillfully captured in illustrations by Academy Award-winner Ralph McQuarrie, production designer of *Star Wars*

(450647—$6.99)

*Prices slightly higher in Canada

Buy them at your local bookstore or use this convenient coupon for ordering.

PENGUIN USA
P.O. Box 999 — Dept. #17109
Bergenfield, New Jersey 07621

Please send me the books I have checked above.
I am enclosing $_____ (please add $2.00 to cover postage and handling). Send check or money order (no cash or C.O.D.'s) or charge by Mastercard or VISA (with a $15.00 minimum). Prices and numbers are subject to change without notice.

Card #_____ Exp. Date _____
Signature_____
Name_____
Address_____
City _____ State _____ Zip Code _____

For faster service when ordering by credit card call **1-800-253-6476**

Allow a minimum of 4-6 weeks for delivery. This offer is subject to change without notice.

R̄O̅C̄ ROC

EXPLOSIVE SCIENCE FICTION

☐ **DEATHSTALKER by Simon R. Green.** Owen Deathstalker, unwilling head of his clan, sought to avoid the perils of the Empire's warring factions but unexpectedly found a price on his head. He fled to Mistworld, where he began to build an unlikely force to topple the throne—a broken hero, an outlawed Hadenman, a thief, and a bounty hunter. (454359—$5.99)

☐ **DEATHSTALKER REBELLION by Simon R. Green.** Owen Deathstalker—"outlawed" with a price on his head and the mighty warrior lineage in his veins—had no choice but to embrace the destiny that befell him. With nothing to lose, only he had the courage to take up sword and energy gun against Queen Lionstone XIV. (455525—$5.99)

☐ **KNIGHTS OF THE BLACK EARTH by Margaret Weis and Don Perrin.** Xris, top human agent of the Federal Intelligence Security Agency, finds himself joining forces with his oldest enemy in a desperate attempt to halt the seemingly unstoppable Knights of the Black Earth—a fanatical group determined to sabotage the current government and revive Earth supremacy. (454251—$18.95)

☐ **FLIES FROM THE AMBER by Wil McCarthy.** An Unuan mining expedition has discovered an alien mineral they name centrokrist—a stone of incomparable beauty. Yet when the Earth scientists at last arrive to investigate, they find a phenomenon eclipsing the centrokrist crystals. For this double-sunned solar system is nestled right next to a black hole. (454065—$4.99)

*Prices slightly higher in Canada

Buy them at your local bookstore or use this convenient coupon for ordering.

PENGUIN USA
P.O. Box 999 — Dept. #17109
Bergenfield, New Jersey 07621

Please send me the books I have checked above.
I am enclosing $_____ (please add $2.00 to cover postage and handling). Send check or money order (no cash or C.O.D.'s) or charge by Mastercard or VISA (with a $15.00 minimum). Prices and numbers are subject to change without notice.

Card #_____ Exp. Date _____
Signature_____
Name_____
Address_____
City _____ State _____ Zip Code _____

For faster service when ordering by credit card call **1-800-253-6476**

Allow a minimum of 4-6 weeks for delivery. This offer is subject to change without notice.

THE ROC FREQUENT READERS BOOK CLUB

BUY TWO ROC BOOKS
AND GET ONE
SF/FANTASY NOVEL FREE!

Check the free title you wish to receive (subject to availability):

☐ **BLACK MADONNA**
Shadowrun®
**Carl Sargent & Marc
Gascoigne**
0-451-45373-5/$5.50 ($6.50 in Canada)

☐ **DARK LOVE**
**Edited by Nancy A.
Collins, Edward E.
Kramer, and Martin H.
Greenberg**
0-451-45550-9/$5.99 ($7.99 in Canada)

☐ **EGGHEADS**
Emily Devenport
0-451-45517-7/$5.99 ($7.50 in Canada)

☐ **ICE CROWN**
Andre Norton
0-451-45248-8/$4.99 ($5.99 in Canada)

☐ **STARGATE™: REBELLION**
Bill McCay
0-451-45502-9/$4.99 ($5.99 in Canada)

☐ **THE WHITE MISTS OF
POWER**
Kristine Kathryn Rusch
0-451-45120-1/$3.99 ($5.50 in Canada)

To get your FREE Roc book, send in this coupon (original or photocopy),
proof of purchase (original sales receipt(s) for two Roc books and a copy of
the books' UPC numbers) plus $2.00 for postage and handling to:

**ROC FREQUENT READERS CLUB
Penguin USA • Mass Market
375 Hudson Street, New York, NY 10014**

Name: _____

Address: _____

City:_____ State:_____ Zip: _____

E-mail Address: _____

RoC **Roc Books**

Offer expires December 31, 1997. This certificate or facsimile must
accompany your request. Void where prohibited, taxed, or restricted. Allow
4-6 weeks for shipment of book(s). Offer good only in U.S., its territories,
and Canada.